The Orchards of Ithaca

Other Books by Harry Mark Petrakis

Novels
Lion at My Heart
The Odyssey of Kostas Volakis
A Dream of Kings
In the Land of Morning
The Hour of the Bell
Nick the Greek
Days of Vengeance
Ghost of the Sun
Twilight of the Ice

Short Story Collections
Pericles on 31st Street
The Waves of Night
A Petrakis Reader—27 Stories
Collected Stories

Memoirs and Essays
Stelmark—A Family Recollection
Reflections: A Writer's Life—A Writer's Work
Tales of the Heart

Biography and History
The Founder's Touch
Henry Crown: The Life and Times of the Colonel
Reach Out: A History of Motorola and Its People

The Orchards of Ithaca

Harry Mark Petrakis

SOUTHERN ILLINOIS UNIVERSITY PRESS

Carbondale

Printed in the United States of America

07 06 05 04   4 3 2 1

Excerpt from C. P. Cavafy's "Ithaca" is from *The Complete Poems
of Cavafy*, expanded edition, translated by Rae Dalven. New York:
Harcourt Brace Jovanovich, 1976.

Excerpts from *The Divine Comedy* by Dante Alighieri, translated by
Louis Birncolli. New York: Washington Square Press, 1966.

Library of Congress Cataloging-in-Publication Data

Petrakis, Harry Mark.
The orchards of Ithaca / Harry Mark Petrakis.
  p. cm.
  I. Title.
PS3566.E78 O73 2004
813'.54—dc22
ISBN 0-8093-2578-0 (alk. paper)   2003025642

Printed on recycled paper. ♻

The paper used in this publication meets the minimum requirements of
American National Standard for Information Sciences—Permanence of
Paper for Printed Library Materials, ANSI Z39.48-1992.♾

For our sons, their wives, and their children
—our grandchildren—
with gratefulness and love

The Orchards of Ithaca

One

THE NIGHT before his fiftieth birthday, Orestes Panos dreamed he had been invited to a reception at the Clinton White House. Clad impeccably in formal attire (since he didn't own a tuxedo, he must have rented one), he moved coolly and with self-assurance among the distinguished guests in the ballroom. In addition to the president, William Jefferson Clinton, and his wife, Hillary Clinton, who were holding court in a corner of the elegant room, Orestes rubbed shoulders with a bevy of celebrities including Wolf Blitzer from CNN and Dan Rather from CBS. He recognized the squat Madeline Albright and tall, slump-shouldered Janet Reno. The stern-faced director of the Justice Department gave him a piercing look as if questioning why a restaurant owner from Halsted Street should have been included on the guest list. Before he could tell her he was as bewildered as she was, he was distracted by the appearance of the courtly, white-maned senator from New York, who spoke in rhetorical flourishes, and whose name escaped his dream. (After he woke, he remembered it was Patrick Moynihan.)

Then, in a corner of the ballroom, Orestes was startled to see the lumpish figure and doe-eyed face of Monica Lewinsky. Her presence suggested the notorious affair with the president had not yet entered its lethal finale.

Orestes suddenly understood the purpose of his visit to the White House was to warn the lascivious leader of the nation of the disaster that awaited him if he continued to pursue the young intern. But every desperate effort he made to approach Clinton was thwarted by stern Secret Service agents who formed an impregnable cordon around the president. Despite all his exertions, they held him at bay.

Frustration woke him. He opened his eyes reluctantly to the first glimmerings of daylight around the rim of the shades. He lay still for a few moments recapturing the images and impressions of the dream, which was more celebrity-riddled than any other dream he could remember. He hoped it wasn't a sign that at fifty, he was succumbing to megalomania.

Dreaming about the White House was understandable because for more than a year, the dominant newspaper and television stories had focused on the Clinton fiasco. Gennifer, Paula, and Monica, Clinton's flexuous troika of either hapless victims or scheming bitches, depending on a Democratic or Republican perception. Months of charges and countercharges and days of debate in the Houses of Congress. Finally, there were the U.S. Senate hearings on the president's perjury and the articles of impeachment.

What Orestes had seen of the political partisanship masquerading as moral indignation had revolted him. The spectacle of the thirteen House managers marching into the Senate for the hearings, their procession led by the portly, egregious Illinois congressman, his flaccid jowls quivering with his fabricated outrage, a man who had himself broken up a marriage by seducing another man's wife, was enough to sour one's stomach. Their brazen efforts to impeach the president had failed in the Senate, but Orestes knew that the residue of the bitter conflict would carry over into the following year's presidential elections. He feared that the whole country would have to pay for Clinton's peccadilloes.

He slipped quietly from beneath the sheets so not to wake his wife, Dessie, still asleep at the other side of the queen-sized bed. As he walked toward the bathroom, he became conscious of a more pervasive stiffness in his limbs than he had felt the morning before. Is that because I am one year older, he thought gloomily? Perhaps the afflictions of age didn't only creep up on a man but enacted a swift explosive mugging on the occasion of a birthday.

In the bathroom, Orestes stared at his face in the vanity mirror, a reflection he had been confronting for half a century. Not even in his youth could it have been mistaken for a handsome face (Tom Cruise need not worry) but, he hoped, a face reflecting some nobility of character.

Feeling the need for reassurance, he made an effort to evaluate his visage as it might be viewed by a stranger. Deep-set dark eyes, forehead furrowed, curly dark hair laced with the first strands of gray, hairline receding slightly. He had good teeth (thanks to his dentist and regular brushing and flossing) and (people told him) a resolute jaw. For some years he had worn a mustache but the great swashbuckling soup-strainer his father, Moustakas, sported while he was alive discouraged him. Any mustache Orestes grew seemed a whimpering imitation of his father's, and he shaved it off.

At fifty, his general health was good. A slight diminishment of eyesight required he wear glasses for reading. His hearing and senses of taste and smell were still good (all three essential functions in the restaurant). He was about ten pounds overweight for his five-foot-ten-inch frame, but he remained active by cycling in summer and swimming indoors in winter. His general health, confirmed by a recent visit to his friend and internist, Dr. Solon Savas, had not revealed any heart or cancer problems. His prostate was slightly enlarged (requiring nocturnal visits to the bathroom) but was also benign.

To keep his mind from stagnating, he still read whenever he

had the chance (he was halfway through David Halberstam's *The Best and the Brightest*). He watched educational programs on PBS, and after returning home at night, following the ten o'clock news, mustering a final effort to concentrate, he watched Ted Koppel on *Nightline* before going to bed.

In the twenty-three years he had been married to Dessie (a diminutive for Despina), they had so far survived all the precipitous entrapments that demolished numerous other marriages. Father Elias Botsakis, their parish priest from St. Sophia's Greek church, called their union an inspiration to the newlyweds in their parish.

Orestes wasn't sure about how inspiring their survival was, but he believed that Dessie and he had a good marriage with very few arguments of any virulence. Meanwhile, unlike so many other married men, for all the years of his marriage he had remained faithful to his wife.

Certainly there had been a few minor scuffles at parties where he had drunk too much, a furtive kiss or two with women who were also emboldened by liquor. But he never followed up on any of these contacts and, since his marriage, had never gone to bed with anyone except Dessie, rewarding her own faithfulness by an unwavering fidelity of his own.

Their family consisted of a twenty-two year old son, Paulie, who had married a little more than a year earlier (after dropping out of city college in his junior year). As a teenager, Paulie had become a follower of one of those Indian fakirs (spending a month in an Ashram in a religious retreat). Afterwards, he had become a Hare Krishna, shaving his head and spending hours chanting his prayers.

Dessie and Orestes made every effort to tolerate their son's quest for faith. They even permitted Paulie to chant Hare Krishna prayers before dinner. That forbearance didn't extend to his own father, Moustakas. Orestes would never forget his father's fury upon hearing Paulie chant a Hare Krishna prayer at the start of a meal. Moustakas unleashed a verbal tirade, punctuated by curses against his grandson that drove Paulie from the room in tears.

Paulie finally escaped from his religious obsessions. With his psyche refocused from religion to sex, he impregnated an attractive Italian girl named Carmela Barzini, the daughter of a neighborhood florist, Mario Barzini. The child, a girl they named Catherine Yoko Ono after John Lennon's wife, was born a scant five months after the wedding.

Dessie had proved more tolerant and sympathetic about the hasty marriage and premature birth than Orestes, who couldn't help feeling that Carmela had trapped their son into marriage by allowing herself to become pregnant. But all that speculation didn't really matter because the child Paulie and Carmela produced was a little beauty who brought a tangible joy into Orestes and Dessie's life.

The youngest member of his family was their daughter, Marika, a fifteen-year-old sophomore in high school. She was a slender, dark-haired, pretty girl who mirrored Dessie's attractiveness.

As sweet and loving as Marika could often be, she spent money as if she were the daughter of Donald Trump. Orestes couldn't make her understand that Citibank and BankAmerica weren't her own personal depositories. On several occasions, he took away her credit cards, only to relent when Marika tearfully reassured him she would mend her ways. Those promises proved feckless beside her compulsion to patronize those two sybaritic gurus, Ralph Lauren and Calvin Klein.

Orestes felt his daughter's obsession with material things wasn't her fault alone. Young people Marika's age were subjected daily to the callow and shallow aspects of society. There were the bizarre and cruel antics of Howard Stern, the dredging up of human misfits by Jerry Springer, the terpsichorean crotch-gripping Madonna, as well as an assortment of rap and rock groups with names like Death, Madness, Rape, Vomit, Mongrels, and worse, whose music assaulted hearing and whose lyrics bristled with references to murder, blood, and death.

Yet Orestes had to admit there were fathers of families with far greater reason for grievance. The son of Mathon Savalas had to drop out of high school because of his addiction to drugs. And, in another neighborhood family, the daughter of Tony Poulos had eloped with a petty hoodlum who was now serving a ten-year term in jail for assault and battery.

There were even more terrifying scenarios such as the massacre earlier in the year at Columbine High School in Littleton, Colorado, when two youths aged seventeen and eighteen, using shotguns and an automatic rifle, massacred a dozen students and a teacher and wounded more than twenty others. As terrible as the grief the parents of the murdered students must have felt, Orestes wondered at the anguish of the parents of the killers. Had there been any hint of those murderous impulses in their sons? He imagined the nightmares those tormented parents would suffer for as long as they lived.

After considering all the somber alternatives, Orestes had to be grateful that his grievances with his son and daughter were minor.

The single remaining member of their household was Dessie's eighty-seven-year-old widowed mother, Stavroula, who had been living in their home for seven years (the seven-year plague) since the death of her husband.

Stavroula was a lean-bodied, wiry woman, steel-jawed and razor-tongued, with beady dark eyes, and lips curled like a scimitar that she used to slash out with one of her barbs. Orestes tried to be compassionate and tolerant because of her advanced age and because she was Dessie's mother, but her merciless and caustic tongue made living with her an ordeal. She had never liked Orestes and took every opportunity she could to deride and demean him to Dessie. Her male ideal was Tom Selleck, the tall, rugged actor she called in Greek "palikari!"—which translated into a strong, virile masculine figure. She'd watch Selleck's old movies and television reruns for hours on the VCR in her bedroom. Orestes could only imagine the obscene and licentious fantasies moving through the old virago's withering head as she watched the palikari.

Stavroula was far too healthy (as well as too mean) to be consigned into a nursing facility (even if one could be found willing to accommodate aging assassins). Any mention of that possibility evoked in the acerbic old woman a rant and rage that included laments about the tragic fate of aging parents and diatribes on the ingratitude and cruelty of heartless offspring.

The only inhabitant of their house who had never caused Orestes a moment of concern had been their dog, Apollo, until the poor creature succumbed to failing kidneys a few years earlier at sixteen (well over a hundred human years) and had to be put to sleep.

Meanwhile, despite some pessimistic rumblings in the economy and on the stock market, Orestes was in fairly solvent financial shape. He owned a portfolio of blue chip-stocks and investment-grade bonds as well as a choice parcel of land in Naples, Florida, where he planned to build a home for Dessie and himself nearer to his retirement. That was years away because he was still active in business, sharing a partnership in the prosperous and upscale Olympia Restaurant on Halsted Street with a good friend, Cleon Frangakis. Despite the problems many downtown Chicago restaurants were experiencing, business on Halsted Street (thanks to a solid customer base of students from the nearby University of Illinois Circle Campus and medical personnel from Rush–St. Luke's hospital) was good.

Meanwhile, the world in which he lived was several months away from the much-heralded millennium. That impending transition had spawned a myriad of plans for extravagant year-end parties, as well as inciting the warnings of zealots who predicted the wicked world's collapse as the century ended. There was also a concern about something called Y2K. As far as his comprehension of the dangers that entailed, at its worst, Y2K would bring about the collapse of the infrastructure of society.

Orestes hoped their predictions would prove baseless, but meanwhile, life around him had become immensely more complicated and intrusive. Nowhere was this more clearly evidenced than in the proliferation of cell phones. It was impossible to ignore them. (He had one himself.) But where there had once remained certain sanctuaries of silence, now the buzzes and rings of the ubiquitous cell phones were everywhere, as was caller ID, call-waiting, take-this-call or don't take-this-call.

Then there were the computers. Under the prodding of Paulie and Marika, who were computer literate, Orestes had finally given in and bought a Gateway PC. But even as he gained a particle of competence in its use, he remained terrified at the way the squat box with the large Cyclopean eye could swallow a letter the way a shark snatched a morsel of prey. Nor could he comprehend the ominous messages that snapped up on his monitor, such as the one that read, THE SYSTEM HAS PERFORMED AN ILLEGAL OPERATION AND WILL BE SHUT DOWN. For the life of him, he hadn't the slightest idea what he had done that was illegal.

Of course the greatest threat mankind would carry into the millennium remained the nuclear bomb that might destroy a considerable portion of the world's population and leave the rest to die slowly in a polluted environment. Any number of countries had the bomb or were developing a nuclear capability. Yet, if a man spent time brooding about the somber prospect of a world held hostage by such dreadful weapons, he'd never muster the will to do any more than lie in bed all day and moan.

Whatever the millennium brought for mankind, Orestes felt a trembling wonder that he had lived to witness a new century. (Of course, there were still a few months he had to get through alive.) He had survived to this point, but the chronology of the half-century mark was merciless. He couldn't help feeling that fifty was a clarion call to get ready for what no one could ever be ready for.

On his way to his room to dress, Orestes listened for a moment outside Stavroula's room. Because his mother-in-law watched Tom Selleck movies at night, she slept later in the morning, sparing him her presence to sour the beginning of his day. He was always careful not to wake her, and when he heard the old lady's sibilant snores, Orestes moved on to his daughter's bedroom to wake her for school.

As he entered the shadowed room, he inhaled the scents of efflorescent youth. Marika slept awkwardly in bed, her body partially concealed under the sheet except for one bare leg visible to the knee. He had a sudden poignant recollection of his daughter as a child, sleeping tangled within her blankets, her face angelic and serene.

Now it was clearly evident that she was no longer a child, the smooth and perfect symmetry of her naked leg emanating an erotic aura. His young daughter was in that awesome transition between girlhood and womanhood, her breasts budding, her thighs curving. He felt he was conscious of those changes not in any prurient way, but because he knew they signified her sexual awakening. He also understood it meant he would have to be more vigilant about those testosterone-glutted despoilers who sought to pursue (and deflower) her. (Sometimes he feared she might be already deflowered.)

Yet his innocent and paternal attitude did not apply to the attractive young girlfriends Marika brought home. Orestes caught glimpses of them lounging on the floor or on the bed in her room, skirts tossed recklessly about their glistening thighs. What was there about teenaged girls that raised a man's blood pressure? The Lolita complex? A child's face on a woman's body. That hint of still unsoiled virginity? (That also was dangerous ground to tread upon.)

When he gently shook Marika's shoulder, she stirred and whimpered a plea for mercy.

"Come on, honey," he said. "Time to get up. You've already been late three days this week."

He waited in the doorway for a sign of movement in the bed.

"Honey, you hear me? Don't go back to sleep now."

Marika raised one slim-fingered, limp hand in a drowsy assent.

After he'd dressed, Orestes walked downstairs to the kitchen and made coffee. By the time he had squeezed oranges for juice and divided the assorted vitamin tablets for his wife and himself, Dessie entered the kitchen in her white terry cloth robe. She came to the table and bent to give him a warm, gentle kiss.

"Happy birthday, my darling."

"I know I'll be reminded of my age many times today."

"Don't be like George," Dessie said, referring to George Darlas, a close friend about his own age. "Mention his birthday and he sulks for days. You're alert, vigorous, with a loving wife, loving children, and a loving grandchild. That makes you very fortunate." She paused. "Did you wake Marika?"

"I did."

"Maybe I better call her again."

"Give her another minute!"

"You'd rather let Marika sleep longer so she won't wake Mama until you leave," she said with a wry smile.

"Let the beloved old diamond get her rest," Orestes said genially. "They say sleep improves one's disposition."

"Mama needs more than sleep for that," Dessie smiled. She returned to the table. "Marika shouldn't be late for school again. That would be the second time this week."

"The third time," Orestes said. "She's getting to bed too late."

"She's only been back in school a week," Dessie said. "After summer vacation it takes time to return to a regular schedule. Besides, girls her age are too excited about life to sleep."

"It might simply be the prospect of a sale at Lord and Taylor that keeps her too excited to sleep," Orestes said, and they both laughed.

They ate a light breakfast of English muffins, cheese, and coffee. Orestes read the *Chicago Tribune* while Dessie watched the morning news on the small screen TV above the refrigerator. She kept the volume low because she knew he preferred to read.

But the same gloomy news prevailed in both mediums. Continued harping by his Republican critics about President Clinton's infidelities. In a more serious vein, there was the murder of ethnic Albanians in Kosovo, and the flight of more than a million refugees including women and children into Albania and Montenegro. Another suicide bombing on a bus in Israel with six people dead and almost a dozen Palestinians killed in the Israeli response. The Iraqi dictator, Saddam Hussein, still rejecting the return of U.N. inspectors. Finally, there was the terrible aftermath of the earthquake in Turkey that had killed forty thousand people. (The month before, Orestes had co-chaired a benefit for Turkish earthquake relief.)

Within their own city, the night had produced several robberies, a car belonging to a prominent minister stolen, a restaurant torched in Old Town, a rape in the Lincoln Park neighborhood.

Reading about these events depressed Orestes and made him feel helpless because he could do nothing about them. He thought, sometimes, that his son, Paulie, was right when he suggested starting one's day by avoiding the news in favor of meditation.

On this morning of his birthday, under the pretext of reading his paper, he studied Dessie, who was intent on the *Good Morning America* program, appraising her as he had earlier evaluated himself.

Four years younger than he was, Dessie had added a little weight but still remained slender and attractive. She had been, as he was, fortunate in having good health. She walked diligently in good weather and exercised vigorously on a stationary bike in their basement when the weather was inclement. Dessie was also scrupulous about their diet.

Despite those inevitable alterations the years had wrought, his wife was still a beautiful woman. Her thick long hair, which had once been raven-black, now revealed only a few vagrant strands of gray. Beneath her large, luminous dark eyes, a web of tiny wrinkles pinched at her flesh. There were times it seemed to him she looked her forty-six years, but when she smiled or laughed, he recaptured glimpses of the lovely, buoyant young girl she had been at twenty.

Orestes still found his wife's nakedness erotic and desirable. She'd had small breasts when they married, and it took a while for him to convince her that he couldn't abide those bulbous-breasted women that filled the pages of *Playboy* and *Penthouse*. Now, the bearing of children had filled out her breasts slightly, and he still found them lovely. Yet in spite of his desire and her own apparent responsiveness, sometimes weeks passed without their finding a chance to make love. He had been reduced to relieving himself as he had done when he was a quivering teenager. Helping him in his periodic need for sexual release were the plethora of sex sites he had discovered some years earlier while surfing the Internet on the computer in the privacy of his office at the restaurant. Heterosexual and homosexual inter-course, sadomasochism, virgins, mature women, transvestism, anal sex, necrophilia, scatophilia, all the bewildering deviations he had read about as a youth in Kraft-Ebbing's *Psychopathia Sexualis*, had numerous Websites in vivid, living color. They catered to every conceivable fetish, including his own fantasies, which involved black garter belts and black silk stockings as well as some playful bondage and spanking. He suspected (and feared) a man could become as addicted to sex on the Internet as he might become enslaved to alcohol, gambling, and drugs.

In the first years of their marriage, he had revealed his sexual fantasies to Dessie, who had indulged him. He still had care-fully hidden some fading Polaroid photos of Dessie in high heels, black garter belt, and black silk stockings.

The unhappy reality was that they had not played those erotic games in at least a dozen years. He still yearned for that sex play, but Dessie had become self-conscious about her body and was reluctant to play out his fantasies. He under-stood her concerns and tried to reassure her that he still found her beautiful.

Dessie noticed him staring at her.

"What are you looking at?"

"The beautiful woman who is my wife," Orestes said ear-nestly. "The woman I love dearly and still desire."

"Isn't it a little early in the morning for that stuff?" Marika asked as she moved sleepily into the kitchen. She wore skin-tight peach-colored slacks, sneakers, and a shapeless yellow vest with fringes on the pockets. Her dark hair was cut short, and she had her mother's lovely, dark eyes and small, shapely ears.

"Do you always have to dress like a refugee from a rummage sale?" Orestes asked.

"Don't be old fashioned, daddy," Marika said. "All the kids dress like this."

"You mean all of them favor tight slacks with torn flaps on their behinds?"

"These are Calvin Kleins, daddy," Marika said. "I bought them at Bloomingdale's."

"Have you ever considered shopping at J. C. Penney? I've seen the clothes in their catalogues, and they seem fine to me."

Marika arched her eyebrows as if the absurdity of his remark didn't warrant a response. Then she crossed the kitchen to give him a hug.

"Happy birthday, daddy!" she said earnestly. "Even if you are old fashioned, I love you very much, and I want you to celebrate many, many more birthdays! A hundred, at least."

"If I'm still hanging on at seventy-five, you'll be begging for mercy."

"Don't forget your father's birthday party this evening," Dessie said. "Paulie and Carmela will be coming, and Mario and Theresa."

"Can I bring Lenny?"

"Is he the skinhead with the pirate rings in his ears?" Orestes asked.

"That was Billy Bob. He and I broke up weeks ago," Marika said. "Lenny is a wonderful new friend I met just last week. Wait till you meet him."

Orestes suddenly heard a clatter from the top of the stairs that indicated Stavroula was descending. He rose quickly to leave. "I'm not going into the restaurant until later today," he told Dessie. "I think I'll stop at the cemetery for a while."

"Do you want me to come with you?"

"You don't have to," Orestes said. "I'll just stop for a few minutes." He smiled to reassure her. "After all, without my parents I wouldn't be here to celebrate fifty."

"Don't let the cemetery depress you for the rest of the day," Dessie said, a soft note of warning in her voice.

He kissed her good-bye and hugged his daughter. She smiled up at him. "Wait until you see the wonderful present I bought you, daddy."

"I hope its something from Ralph or Calvin," he teased her and left.

Two

As Orestes walked from the house to the garage, the early September air retained the moistness of summer with clusters of hibiscus and dahlias still in bloom. The only intimations of autumn were a few yellow leaves on the poplar in their yard.

As he drove from the shadows of the garage into the light, he noticed the tiny liver spots of aging on the backs of his hands gripping the wheel. He couldn't believe they had appeared overnight, but he hadn't noticed them before. He felt a tremor of apprehension.

"Snap out of it, boofo!" he said loudly, using the derogatory epithet his father had often used against him. "You're just fifty, not a hundred!"

He drove north on Seeley Avenue through the Beverly neighborhood, passing the spacious houses and sloping lawns on Longwood Drive. He couldn't shake off the nagging unrest he had felt upon rising. He had read somewhere that in the journey of one's life, midpoint could become a time of crisis. He was suddenly afraid that Dessie was right and that visiting the graves of his parents would depress him for the remainder of the day. He didn't want to dampen the festivities planned for his birthday party that evening.

As a precaution, he decided to stop briefly in the neighborhood library. He used his cell phone to call the Olympia and left word for his partner, Cleon, that he wouldn't be in until later in the morning.

At Longwood Drive and Ninety-fifth Street, he turned west to the library. He parked in the lot and walked into the old stone building he had frequented so many times. Mrs. Kohn, the gray-haired, gentle-voiced librarian, greeted him.

"Good morning, Mr. Panos," she smiled.

"Good morning, Mrs. Kohn."

"You're not usually here this early."

"I'm just stealing a little time away from work."

"Good for you," she nodded in approval.

That time of morning the library was quiet, its only occupants several old men reading newspapers, or dozing in the armchairs. Orestes walked slowly along the shelves, immersing himself in the beguiling aura of books. As he turned a corner, he noticed a girl in an armchair bent over a book.

The most striking thing about her was the blondness of her hair made even brighter by the morning sun streaming through the window across her bent head. The thick, golden waves looped in back and fastened in a glittering pearl comb cascaded in a silky mane down across her shoulders.

Orestes moved away, and, as he drew down a book from the shelf, an image of the girl returned to him. He felt a curious impulse to see her again. He walked casually toward the alcove where she'd been sitting, but she was gone. He sighed and returned to his browsing.

From boyhood he had loved libraries and the multitude of books they contained. He recalled his awe before the sheer number of volumes, amazed that so much had been written during the preceding centuries. When he was much younger, he recalled a librarian telling him the books contained the collective wisdom of the past.

At one time in his youth, he had thought about writing himself, and somewhere, shuffled in among boxes of old magazines and correspondence, was a slim packet of poems and a couple of stories he had written. But the task of putting words coherently on paper proved too arduous, and he gave up any effort to write.

Yet he still loved the sight and feel and yes, particularly, the smell of books. Not old books that had been handled by many hands but new books, their jackets bright, the fresh paper and ink emanating a fragrance hard to describe but palpably pleasurable.

He browsed in the fiction areas, found the work of Nikos Kazantzakis, and took down *Zorba the Greek*. Sitting in one of the armchairs, he began to reread the opening chapter. As much as he loved the work of Kazantzakis, the melancholy introspection he had begun upon rising made it difficult for him to concentrate, and his thoughts wandered over the terrain of his life.

His love of books had been nurtured during a two-year period of illness that began when he was eleven. Prior to his visiting the doctor, he had been listless for months, his appetite diminished, his energy curtailed. His mother finally took him to their family physician, Dr. Ioannides. A set of chest x-rays revealed lesions on Orestes' lungs that the doctor diagnosed as tuberculosis. In those days before medications were discovered for that disease, the prescribed therapy was rest, and the doctor ordered Orestes to bed for a month. That was followed by another month, and those months grew to become a year, and the year became two years.

In the beginning, Orestes exulted in his good fortune at escaping school, lounging lazily beneath the sheets, his solicitous mother bringing him food on a tray, pleading with him to eat.

During this period of his illness, he rarely saw his father, who worked long hours at the restaurant. On those infrequent occasions when Moustakas was home, he would come to stand briefly in the doorway of the room. Orestes believed his father feared being infected by his illness because he never lingered in the room, never approached his bed or touched him. He'd stand staring at his son for a few moments in silence.

"You eat your food, you hear?" his father might say.

"I will, papa."

His father continued staring somberly at him and then turned and left the doorway.

As the weeks wore on, Orestes' initial exhilaration at loafing in bed all day became boredom and frustration. His father had been adamant against allowing a television set in their house, but, defying him for the only time Orestes could remember, his mother bought a small, used black-and-white set from a neighbor that she placed in Orestes' bedroom. As a precaution against his father's anger, he only watched it during the day when Moustakas wasn't home.

But the cooking programs and soap operas held no appeal for Orestes. His salvation rested in books. At first he read his school books, which classmates brought him, and then he read the books brought to him by friends of his parents. A cousin of his mother who taught high school in the city brought Orestes a twenty-volume set of the *The Book of Knowledge*, which he read from the first volume to the last.

Orestes loved the stories of adventure most of all. *The Count of Monte Cristo, White Fang, Captain Blood, The Call of the Wild* he read with growing delight, at the same time assembling a vast array of diverse information regarding myths, geography, history. His mind became a sea into which flowed the fertile rivers of hundreds of books.

Near the end of his first year of illness, his condition became critical. On several occasions his coughing brought up particles of blood. One night he heard Dr. Ioannides in the adjoining room telling his parents that it might be necessary to send him to a "sanatorium." Orestes had never heard the multisyllabled word before, and it suggested something dreadful, much like the labyrinth of the monster, the Minotaur, he had read about in the books on Greek myth. Despite his mother's assurances that he wouldn't be sent away, he fought going to sleep, terrified that while he was unconscious he'd be transported to the dreaded "sanatorium" to die.

Each night for weeks, his weary mother sat beside his bed until he fell asleep. Even after sleeping, his nights were lashed by terrifying dreams of demons and dying. When he sometimes woke screaming, only his mother came to reassure him.

His condition slowly improved, the passing of time dispelling some of his fears about dying. His mother, who helped his father in the restaurant by cooking some of the entrees on the menu, returned to work part of the day in the restaurant kitchen. In her absence, a variety of caretakers were brought in to look after Orestes. These included several stern, somber-cheeked old women who smelled of stale coffee grounds and spoiled fruit. There were also two girls, each one no more than seventeen or eighteen years of age, conscripted from an orphanage where they had been confined since childhood. Orestes had long since forgotten their last names and remembered them only as Olga and Mary.

Olga came first, in the spring of the year. She was a stocky, robust-armed Russian girl who walked with a limp because one leg was an inch shorter than the other. A large, discolored birthmark stained one side of her throat. She had a habit of rubbing her fingers roughly against the mark, as if trying to scrape it away.

Olga was a powerful girl whose strength, at first, frightened and then fascinated Orestes. When she changed the linen on his bed, he'd sit in an armchair and marvel how easily she lifted and flipped the mattress. He was especially intrigued by her big ugly hands with stubby, broken nails that she chewed down to her fingers.

From time to time, Olga would light a cigarette that she smoked near an open window, brushing vigorously with her hand to disperse the smoke.

"You don't say nothing to your father or mother now, you hear?"

He would nod that he understood.

"If you do talk, you know what I'll do to you?"

He nodded once again, feeling an excited tightness in his belly.

She chuckled, winked, raised one broad, ugly palm.

"You'll get this," she said slowly, relishing the effect she was having on him. "You'll get it you know where . . ."

"I know," he said and released his pent-up breath.

She bullied him and teased him, never with any cruelty but in a playful demonstration of her dominance. She'd lift him from the bed in her strong arms, and he'd see the glaring birthmark on her throat and the small hairy moles on her cheeks. On one occasion when she was putting him back in bed, she gave him a light teasing smack on the seat of his thin pajama trousers.

He encouraged her disapproval, relishing her mastery and control over him. She began threatening him with spankings if he "wasn't a good boy." With a mixture of excitement and fear, he went out of his way to disobey her. She obliged by spanking him, first on his pajamas and, finally, on his bare buttocks. The light spankings seemed to fulfill a strain of dominance in her own nature and also satisfied a submissiveness in him. In the grip of her excitement, he smelled the sour stench of her sweat and saw her glowing eyes. The spankings also evoked erotic feelings in him he had never experienced before.

Then, one morning at the beginning of autumn, Olga was gone, replaced by Mary, a plump, sweet-faced girl who smelled of lavender. There was nothing strong or assertive about Mary, who was feminine and soft and evoked in Orestes different feelings than those he'd felt with Olga. He became conscious of the soft sheen of Mary's skin, the mounds of her breasts with their nipples visible against her blouse, and the tantalizing glimpses he caught of her bare thighs when she bent to make his bed.

As they became more familiar with one another, he couldn't resist reaching out and touching her, caressing her hair and stroking her arms. She asked him if he liked touching her, and he told her yes.

"Do you think I'm pretty?" she asked.

"Yes."

"Do you think I have nice skin?"

"Yes."

"Do you like my eyes?"

"Yes . . ."

"Do you like my . . ." she left the word unfinished, but one of her slender hands fumbled to touch her breast.

"Yes!" he said fervently. "Yes . . . yes."

His caresses became more intimate, and, when she didn't object, excitement made him bolder. Sometimes she lay in bed beside him, let him touch her breasts and press his lips lightly on her mouth. She guided him gently into the first kisses he had ever known.

Their games grew more brazen, and there were times during the day when they were alone that Mary stripped to her slip. After a while she peeled off that garment, as well. Wearing only drab cloth panties and brassiere, she snuggled into bed beside him.

She talked to him sweetly, her scents making him dizzy. She stroked him and encouraged him to caress her. Mary's breasts were the first he had ever seen naked, and he marveled at their symmetry and at their resilience, the way her nipples sprang back against his awkward, groping fingers after he'd pressed them in. When she fondled his genitals, her touch light as a bird's wing, he felt a tingling and surges of heat all through his body.

Then Mary was gone, as well, replaced by a prune-faced old woman appropriately named Barboonis, sexless and humorless, who made his room appear darker no matter what the time of day. From that period until his recovery and beyond, he thought with great longing and excitement of the two girls.

In later years, he came to understand how those dualities of his confinement, books and the sexuality of the girls, had blended. Perhaps that was the reason he was drawn so strongly to libraries.

Lost in the recesses of memory, the book he had been reading slipped down to his side. He became aware of the faint noises of the library around him, an old man clearing his throat, Mrs. Kohn at the reference desk responding on the phone to some query. As reluctant as he was to leave the warm sanctuary of the library, he knew he had to go. He checked out *Zorba the Greek*, and, as he left the library, he girded himself for the visit to the graves of his dead parents.

Driving east on Eighty-seventh Street to Kedzie, he passed between the iron gates of the Evergreen Cemetery, and the sign that read, HOURS: 8 A.M. TO 8 P.M. He stopped in the cemetery greenhouse and bought a bouquet of fresh flowers.

He drove into the Greek section of the cemetery, passing the graves on the slopes that grew more crowded year after year. The stones and markers bore the names of families he had known, CAPPAS, CHRISSIS, LAMBESIS, STAMOS. The graves held the parents of boys and girls who were his classmates in the parochial school.

Near his family's gravesite, he passed a mound of fresh wreaths and garlands that marked a new grave. He wondered if he knew the person who had died. He parked, finally, on the road beside the large, brown, granite cross that bore his family's name of PANOS.

At that midday hour, the cemetery was silent and deserted, a light wind fluttering the neatly trimmed shrubs and patches of flowers decorating the graves. A solitary oak tree whose thick branches shaded a score of graves rustled its foliage.

Three of the six graves in his family plot were occupied. One belonged to his father, Moustakas, one to his mother, Kanella, and one to Manolis, the brother born before him, who had died of meningitis at the age of four. Orestes felt sure his mother's lifetime sadness resulted from the early death of her first child. Perhaps his father's relentless cruelty and anger stemmed from the child's early death, as well. Each time Moustakas looked at Orestes, he must have been reminded of the son he had lost.

Orestes thought often of the brother he had never known. If he had been allowed to live and grow into adulthood, Orestes might have been able to turn to him for counsel. His brother might also have become Orestes' ally against the harshness of his father.

Orestes spread the flowers, placing a few petals on each of the graves. His family gravestone had once held two small cameo photos of his father and mother, but they had been defaced by vandals with air guns. He had replaced the small photos several times, but each time the vandals destroyed them again. When Orestes complained to the cemetery management, they told him apologetically they couldn't possibly patrol the vast acreage of the cemetery. He finally stopped replacing the photographs.

Now, standing above the graves, Orestes recalled his mother's patient, impassive face. A melancholy, resigned woman, she had died in 1993 at the age of eighty-two, as quietly and uncomplaining as she had lived, slipping seamlessly from pneumonia into death in the space of a weekend.

His father's dying in 1997, at the age of eighty-eight, had been a savage battle pitting Moustakas against the forces of death. In the hospital in his last weeks of life, the old man not only berated his son but spit at the doctors and nurses who attended him. When his raging heart finally succumbed to the assorted liver and heart ailments that killed him, Orestes knew every nurse, orderly, and doctor on the floor breathed a sigh of relief.

Orestes made the arrangements for both his mother and father's funerals, picked out their caskets, arranged for the vaults and the opening of the graves.

Remembering how his parents looked in their open coffins, his mother's stillness seemed compatible with her passive nature. For the first time he could ever remember, she appeared finally at peace. His father was a different story. For all the efforts of the undertaker, a tranquility couldn't be fashioned on Moustakas's face. Even in death, there seemed a grimace on his cheeks, a snarl around his mouth. A family friend passing his coffin remarked, in an awed voice, "My God, he still looks angry!"

It was true that even in death his father radiated the same fury and harshness that had characterized his life. He had been boorish, brutally outspoken, saying what he wished, doing what he wanted, his voice mocking or bellowing, lashing and intimidating the waitresses, busboys, and cooks in his restaurant. Behind his back they referred to him as "Moustakas, the beast!"

Everyone around him was subjected to his anger or to his insatiable appetite. He ate and drank voraciously and pursued the waitresses in his restaurant with relentless lust. Many rebuffed him, and, soon afterwards, he found a pretext to fire them. The exceptions were the older, experienced waitresses his partners would not allow him to discharge.

Orestes first learned of his father's sexual infidelities when he was fourteen, the year following his recovery from his illness. After attending a basketball game at school one evening, he had stopped by the restaurant to go home with his father. The cook who had since died was cleaning his grill and, with what Orestes later recalled was a malicious glint in his eyes, told him his father was in the storeroom. When Orestes opened the door, he saw his father, pants crumpled around his ankles, crouched between the naked, thrashing legs of one of the waitresses.

For an instant Orestes stood frozen, as much anguished at what his father felt about being caught, as at his own shock. Then his father snarled, "What are you looking at, boofo? Go and wipe your snots!"

Orestes closed the door and stumbled out of the kitchen, the memory of his father crouched between the naked thighs of the waitress searing his heart all the way home.

His father never mentioned the episode, never asked him not to say anything to his mother. Orestes felt his father wouldn't have cared if he had told her. But even as he remained silent, carrying the burden of that revelation with him all through the years he attended high school, he suspected his mother knew of his father's infidelities.

There were other waitresses his father pursued beside the one Orestes had seen him crouched over in the storeroom. Young ones and older ones, fair-haired and dark-haired, skinny and plump, bold and shy. Moustakas played no favorites but graced all with his ubiquitous cock.

All through Orestes' childhood and into adolescence, the image of his father's great cock and massive dangling testicles he had first seen in the bathroom when he was a child, seemed those of a giant, far out of proportion to his bony, lean-fleshed frame. Orestes imagined the cock in full erection, a battering ram invading the loins of the waitresses and unloading in them a flood of rancid semen.

As a boy, there were nights Orestes sat in the locked bathroom, studying his own genitals, despairing at their inadequate size beside those of his father, hoping and praying they would grow as the rest of his body grew.

The shadow of his father's proportions lingered over him through his first sexual explorations so that he feared girls would reject him because his organ was inadequate. But the few girls with whom he had sex seemed satisfied, and that was also true of Dessie after they married.

Nothing more fittingly exemplified the retribution fate exacted on his dying father than the withering and shrinking of his genitals. In the hospital, in his father's last weeks of life, when Orestes had to wash him and change the diapers he wore for incontinence, he saw his father's huge genitals had become a dried, rotting clump, his cock a small and wrinkled turnip, his testicles a pair of withered olives eroded and drained by a lifetime of copulation.

A bird flew overhead, trailing its throaty cry across the cemetery. At times in the past when Orestes visited the graves, he had felt driven to curse and rebuke his father.

"Goddam you, Moustakas," he'd cry in the silence and solitude of the cemetery. "Goddam you for the things you did and goddam you for the things you should have done. I hope you're burning in hell for eternity!"

That day of his birthday, he felt only a melancholy, an awareness that each passing year brought him closer to the time when he'd take his place in one of the graves beside his father. They'd have eternity to settle their quarrels then.

"Let bygones be bygones, pa," Orestes said. "It's my birthday. Today I'm fifty. I thought you might want to wish me 'happy birthday.'"

He saw the flowers flutter above his mother's grave and could almost hear her sad, quiet voice saying, "Happy birthday, my son." But he waited in vain for any sign that his father might have heard him or that he even cared.

After Orestes received his bachelor's degree from Roosevelt University in downtown Chicago, he told his father he wanted to work in the restaurant full time. He had worked there as a busboy after school and as a waiter during the summers, but his father vehemently objected to Orestes' making the restaurant his life's work.

"What the hell you want to spend your time in here for?" his father cried. "I don't need you! Why don't you go be somebody, maybe a doctor or a lawyer! Not another hamali, a Turkish beast of burden!"

"You've been in the restaurant all your life," Orestes fought back. "It was good enough for you!"

"Because I was ignorant!" his father stormed. "Because I was barely able to read and write! I never had the chances you got! I paid for your goddam education, so you could make something of yourself!"

What tormented Orestes most was the way his father used his dead brother to attack him.

"Why couldn't your brother have lived!" his father cried. "He would have made something of himself, made me proud! He wouldn't have shit up my life the way you do! He wouldn't have been a lazy, worthless boofo like you!"

Now, years after his father hurled those words at him, Orestes still felt their sting and bite.

"I wasn't lazy or a boofo, pa," Orestes said. "I worked as hard and even harder than you. After you were gone, I made the restaurant more successful and more profitable than it had ever been. Then I bought a bigger place that I turned into one of the finest establishments on Halsted Street. And I did all this without tongue-lashing the busboys, abusing the cooks, or fucking the waitresses."

But as it had been when his father was alive, Orestes knew

he could never convince the old man of anything he didn't want to believe.

He turned slowly to leave and paused.

"You never listened to me before, pa," he said slowly. "So why the hell should I expect you'll listen to me now that I'm fifty? I never became a doctor or a lawyer because I had no confidence that I could do anything else besides work in the restaurant. All the years of your cruelty and your mockery cut out part of my heart and maybe my balls, as well. By the time I could pull together any courage or confidence, it was too late for me to change." He paused and shook his head. "You never understood that, pa, you never understood something as simple as that."

The cemetery remained silent, the gravestones unmoving, the flowers fluttering in the wind.

Among the throngs of the dead in the graves about them, there may have been fathers who believed his words and who understood his grievance. But Moustakas Panos was not one of them. As Orestes started for his car, he thought he heard the mocking laughter of his father spiral into the summer sky above his head.

Three

ACH TIME Orestes entered the Olympia Restaurant, he was hurled into smells and sounds that melded America and Greece. Depending on the time of day, the restaurant was lively over lunch, quiet through mid-afternoon, the tempo of activity intensifying to a peak of hustle and clamor through the evening. On Friday and Saturday nights, the line of people waiting for tables would stretch out to Halsted Street while cheerful young waiters poured the patrons small tumblers of ouzo as a consolation for the delay.

During the crowded, boisterous evenings, the atmosphere in the Olympia would be singed with the cheese and brandy scents of saganaki, the garlic aromas of roast lamb, the pungency of assorted brandies and wines.

Joined to the smells were the treble tones of women, the deeper, hoarser voices of men, the shrill bursts of laughter, the buoyant calls of waiters placing orders, the harsh responses of cooks. Meanwhile, loudspeakers throughout the restaurant emitted the ebullient strains of Greek music.

All of this ambience was so familiar to Orestes that he could graphically recapture it no matter where he was. Even when he was away from the restaurant, the smells and sounds lingered in his nose and ears.

His partner, Cleon Frangakis, standing at the register caught sight of him.

"Because it's your birthday," Cleon called with mock sternness, "you think you can just take the day off?"

"I wanted you to see how much you need me," Orestes laughed. "How was lunch?"

"The main room was half full including the thirty ladies from the Philoptochos Society." Cleon turned to service a waiter bringing him a check and a credit card. "They asked about you and I told them you had run off with the bearded lady in the circus."

Cleon was a stocky, swarthy man in his sixties who'd worked in restaurants all his life. He'd been managing another restaurant on Halsted Street when Orestes hired him. Cleon quickly became a diligent employee as well as a loyal friend. Realizing that he would be an even greater asset as a partner, Orestes worked out a generous arrangement allowing Cleon to acquire part ownership in the Olympia. The association had greatly benefited both of them.

Cleon finished the credit transaction and then hurried around the register to clasp Orestes in a great bear hug.

"Happy birthday, partner and friend!" he said earnestly. "Today I wish you the love and best wishes I'd wish my own brother."

"Thank you, partner and friend."

In the hours that followed, Orestes accepted birthday greetings from waiters and busboys, from dishwashers and cooks, from vendors delivering produce, from a few customers, and, finally, from other merchants on the street. Sophie Kalamas hurried in from the Hellenic Bakery with a freshly baked tray of baklava, and Jim Spirou came from the Salonika Candle Shop with a small icon of his patron saint.

"My God," Orestes exclaimed to Cleon after several additional well-wishers had gone. "Does everyone in the city have to know I'm turning fifty today?"

"That isn't all!" Cleon spoke with the delight of a child revealing a secret. "I haven't told you yet that our distinguished county treasurer, Maria Pappas, phoned her best wishes and so did Christos Panagis, you know he's one of the aides to Mayor Daley. He's trying to get the mayor's office to issue a proclamation making this 'Orestes Panos Day in Chicago.'"

"You're all crazy," Orestes sighed. "I should have taken the rest of the day off and driven to one of the riverboat casinos."

In the next few hours Orestes reviewed the evening's menu with Kyriakos, the master chef, and called the Hellenic Packing Company about an overdue shipment of steaks. He mediated a complaint between a pair of young waiters. He spent an hour with a liquor salesman replenishing the Olympia's extensive supply of wines. In all these contacts, while he remained resolute about what he wished done, he remembered his father's harshness towards employees and associates, and his demeanor was quiet-spoken and courteous.

Later in the afternoon, a few old friends who were also regular patrons drifted in. They gathered at the large round table Cleon set aside for them in a quiet corner of the restaurant.

"Happy birthday, Orestes," George Lalounis said. He was a handsome, neatly dressed man in his early forties, who owned the Crown Realty Company. ("Buy a Crown home and live like a King.") He handed Orestes a small wrapped gift.

"A small token of friendship," he said.

"The keys to the kingdom?" Orestes smiled.

"Happy birthday, my friend," the greeting came from Nikos Karvelas, a tall, sixtyish undertaker who owned the Santorini Funeral Home. He shook Orestes' hand firmly. "I too have brought you a modest present."

"Probably a certificate allowing Orestes ten percent discount on his funeral expenses," Dr. Solon Savas, a white-haired general practitioner in his late seventies who had just walked up, laughed.

"To joke about death and funerals is callous and boorish," Karvelas scowled. "And coming from a man whose medical blunders probably dispatched scores before their time is an added blasphemy."

"If that's the way you feel," Dr. Savas sneered, "I'll be happy to give you back the diseased gall bladder I removed last year from your worthless carcass!"

"Stop this bickering!" Cleon cried brusquely as he carried several bottles of wine to the table. "Today is Orestes' birthday, and we should offer him our good humor and good cheer. If you can't do that, then go eat those abominable burgers they serve under the golden arches!"

"I'll wish Orestes well, but why should we have to be cheerful and good humored about his birthday?" Ted Banopoulos, lean-framed and acerbic-tongued, approached the table. He was a notary public, as well as editor of a small neighborhood newspaper, the *Hellenic Daily*. "His birthday means all of us become a year older. Should I be cheerful about that?"

Professor Achilles Platon joined the group in time to overhear the editor's question. He was a heavyset, florid-faced man, a former high school teacher, who delivered every utterance in the sonorous voice and rhetorical style of a commencement speaker. He waved a stern finger at Banopoulos.

"Our revered ancestor Socrates said that a man who has lived a worthwhile life doesn't need to fear age."

"Never mind the ramblings of Socrates," Dr. Savas responded grimly. "As the dinosaur in this herd, I can tell you old age is an irreparable disaster."

The last person to join the group was Father Anton Stephanos, the young, unmarried assistant priest from St. Sophia's Orthodox Church. He was a pale-cheeked, slightly built man in his early thirties, who seemed at times to be wearing the clerical collar circling his throat as if it were a noose. A few of the men attributed his chronic nervousness to his being unmarried and without any sexual release. Others felt it the result of the young priest being harassed by his superior, Father Elias Botsakis, and, on numerous occasions, harshly criticized by the church's parish council.

The most rabid of Father Anton's critics was Sam Tzangaris, a pasty-faced, mean-spirited owner of a meat packing company, who ruled the parish council of St. Sophia's church like a despot. His persistent, acrimonious criticism of the young priest, abetted by other parish board members intimidated by Tzangaris, were among the reasons Orestes had resigned from the council. For three years, he had fought Tzangaris on numerous church issues until, finally, the man's unending reserve of sheer malice wore him out.

Tzangaris not only criticized the young priest in the privacy of parish council meetings but in the open church, as well. Just the previous Sunday, Orestes had heard him denouncing Father Anton to a small group of parishioners in the nave of the church.

"I think he's lazy," Tzangaris said harshly. "He should have had all the advertisers for the Memorial Album committed to buy their ads by now."

Orestes couldn't resist speaking up in the priest's defense.

"Father Anton is a priest whose purpose here is to serve our spiritual needs," Orestes said. "He's not an advertising salesman."

"How fortunate Father Anton is to have you as his champion, Orestes," Tzangaris sneered. "Perhaps you can explain to us what he does to earn the wages we pay him?"

"I wouldn't boast too loudly about his wages," Orestes snapped, "since they are barely enough to allow a man to live on decently."

Dessie, standing beside Orestes, tugged urgently at his arm. As he turned away, he heard Tzangaris say something in a low, caustic voice that caused those standing around him to laugh.

Whatever problems he might have had with the council, Father Anton was well liked by the group in the Olympia, and they greeted him warmly.

"Welcome, young Father Anton," Professor Platon said. "Your presence brings some badly needed spiritual balance to this rag-tail assembly."

Father Anton smiled gratefully.

"I'm honored to spend time with this distinguished group," he said a little shyly.

"Be careful, Father!" Dr. Savas said. "You're giving these pontificating elders another dose of vitamin P, the deadliest of the vitamins."

"I've never heard of vitamin P," Karvelas said.

"P for praise . . ." Dr. Savas smirked.

The young priest spoke to Orestes.

"Father Elias asked me to extend his best wishes on your birthday, Orestes," Father Anton said. "Of course, I offer you my warm best wishes, as well. Father Elias would have come himself but he had a meeting with his grace at the diocese."

"I'd like to eavesdrop on what they talk about," Banopoulos said. "Put two monks together and they can hatch more schemes to bleed money out of people than a bunco artist."

Father Anton stared at Banopoulos in dismay.

"Please thank Father Elias for me," Orestes said to the priest. "Now sit down, Father, and join us for an appetizer and a glass of wine. Cleon has foraged in our cellar and brought up some wonderful wine from Samos."

"I'm afraid I can't stay," Father Anton said with regret. "Father Elias told me to be sure to stop only long enough to extend his best wishes and then go on to make an urgent sick call. One of our parishioners, Mrs. Placouras, called for communion to be given to her husband, Andreas. The poor man is dying."

"That grizzled old goat has been on his death bed for years," Dr. Savas scoffed. "Another hour won't make any difference. Sit down, Father, and join us for a glass of wine and some sparkling dialogue you're not likely to hear in church."

Father Anton wavered. "Father Elias won't be pleased if I delay answering a call for communion." He sighed. "To tell the truth, I'm not exactly in his good graces just now."

"I'll tell him you were soliciting a larger Christmas offering from me," Orestes smiled. "And to confirm it, this Christmas, I'll make my pledge much larger."

"In that case perhaps I will stop for just a moment!" Father Anton smiled gratefully. "But I must leave very soon."

In the following hour, waiters kept returning to the table with trays of appetizers and bottles of wine. Meanwhile, Orestes endured the group's good-humored though sometimes biting banter about his birthday.

"This is the beginning of the end for you, Orestes," Banopoulos said somberly. "From fifty to sixty is a short step, from sixty to seventy, an even quicker leap."

"So glad you could join us today, Banopoulos!" Cleon glared at the editor. "Your cheerful message is just what we need!"

"I am a journalist and a realist!" the editor said sternly. "If you're expecting to get simpering nonsense from me, I'll send Orestes a card from Hallmark!"

Three glasses of wine had emboldened Father Anton, and he spoke firmly.

"It seems to me that the length of a life is not as important as the spiritual quality of a life."

"Well spoken, Father!" Cleon cried. "Put all these aging doomsayers to shame!"

The men's dialogue and arguments flowed easily from topic

to topic, from national politics to world affairs, from dismembered Cyprus to economic problems in Greece, from the benefits of kalamata olives to the merit of wines from Samos and Crete, from the mayor's office in Chicago, to the White House in Washington. For a while, the conversation lingered on the foibles of William Clinton.

"Remember the editorial I did on that White House satyr last April?" Banopoulos said. "I confessed then that I simply didn't understand what motivated him. He could have his pick of a hundred attractive women and he chose this starry-eyed, simple-minded intern right in his own house. The man's not only sexually promiscuous, he's a fool."

"You just can't write him off as a fool," Orestes said. "He's been a good president in many ways. Look at the strategic diplomacy he accomplished to bring Yitzhak Rabin and Yasser Arafat together."

"If a man is stupid about the affairs of sex," Karvelas said, "nothing else he does can redeem him."

"Are you speaking from personal experience?" Dr. Savas grinned at Karvelas who glared back at him.

"The unhappy truth is that every president since George Washington has philandered," Professor Platon said gravely. "Jackson, Garfield, Wilson, Eisenhower, Kennedy, Johnson, the roll call of fornicators who occupied the White House goes on and on."

"Were all of those presidents really unfaithful?" Father Anton asked in alarm.

"Yes, Father," Professor Platon nodded somberly. "It proves only that however exalted the position, these leaders were also men of flesh and blood."

"I tell you what Clinton should have done," Lalounis, the realtor said. "He should have had his secret service guys find him some elegant call girls for a rendezvous at hotels outside of Washington."

"That would have been immoral!" Father Anton broke in. "And our national leader must set an example for the young people of our country!"

"With Hillary as a wife, the man had to be especially careful," Banopoulos snapped. "There's something sinister about that woman. She's to blame for this whole mess."

"Don't you think that's a leap of illogic even for you?" Karvelas asked sarcastically. "Blaming the man's poor wife for his indiscretions?"

"She should be blamed!" the editor said sharply. "She's lived with this man in the governor's mansion in Arkansas and then in the White House. She had to be familiar with his phenomenal sexual appetite and should have had sense enough to understand that if he wasn't getting his sex at home, he was certain to wander."

"Sometimes the problem of sexual compatibility is much more complex," Dr. Savas shrugged.

"We poor devils are at the mercy of our appetites," Cleon said somberly, "but if God didn't want us to unload our jiggers, he'd have given us a slit instead of a cock."

Father Anton, his wine glass near his lips, flushed and lowered his head.

"In deference to good Father Anton, we should abandon this bawdy topic," Professor Platon said.

"He's still a young priest and should be grateful for anything he learns from us," Banopoulos said. "This table contains enough knowledge and experience to fill a library."

"I do feel it's important to listen to my elders." Father Anton said earnestly.

"Listen only if your elders aren't idiots," Dr. Savas said. "Unfortunately, Father Anton, I can't reassure you that everyone here eludes that category."

"Anyway, the truth is we're spending too much time on our

randy president," Banopoulos said. "His sad story will end as a pimple on the rump of history. There are more important battles to be fought. Tomorrow morning I'll be running an editorial on the reasons the Parthenon marbles should be returned from England to Greece."

"You ran an editorial on that issue last week," Karvelas said impatiently. "Since all your readers are Greeks who support your position, why keep writing them?"

"Because the bloody English descendants of that pirate, Lord Elgin, still have those marbles imprisoned!" Banopoulos snapped. "This year will mark the two hundredth anniversary of the theft!"

"My wife, Dena, and I saw them in the British Museum a few years ago on our trip to England," Lalounis said. "They're displayed magnificently, and hundreds of thousands of visitors view them each year. I wouldn't call that imprisoning them."

"Throughout history the treasures of Greece have been looted by thieves from other countries," Professor Platon sighed. "The museums of Europe are filled with Greek antiquities. I'm afraid that unhappy situation won't be corrected soon."

"You haven't written anything on the Cyprus problem for months now," Lalounis, who had been born on that partitioned island, complained. "That's a more timely topic than the business of the marbles."

"I am presently writing another editorial on Cyprus," Banopoulos said. "Rest assured, it will appear in the near future."

At that moment the conversation was interrupted by a group of smiling waiters who surrounded the table. A grinning Cleon appeared carrying a large birthday cake with several circles of candles flickering on the frosted surface.

"My God," Orestes protested. "Cleon, you promised me there'd be none of this damn nonsense . . ."

"I count only twenty-five candles," Dr. Savas said after Cleon placed the cake on the table before Orestes. "Is this establishment too cheap to provide its owner the full complement?"

"The cake wouldn't hold fifty bloody candles!" Cleon scowled. "Now, hurry up, Orestes, make a wish and blow because the candles are burning down . . ."

Making a wish over a birthday cake was a relic of childhood, but Orestes felt there wasn't any harm in indulging the ritual. Perhaps his wish should encompass those troubled areas of the world such as Africa and the Middle East where wars and famine existed. He might offer good wishes to the survivors of the Turkish earthquake. He might even oblige Banopoulos by wishing that the Parthenon marbles be returned to Greece and for Lalounis that the partition of Cyprus be ended and the island united.

"Orestes, please!" Cleon pleaded. "The candles!"

In the end, Orestes made a small personal wish for Dessie and his children and grandchild to remain healthy and out of harm's way. Then he bent forward, sucked in his breath, and exhaled in a strong burst of air. The candles snapped out neatly, leaving twenty-five tiny tentacles of smoke spiraling toward the ceiling. The men clapped and cheered loudly, and then, led by Cleon and joined by the waiters, they sang Orestes a rousing and discordant happy birthday.

As Orestes began cutting the cake, Karvelas, who had been called from the table for a phone call, returned. The undertaker, his face tense and distressed, bent to speak to Orestes.

"Orestes, I have bad news," Karvelas said in a low, grave voice. "A niece of Mrs. Placouras phoned the church, and they called the funeral home. Mrs. Placouras's husband, Andreas, just died."

Orestes stared quickly at Father Anton, who sat relaxed and smiling across the table. The young priest had been drinking for several hours, and his cheeks were flushed, his eyes bright.

Orestes handed Cleon the knife to continue cutting the cake.

He walked around the table and placed his hand gently on the priest's shoulder.

"Father Anton," he said quietly. "Will you please come outside for a moment?"

The priest rose a little unsteadily from the table. Orestes took his arm and, with Karvelas following behind them, walked to a nearby alcove.

"Father Anton," Orestes said. "Karvelas has just received word that Andreas Placouras has died."

The priest stared at him numbly, as if unable to comprehend what Orestes was saying. He shook his head to clear away the haze of wine.

"Andreas Placouras?" Father Anton appeared finally to understand. "The dying man who was waiting for me to give him communion? Oh my God, no!" he spoke in a low, shocked voice. "No . . . no!"

"It isn't your fault, Father," Orestes said urgently. "We all urged you to stay! Dr. Savas said the man has been hanging on for years! It's not your fault!"

"I must go see Mrs. Placouras," the priest spoke in a shaken whisper. "I must ask her to forgive me."

"That won't do any good now, Father Anton," Karvelas said earnestly. "I'll arrange to have the body picked up and you'll see Mrs. Placouras at the wake. You can offer her your condolences then."

"That makes sense," Orestes agreed.

"You don't understand!" Father Anton cried. "The woman was waiting for me to give her husband communion! While I sat here swilling wine, the poor man was dying! I must go to see her now!"

Karvelas shook his head at Orestes, suggesting there was nothing they could do to dissuade the priest.

"If you feel you must go, Father," Orestes said, "I'll drive you."

"Let me drive Father Anton," Karvelas said. "It's your birthday, Orestes, and you should remain here with your friends.

"I can drive myself," Father Anton said. "I'll be fine . . ." He fumbled in his suitcoat pocket and pulled out a slip of paper. "You see I have the address right here in my pocket. I planned to stop for only a minute . . ." He paused, his face still raw with shock. "Oh my God, what have I done!"

In the next few minutes, Orestes called Cleon aside to tell him what had happened. Cleon stared with pity at the priest.

"This is the last thing the poor devil needed," Cleon said somberly. "Tzangaris and the carrion on the council will eat his liver."

"We pressed him to stay," Orestes said remorsefully. "I probably made the difference with that stupid bribe about the Christmas offering."

"Don't start thinking its your fault," Cleon said sternly.

"Phone Dessie for me, please, Cleon," Orestes said. "Tell her what happened and that I'll be late getting home. Tell the others why Father Anton and I had to leave. I'll let you know later what's happening."

Orestes walked with the priest to the lot behind the restaurant for his car. As they started driving north on Halsted Street, Father Anton, in the front seat beside him, leaned wearily against the window.

"How could I have done such a thing?" The words came burned from his tongue. "Sitting there drinking and eating while the poor man was dying. Oh dear God, what have I done!"

"Father Anton, it isn't your fault!" Orestes said earnestly. "Remember that we don't really know when the man died. Even if you'd left the Olympia right away, you still might not have gotten there in time."

But the priest would not be consoled. He slumped in his seat, whispering words that Orestes couldn't understand.

Orestes located the old brownstone apartment building on Armitage where Placouras lived. He parked and walked around to open the door for the priest, who stumbled slightly as he lurched out of the car.

"You don't need to come up with me," Father Anton said. "This is my responsibility."

"You're not going up there alone, Father!" Orestes said firmly. "I'll come up and express my condolences to Mrs. Placouras, as well."

In the building foyer, before the row of mailboxes they located the name and rang the bell. When the buzzer sounded, they started up a narrow flight of stairs, Father Anton walking slowly before Orestes, leaning heavily on the banister for support. On the second floor landing, a stern-faced young woman confronted them.

"I've come to see Mrs. Placouras," Father Anton said in a low, tremulous voice.

"My aunt is resting," the woman said coldly. She glared at the priest. "She waited for you for hours."

"I'm so sorry." The words came falteringly from the priest's lips. "I'm so sorry . . ."

Mrs. Placouras suddenly appeared in the doorway and pushed her niece aside. Orestes remembered seeing her in church on Sundays, an unsmiling, stocky-bodied woman in black, indistinguishable from so many other somber old women who seemed in perpetual mourning.

"Mrs. Placouras, we're sorry for your loss," Orestes spoke quickly to deflect her attention from the priest. "I delayed Father Anton for which I sincerely apologize."

The old woman ignored him, her eyes clamping like teeth on the priest.

"I phoned the church!" she said, her voice harsh and unyielding. "They said you left to come here more than three hours ago!"

"Please understand, I was the one who delayed Father Anton," Orestes said again. The priest pressed his arm.

"The delay was my fault!" Father Anton said, his voice little more than a whisper. "Please forgive me, Mrs. Placouras, forgive me."

"Forgive you!" The woman's face grew dark and swollen with rage. "I won't forgive you and neither will God! My poor husband died without the holy sacrament! You sent him to purgatory for eternity! He'll never find his rest now! Forgive you? All you'll get from me is my curse, which I pray scourges you for as long as you live! That's what you'll have! My curse!"

Gathering her body into a misshapen clump of fury, the woman spit fiercely at the priest.

Orestes was stunned at her ferocity while Father Anton could only stare at her in shock. Mrs. Placouras turned and pulled her niece into the apartment. The door slammed closed.

Orestes and the priest stood in dazed silence for a moment, and then both men turned wordlessly and started down the stairs.

On the drive to Father Anton's apartment, the priest sat trembling beside Orestes, mumbling what sounded like a prayer. From time to time, a great shudder pillaged his body. Orestes made several efforts to console him, but his words rang hollow against the merciless force of the old woman's curse.

Orestes pulled up before the building where the priest lived in a basement apartment.

"First thing in the morning, I'll go to church and pray," Father Anton said as he emerged from the car, his voice low and slurred. "I will talk to Father Elias . . . explain to him what took place."

"We'll both talk to him, Father," Orestes said. "Now lets get you inside so you can get some rest. I'll have someone bring your car over first thing in the morning, and then I'll meet you at church."

Orestes had dropped the priest off before his building in the past but had never been inside. When the lights were turned on in the basement apartment, he was dismayed at how small and gloomy the dwelling appeared. Is this the best we can provide our parish priest? he thought bitterly

The apartment was a single large room. One wall held a sink, stove, and refrigerator. There was an armchair, a table, and a small television set. A twin-sized bed occupied one corner, the covers on it rumpled and unmade. Beside the bed was a lamp table and a bookcase filled with books.

"Why don't you rest now, Father," Orestes said. "Would you like me to make you some tea?"

The priest shook his head. He pulled off his suit coat and fumbled to unhook his collar.

"I am tired," he said wearily. "I think I will rest for a little while."

He walked slowly to the bed, pushed aside the covers, and sat on the edge. He swayed there for a moment and then slipped heavily down on his back. When he looked at Orestes his cheeks were pale and his eyes moist.

"You'll be more comfortable with your shoes off, Father." Orestes said.

The priest didn't speak as Orestes unlaced and removed his shoes. Afterwards, he sat in an armchair near the bed.

The priest lay with his eyes closed, from time to time a tremor sweeping his body.

"God of our lives," the priest whispered, "through all my anguish, I trust in thee." He opened his eyes and looked at Orestes.

"It will be all right, Father," Orestes spoke in a low, reassuring voice. "This wasn't your fault, and no one can blame you."

"I blame myself." The priest released a long, heavy sigh. "I am a failure as a priest. God gave me a chance to be of some use, and I failed him."

"You're not a failure, Father!" Orestes said urgently. "You're loved by many people in our parish. That is the honest truth!"

"They don't know," the priest's voice trembled. "Failing that family today wasn't my first sin. God knows I am burdened with mortal sin."

The priest stared beyond Orestes, as if he were seeing some stark apparition visible only to him.

"They don't know how wretched and how guilty I am," the priest whispered. "They don't know how many times I have looked at a young boy or a girl and had sinful thoughts. They don't know the sins I have committed in my thoughts and in my dreams. But God knows I have sinned, God knows I am lost."

Orestes felt suddenly as if he were witnessing the stripping away of flesh and blood to reveal the nakedness of a soul. Part of him wanted to flee the cramped, close room, but he didn't move.

"I often think of the death in the sea of that young John Kennedy," the priest said, his anguished voice echoing from the hidden corners. "How could God take so vibrant a young man and his beautiful wife and leave a worthless creature like me to continue to draw breath on his earth. I don't understand . . ."

After a while, the priest fell silent, and his body ceased trembling. His breathing grew more even, and it seemed to Orestes that he had fallen asleep.

Orestes didn't know how long he sat in the small apartment, shivering as the dampness of the room seeped into his body. In the drawn-out silence, he became conscious of the slow, heavy throbbing of his own heart.

He reviewed the course of his day beginning with his visit to the library, then to the cemetery, and, finally, the party with his friends in the Olympia. If it had not been his birthday, the young priest would have gone directly to give communion to the dying old man. There would have been no curse from the vengeful, merciless woman, no need for Orestes to hear the priest's lament.

Yet, perhaps his presence in the small apartment served a purpose. In that shattered moment of remorse and grief, the priest might have needed another human being to hear his confession.

If there had been anywhere but the floor to lay down as a resting place, Orestes would have slept in the apartment. He rose and bent once more over the priest, who had fallen into a deep, exhausted sleep. He pulled a quilt from the foot of the bed up carefully over the sleeping figure, and then he left.

Outside on the street, he breathed in the bracing night air, grateful to be free of the damp, oppressive apartment. Above his head, he saw the outline of stars that were only a fraction of those multitudes that existed beyond human sight.

Orestes drove into his garage, parked, and entered the dark house. Passing the luminous dial of the clock in the kitchen, he was startled to see it was almost 3 a.m.

He walked upstairs, undressed quietly, and washed. When he entered the bedroom, a fragment of moonlight through the windows outlined Dessie's figure under the sheets. He slipped carefully into bed beside her.

"I'm awake," Dessie said quietly.

"I'm sorry I'm so late," he said. "I went with Father Anton to see Mr. Placouras's wife."

"Was it very bad?"

"She was enraged about the delay and cursed Father Anton. It was a terrible thing to hear. I drove him home and stayed with him for a while."

"Poor, poor man," Dessie said softly.

"What happened here?"

"Paulie and Carmela stayed for a while, and then the baby became restless and they left. Tommy came, and Mario and Theresa were here, as well. Everyone understood, of course, except mama. She thinks you stayed away on purpose."

"Stavroula never fails my expectations," Orestes sighed.

"We saved your cake in the refrigerator," Dessie said. "We'll cut it another time."

"Was Marika very disappointed?"

"She was anxious for you to see her present."

"I'll open it in the morning . . ."

"What a sad way to end your birthday." Dessie's voice sounded sleepy and distant.

"A more dreadful day for Father Anton," Orestes said. "I want to get to church first thing in the morning and talk to Father Elias before the news spreads through the parish. You can be sure Tzangaris will be one of the first to hear."

Dessie murmured assent. A few moments later, he could tell by her breathing that she was asleep. He drifted for a while in a web of weariness. His last thoughts were of the anguished young priest whose life had now been darkened by the old lady's curse.

Four

ORESTES SLEPT fitfully for the remainder of that night. When the first light appeared around the shades of the windows, he slipped into a deeper sleep. Later, a rattling of cans in the alley behind the garage woke him. He was alone in bed, and, by the intensity of daylight streaming in through the windows, he knew it was late morning. He put on his robe, walked downstairs, and found Dessie in the kitchen.

"Why didn't you wake me?"

"I tried, but you were so exhausted, you just wouldn't wake up. Are you still going to church?"

"I'm sure the trial and sentencing will already have taken place," Orestes said, "but I can still have a few words with Father Elias." He paused. "Was Marika expecting me to open her present this morning?"

"I told her how late you came in. I've rescheduled your birthday dinner for tomorrow evening because Paulie and Carmela can't come over tonight. We'll open your presents then. Do you want me to phone Mario and Theresa and Tommy again?"

"Let's just keep it small with the kids," Orestes said. He smiled wryly. "And of course your blessed mother. By the way, where is she?"

"On the terrace reading the Greek paper," Dessie said. "When we open the presents, I think mama has one for you too."

"A cup of the hemlock they gave Socrates?"

Dessie laughed, and Orestes went upstairs to dress. On his way out of the house, he kissed Dessie good-bye.

"Don't let yourself get all torn up about this," she said. "You know what Sam Tzangaris and the others are like. What they do to Father Anton will be worse than the old woman's curse."

"I know what the bastards are like," Orestes said, "but I can't help feeling responsible. I was the principal reason that poor priest delayed his communion call."

Orestes left the house and walked to his mother-in-law, Stavroula, sitting in a patio chair hunched over her paper. He had a sudden chilling vision of a bony-plated lizard clad in sweater and scarf. Unable to resist a surge of apprehension at having to face the whip of her eyes and sting of her tongue, he couldn't help thinking how miserable life must have been for her late husband. The poor wretch had probably found hell a welcome sanctuary.

When he paused beside her, her eyes glowered at him over her paper.

"Good morning, Stavroula," he said pleasantly.

She ignored his greeting.

"You kept everyone waiting last night!"

"It couldn't be helped," he said. As she continued glaring at him, he gave her a benign smile and started toward the garage.

"You spoiled Despina's dinner!" she hurled after him. Without looking back, he gave her a final, amiable wave.

Orestes parked in the lot behind St. Sophia's church. When he entered the silent, thickly shadowed nave, he breathed in the familiar scents of candles and incense.

The office door of Helen Vranas, the parish secretary, was open. As Orestes entered, she looked up from her desk.

She was a thin, wiry woman in her sixties who had been parish secretary for twenty-five years. Through years of bitter internecine warfare, she understood well the hypocrisy and intrigue surrounding church politics.

As soon as she saw Orestes, she answered his unspoken question.

"First thing this morning, they were all here about Father Anton," she said quietly. "You know, Tzangaris and the others."

"Was Father Anton here?"

She answered with a somber nod.

"How did he seem to you?"

"Like a fly caught in a spider's web."

"Is he still here?"

"Father Elias sent him on a hospital call."

"Is Father Elias in his office?"

Helen nodded, and Orestes crossed the church foyer to the office of the priest. He knocked, and, when the priest answered, he entered.

Father Elias had been pastor of St. Sophia's for twenty-two years. He was a short, gray-haired, dark-complected cleric in his mid-sixties. Parishioners complained that he sometimes seemed cold and unsympathetic, but Orestes suspected that the reserve was a defense against the endless demands of his parishioners as well as the relentless carping of Tzangaris and the parish council.

"Good morning, Father."

"Good morning, Orestes," the priest smiled wryly. "I thought you'd be coming in this morning. Sam and a few of his cronies were here bright and early."

"I planned to be here earlier," Orestes said. "So I could tell Tzangaris and the council members that Father Anton's delay yesterday in going for the communion visit was my fault."

"They knew all about it," Father Elias said. "I had calls first thing this morning from Cleon and from Karvelas, both trying to convince me they were to blame. But it didn't make any difference. Father Anton should have only stopped briefly and then gone on to administer the communion. I knew that all of you at the Olympia would be urging him to stay. I warned him. The responsibility for the delay was his."

"How bad was it with Tzangaris?"

"No worse than we've seen before," the priest shrugged. "You know Sam. If he had been a monk and lived in the Middle Ages, he'd have gleefully been one of the torturers of Savonarola."

The priest fell silent. Orestes sat down in a chair across from his desk.

"You're a good man, Orestes," Father Elias said quietly. "And you must wonder why I ally myself with men like Sam Tzangaris when I think he is a pestilence in the church."

"You must have your reasons, Father."

"I have, Orestes," the priest said earnestly. "It is a working pact with the minions of the devil. If I fought them every step of the way, I'd be exhausted, and none of the work of the church would get done. Now you need to understand this problem isn't unique in our parish. I'm in contact with other priests, and an unhappy number of them have similar problems. You see, I have come to believe every parish council holds at least one or two disciples of Satan. They must be dealt with or they will devour the church."

"You think San Tzangaris is one of those disciples?"

"I trust you to keep my confidence," Father Elias said, "so I can tell you that of course he is. He has been put into this church for the purpose of destroying the spiritual fiber of this parish . . . if I let him."

"Then why not challenge him openly, Father?" Orestes asked urgently. "You'd have a group of us who would join you."

"If it weren't Sam, it'd be some other minion of Satan," Father Elias sighed. "I know this man, all his sordid conspiracies and intrigues. He is ruthless and immoral. He is also wealthy and intimidates other council members into doing his bidding."

The priest smiled wryly. "But at least, he's the devil I know instead of some new devil I don't understand."

"Where is Father Anton in all this maneuvering?"

"Father Anton is my decoy," Father Elias said. "He is my buffer, a weapon in my strategy. If I didn't have him to hurl from time to time into the battle, I'd have to face the full wrath and force of Tzangaris and his toadies on the council."

"Father Elias, that seems cowardly," Orestes said grimly.

"Cowardly, perhaps," the priest agreed somberly, "but pragmatic, as well, and, in the long run, beneficial for the church." He paused. "Besides, it's good training for Father Anton. Someday he may have his own church and his own parish council to deal with. He needs to be toughened, needs to learn things about dealing with the evil they don't teach in the seminary."

After Orestes left the priest's office, he sat for a while in a pew at the rear of the church. The sunlight streamed through the stained-glass windows, illuminating the lean, ascetic figures of the sorrowful-eyed saints in the icons. On the ceiling of the church loomed the great painted figure of God, the Creator. As a child Orestes trembled when he looked up at the fierce-eyed deity, robes swirling around his massive body, one immense finger pointing sternly at the worshipers below, his piercing eyes stabbing into every soul, exposing every venal sin.

Despite the fear the giant figure in the painting evoked in him, his childhood memories recalled the church as a refuge from the loneliness and unhappiness in his own life.

He attended the parish school and also served as an acolyte in church. Every Sunday morning, he'd rise early and join the other acolytes clustered in the room back of the sanctuary, giggling and whispering until the stern-faced altar master hissed at them to hush. Wearing their white, brocaded robes, the boys would sit in a restless, squirming row from which half a dozen

were summoned at a time to carry out the lambades, the long
candlesticks. When Orestes took his turn, he'd stand before the
crowded church, clutching the flickering candle in his hands.
With the vapors of incense seeping into his nostrils, he felt himself part of a consecrated and exalted faith.

The highlight of the church year were the holy days of Easter. The excitement and anticipation permeated the parochial
school, the teachers stressing the importance of fasting, and of
the repenting of transgressions. The Monday following Palm
Sunday was the beginning of Holy Week, each day building
emotionally toward the Saturday night of Anastasis when the
entombed Jesus C`rist was resurrected. On that holiest of
nights, the acolyte duties were conducted by older boys, and
Orestes stood with his parents in the crowded church.

At the stroke of midnight, the great vaulted church was
hurled into darkness. Into that raven-winged blackness, a single
lighted candle would be brought from the sanctuary, and from
that solitary flame, hundreds of candles would flare into light.
Orestes felt his heart bursting with the glow of that sacred
illumination.

The liturgy finished about two in the morning, and, as the
parishioners left the church, they'd exchange the joyful greeting "Hristos anesti!" "Christ is risen!" And then the response,
"Alithos anesti!" "Truly he is risen!" That night of Easter was the
only time during the year that Orestes saw his father smiling.

They'd return home in the middle of the night, joined by a
few of his father's friends and several children about Orestes' age,
for the Easter dinner his mother prepared. After the weeks of
fasting, Orestes ate ravenously until, glutted with food, he'd fall
wearily into bed at dawn.

For Orestes, those memories of the Easters of his childhood
remained fruitful and satisfying. Yet that bond to faith wasn't true
for his son and daughter or, he suspected, for many other young

Greeks. As each generation moved further away from its immigrant roots, assimilating more completely into the new country's culture, the links between family and church were weakened.

Much of the church ritual had become secularized, the liturgy performed more and more in English, an increasing number of converts appearing in the clergy and among the laity. Despite these efforts at renewal and accommodation, young people like his son sought solace in other religions or, as with his daughter, felt no need of any religion at all.

Orestes feared all that would someday remain of the once-vibrant Greek immigrant church would be services attended only by the very old and the converts. There would also be the ubiquitous Greek festivals crowded with people eager to sample Greek food, Greek pastries, and Greek music.

While he understood this transition into a broader and more diverse society was part of the process of integration into American life, the loss of the church as he remembered it from his childhood saddened him, as well.

Orestes left the church and walked slowly to his car. The still-balmy September air carried only the faintest intimations of autumn. Once again, the prospect of entering the tumult of the restaurant disheartened him. He had delayed going in the day before because of his visit to the library and the cemetery. He had no reason for delaying again except for a certain restlessness and the distress he felt about Father Anton's plight. He wondered uneasily if those feelings were compounded because of his fiftieth birthday. Whatever the reason, he decided to stop briefly by the library once more.

"Two days in a row, Mr. Panos?" Mrs. Kohn said in surprise.

"I'm rehearsing for my retirement," he smiled.

Once again, he wandered among the stacks, took down several books, leafed idly through the pages, and put them back.

For some reason not totally clear, he longed once again to see the young blonde girl who had been in the library the day before. But all the chairs under the windows, including the one in the alcove where she had been sitting, were empty, and he reconciled himself that she wasn't there. On his way out of the library, he walked through the larger reading area where the old men sat dozing over newspapers. Then he saw the girl sitting at one of the tables. He was startled by the leap of elation he felt at the sight of her.

Walking casually past the table where she sat, below the lovely flow of her hair, he was surprised to see the book she was reading was the imposing *Odyssey* of Kazantzakis, the long, epic poem that was the Greek writer's sequel to the *Odyssey* of Homer. That she would be reading Kazantzakis in some way sanctioned the attraction he felt toward her.

Trying to untangle his emotions, he busied himself at a nearby magazine rack, furtively watching the girl. She bent intently over the book, one slim finger drumming silently upon the wood of the table. Once she raised her head unexpectedly and caught him staring at her. His cheeks flushed and he turned quickly away. She must think me another lascivious middle-aged man peering at a young girl, he thought ruefully.

He fled to the concealment of the stacks and pulled down a book, forcing himself to concentrate. When he mustered the courage to look once more toward the table where the girl had been sitting, he saw she was gone. While berating himself for having driven her away, he turned a corner and found himself face to face with her.

In the first quick glimpse, he saw that her face fulfilled the loveliness of her hair. Her eyes were a shade of light blue, her lips full and moist as though she had just eaten a grape, her cheeks pale and smooth. She was smaller than he'd imagined, the top of her head coming only to his shoulders. When she smiled up at him, he was charmed at how the smile illuminated her face.

"Excuse me," she said, and her voice was soft and pleasing.

She moved to raise the heavy volume of the *Odyssey* to the shelf.

"Let me help you," Orestes said quickly. He took the book from her hands and slipped it onto the shelf. He turned to her again. "I'm impressed that you're reading the *Odyssey*," he said. "It's a very difficult book."

"I love Kazantzakis," she said. "And the *Odyssey* is the only creation I've ever read that comes close to Dante's *Divine Comedy*. Have you read that work?"

He didn't want to confess that he'd never read it.

"A long time ago," he said. "Not since my days in school."

"It is a majestic book," she said. "I have read it many times."

"I must go back and try to read it again," he said. "Have you read any of the other work of Kazantzakis? Any of his novels? The best known, of course, is *Zorba the Greek*."

"I've read *Zorba*," she said, "but I like *The Greek Passion* more. Another of my favorites is his autobiography, *Report to Greco*."

"That's amazing!" Orestes said. "I mean, you're so young to be drawn to Kazantzakis."

"I first discovered him a few years ago when I lived for almost a year on the island of Crete," she said quietly. "He has a great deal to say to young people." She paused, and he felt the lambent warmth of her eyes. "Are you Greek?"

He told her he was.

"I thought so," she said. "Have you been to Crete?"

"Many years ago," he said. "When we cruised the Greek islands, Crete was one of the stops."

"Have you visited the grave of Kazantzakis?"

He was sorry to admit that he hadn't.

"It is a moving experience," she said earnestly. "The grave covered by three great stones is set high on a fortress above the city of Irakleion. There isn't any name on the grave, no date of birth or date of death, just a stark wooden cross and a simple inscription."

"I know the inscription," Orestes said. "'I fear nothing, I hope for nothing, I am free.'"

"That is very profound," she said quietly.

They stood in silence for a moment longer and then she smiled again and he moved aside to let her pass. He watched as she walked by the librarian's desk and out the door. He reproached himself because he hadn't been quick-witted enough to even ask her name.

After she'd gone, he pondered why he should feel so attracted to a girl he had first seen in the library only the day before. He also found it felicitous that she should love Kazantzakis and that she had spent a year living on Crete. At the same time he could not help feeling a certain futility because she appeared to be in her early twenties, not that many years removed from the age of his daughter.

A day earlier, he had been smugly congratulating himself for his lifetime of fidelity to Dessie. Now, in the grip of a turbulence set off by the golden-haired girl who read Kazantzakis, his self-righteous feeling vaporized like smoke in the wind.

As he drove downtown to the Olympia, the turmoil of his feelings had coalesced into a heavy depression. He understood it was depression, although he felt it as a physical malady, his breathing shallow and a muscular tension in his chest and shoulders.

Cleon had greeted him jubilantly the day before, but that afternoon when Orestes entered the restaurant, his partner greeted him with concern.

"Are you all right, Orestes?"

"I'm fine. I stopped by the church this morning."

Cleon seemed to accept that the affair of the young priest was behind his dark mood.

"You probably heard how that bastard, Tzangaris, raked Father Anton over hot coals," Cleon said angrily. "I phoned Father Elias! I tried to explain that it wasn't the young priest's fault!"

"Father Elias told me he spoke to you. I'd hoped to be there in time to speak up for him, but I was too late."

A waiter interrupted them with a message from the master chef, Kyriakos, who wanted to see Orestes in the kitchen.

"He wants to talk to you about the menu for the Ahepa party on Saturday," Cleon said gruffly. "I offered my suggestions, but he wanted to speak to you. That arrogant and beef-headed prima donna feels only you truly understand the artistry of his cuisine."

"We've got to humor him, Cleon," Orestes said and started toward the kitchen. "Half a dozen restaurants on this street would love to have him in charge of their kitchen."

In the kitchen, Orestes consulted with Kyriakos, a tall, somber-faced culinary specialist who had worked in fine tourist hotels in Greece before journeying to America.

"As an appetizer," Kyriakos said, "I suggest bite-sized pieces of lamb skewered on toothpicks with fresh mint leaves in a light yogurt and mint sauce."

"Excellent."

"A grilled eggplant, cucumber, and black olive salad."

"Splendid. What about the main course?"

"We'd been talking about roast lamb, but I want to give them something different. I suggest a sweet and sour stuffed chicken, basted in honey and vinegar, filled with Cypriot haloumi cheese." He paused and, as if to allow Orestes the option of selecting the least important part of the dinner, he asked, "What about the dessert?"

"Let them choose from the tray of baklava and galato-bouriko," Orestes said, "and then have Korelis prepare his honey, nut, and butter cream mousse. Let's include some Montofoli wine to go with the dessert, as well."

Orestes spent the balance of the afternoon attending to other chores in the restaurant. That evening, he was checking invoices in his office, when Cleon entered.

"Are you still here? Dessie will be blaming me for delaying you."

"Considering the time I came in, I've only been here half my usual hours."

"To hell with the usual hours!" Cleon said brusquely. "You're a senior partner and don't have to punch any damn time-clock. I've been telling you for months now that you should be taking more time off. Leave the Olympia to me."

"I'm fine, Cleon."

Cleon stared at him for a moment in silence.

"If you don't mind your partner telling you what he's thinking," he said somberly, "you're not fine. I know the business with Father Anton was a kick in the balls. Then there's the other thing."

"What other thing?"

"You know," Cleon said gravely. "The big half-century mark, the big five-o . . ." He uttered the words as if they were a dirge.

Orestes couldn't restrain a laugh.

"I'm only fifty, not eighty, Cleon, for God's sake!" he said. "The world is going up in flames. Young men and women are dying in the Middle East and Africa. Why should I develop severe hypertension about reaching fifty?"

"I'm just saying it can be traumatic," Cleon said. "I know how I felt at fifty. A damn sight worse than I felt at sixty."

"How do you think you'll feel when you reach seventy?"

"I'm not far from that bloody milestone so maybe just getting there will be a relief," Cleon sighed. "But if that papal pill pusher, Dr. Savas, doesn't start paying a little more attention to my complaints, I'll never reach that eighth decade. When I try to tell him the things bothering me, the old Minotaur seems to be sneering. He makes me feel like I'm out of focus."

"He doesn't want to waste time with a man as healthy as you."

"I'm healthy all right," Cleon said gloomily. "I think about how healthy I am all night long when I have to get up a half dozen times to relieve myself." He paused and chuckled. "You're a slippery one. I start off talking about your problems and we end up talking about mine."

Later that night at home, after he'd had a cup of tea with Dessie, they sat quietly in the living room. Orestes endeavored to read the Halberstam book while Dessie leafed idly through a magazine. Marika was at a girlfriend's house doing homework, so the walls around them weren't vibrating with the deafening clatter of a rock group. Stavroula was upstairs in her room, salivating over a Tom Selleck movie.

From time to time, Orestes glanced over his paper at Dessie. With her dark hair and large dark eyes, she had been a beautiful young girl and she was still beautiful. Any number of men would have to be proud and grateful to have her as a wife.

That evening she wore a light print house dress, her legs bare, her feet in sandals. She had one knee curled beneath her, and he caught a glimpse of her naked thigh. He was conscious of the contour of her breasts against the dress, and the light beads of perspiration glistening on her cheeks. A sandal had slipped from her foot, and he saw her lightly tinted toes gleaming against the carpet.

He was suddenly remorseful because they made love so infrequently. He imagined his neglect driving her into the arms of another man who would be taken with her beauty. The possibility of a man seeing Dessie naked, making love to her, imbued him with a storm of both jealousy and desire, unlike any-thing he had felt in a long time.

He rose and walked to where Dessie was sitting. He stepped behind her, placed both his hands gently on her shoulders, then bent and lightly kissed the crown of her dark, fine hair. She put her book aside and looked up at him. Gazing into the depths of her eyes made him feel as if he were being given a glimpse of her soul.

"I love you, Dessie," he said, and he heard the words echo from the corners of the room. "You're such a beautiful woman and I know I don't tell you often enough . . . I mean, tell you how much I love you."

She rose slowly from the chair to face him.

"Are you trying to tell me you're horny?"

"I know its been a while," he said ruefully.

"It has been quite a while," she said, and a trace of a wry smile curled her lips. "I thought perhaps you were finding your plea-sure on the Internet."

"They're all the same," he said firmly, hoping his voice did not recant the lie. "The women have breasts like the udders of cows. It's more of a turn off than a turn on." He paused. "Has it really been very long?" He was sorry as soon as he asked the question because he knew how long it had been.

"Almost two months."

He feigned surprise.

"My God, really that long!"

"Time flies when you're having fun," she smiled, and the teasing glow in her eyes aroused him even more. "If we're go-ing to do it, we better get upstairs. Marika could be home any moment."

"She's old enough to understand that her parents still desire one another," Orestes said. "Besides, I don't want to go up to the bedroom. We always do it in the bedroom."

"Where do you want to do it?"

"Right here on the living-room floor!"

She looked at him in surprise.

"Have you been drinking?"

"I haven't been drinking!" he said. "I just desire my wife. Is that so hard to understand?"

"The drapes are open. Marika could come in with her friends at any moment. Now, Orestes, don't be foolish."

He reached for her then, pulling her into his arms. He felt the pressure of her breasts against his chest and he reached behind her and urgently fondled her buttocks. He struggled to draw her down to the floor.

"Orestes!" her voice was suddenly tight and flustered. "What's the matter with you? Orestes . . ." She paused. "Let's go upstairs, please. Anyway, I have to wash up. Give me a couple of minutes."

"To hell with washing up! Lovers in the movies don't stop to wash up!"

They slipped down to their knees on the carpet, their bodies braced awkwardly against one another. He kissed her again, tasting her breath, inhaling the familiar, moist scents of her body. She struggled against him for a moment and then he felt her resistance yielding, her body slowly responding. He tugged down her panties and as he stroked her naked thighs he sought to push her down on her back. He unzipped his fly, unbuckled his pants and peeled them down to his knees. He crouched down between Dessie's legs.

"Despina!" The harsh voice of his mother-in-law erupted from the hallway.

His blood froze and, under him, Dessie loosed a low cry of despair! He hadn't heard the old harpy coming down the stairs, and yet she had somehow reached the hallway. He scrambled off Dessie, tugging frantically at his trousers which imprisoned his legs.

"Despina!" The old lady's strident voice rang through the room once more.

He struggled desperately to pull up his pants as Dessie rolled over on the floor, tugging down her dress, fumbling for her panties that she bunched in her hand. Orestes lurched to his feet and, clutching his pants a little above his knees, he catapulted himself out of the living room. Stumbling toward the kitchen he tripped once, banged down on one knee, groaned and scrambled back up.

He collapsed against the sink, stuffing his shirt into his pants, zipping up his trousers, his heart beating so wildly he was certain it would burst out of his chest. He felt like a rabbit flushed out of the brush by a rabid fox.

"Goddam it to hell!" he whispered hoarsely. "Goddam it to bloody hell! The witch must have ridden her fucking broomstick down the goddam stairs!"

"Where were you?" he heard Stavroula's querulous voice speaking to Despina in the living room. "I've been calling and calling till my throat is hoarse! It's time for my medicine. What are you doing in here in the dark?"

Dessie answered in a low, shaken voice. For several minutes longer Orestes stood there, braced against the sink, waiting for the drumbeats of his heart to diminish.

"Goddam it to bloody hell!" he kept senselessly whispering the curse. "Goddam it to bloody hell!"

Later, after he'd showered, he rested in bed while Dessie showered. Marika had returned home and was in her bedroom, the sound of music carrying in a low rumble down the hall. Stavroula had returned to her lair. Dessie came out of the shower in her nightgown, her feet bare, traces of water glistening across her naked shoulders. She stared wistfully down at Orestes and shook her head.

"I still don't know whether to laugh or cry," she said. "She could have walked in . . . walked right in."

"She would have screamed I was raping you and called the cops," Orestes said. "I still don't know how the hell she got down the stairs without either of us hearing her. She generally sounds like a tractor." He sighed. "She must have sensed us feeling loving and happy, and she couldn't abide that."

Dessie came to sit on the edge of the bed. She reached out and gently stroked his calf.

"Poor Orestes," she said gently. "The first time in months you feel horny, and all you get is mama." She paused. "Do you want to try again now?"

"I'd like to, my darling," he said pensively, "but my cock is still so frozen with shock it may take days to thaw out!"

"We'll do it tomorrow evening," Dessie said. "We'll come up after dinner and lock the door. I promise we'll do it then."

She slipped into bed beside him. He turned on his side toward her, her face close to his own.

"Was it the fiftieth birthday?" she asked softly. "Are you melancholy because we're both growing older, and you feel that time is growing shorter? Was that the reason you became horny tonight?"

Even as he assured her that it was unquestionably the milestone of the birthday, he wasn't sure she believed him. They were so attuned to the feelings of one another that Dessie might have suspected something else had aroused him. Long after they had turned off the light, he lay sleepless in the dark room, and, by the fitfulness of her breathing, he knew Dessie also lay awake beside him.

Five

ORESTES WOKE early in the morning, still angry and frustrated at the humiliating debacle of the night before. As he rose from bed, Dessie spoke in a drowsy voice.

"Do you want some breakfast?"

"I'll have something at the restaurant," he said. "Go back to sleep now." As he bent to give her a fleeting kiss, she reached up to gently touch his cheek.

"My darling, don't forget our date this evening."

"I'll remember."

After leaving the house, he drove directly to the ramp leading onto the Dan Ryan. Driving the expressway downtown, he recalled the absurdity of the scene in the living room, Dessie and he, both nearly naked, scrambling like delinquent adolescents to escape exposure.

"We should have kept fucking!" he cried at his reflection in the rear-view mirror. "Give the prune-faced old hag an eyeful she would never forget!"

Yet he knew how painful the confrontation would have been for Dessie and how Stavroula would have reminded her of the episode countless times.

As he grew calmer, he recalled that he hadn't spoken to Father Anton since the night he drove the young priest home. His own humiliation seemed suddenly trivial alongside the priest's anguish. He dialed a call on his cell phone to the priest's office in church and, when there wasn't any answer, left a voice-mail message.

Once in the Olympia, he was grateful for the activity and sounds of people. Late in the morning, he met with Cleon and Kyriakos, to plan their year-end millennium party. Cleon's plans for the affair were ambitious and grandiose, and he waved aside the suggestion of Orestes that they plan a less ostentatious affair.

"It's a millennium, partner!" Cleon cried. "This comes around once in a thousand years! They're planning gala celebrations all over the world. I was reading the other day that in Edinburgh, they're expecting half a million revelers to attend the most elaborate street party held this century! In Vienna, twenty classical and popular music orchestras will perform on stages set up for them across the city! Rome is preparing for thirteen million visitors! They're asking the old Pope to bless them all, heathen as well as Christian!"

"This isn't Edinburgh, Dublin, or Rome, partner," Orestes said amiably. "And you and I are not granting papal audiences. This is the Olympia Restaurant on Halsted Street. Every restaurant and night club in the city is planning a major party. The competition for patrons will be intense."

"I know that!" Cleon cried. "I'm not suggesting we launch a satellite from the roof of the Olympia, but what we finally do must surpass anything else done on this street!" He appealed to Kyriakos. "Don't you agree?"

"Do whatever you want," the old chef said somberly. "Big party or little party, my food will be the highlight."

"What about Y2K?" Orestes asked.

"What about it?"

"Suppose we've got a gala party planned and then everything goes black, power broken off, clocks stopped, it could be a catastrophe."

"Do you understand what Y2K means?" Cleon asked Kyriakos. The chef looked at him numbly.

"Is it a recipe of some kind?"

"How about you?" Cleon asked Orestes.

"No," Orestes laughed, "I don't know what the hell it means."

"I don't either, nor does any one else in the whole country!" Cleon cried triumphantly. "And we damn well shouldn't make our plans based on a couple letters from the alphabet and a number!" Cleon paused and then continued excitedly. "To show you how hard I've been working, just this morning I spoke to Plato Lembesis, the impresario in Detroit! He told me we could get Bakalakis, the finest lyre player in the country, maybe in the world, for ten thousand plus expenses!"

"Dollars or drachmas?" Orestes asked.

"You're trying to be funny, partner," Cleon said reprovingly, "but I'm dead serious."

"Other restaurants and clubs are bringing in rock bands," Orestes said. "Why would we bring in a lyre player?"

"Because he's a great artist!" Cleon said. "I heard him, maybe ten, twelve years ago at a festival in Toronto. When he played, I swore I could see my father's village above Tripoli, the mountains and the sun. The man's music paints pictures!" He paused. "Of course, if you're looking for cheap entertainment, we can get a Middle Eastern belly dancer like Saranitsa for $500."

Orestes gestured at the chef.

"Which one would you choose, Kyriakos?"

"Get all the fiddlers, and rump-wigglers you want," Kyriakos growled. "My food will be what draws them in."

In mid-afternoon, Father Anton came into the Olympia. Orestes greeted him warmly. The priest looked pale and his eyes red-rimmed as if he hadn't slept. Father Anton asked only for a cup of tea and the two sat at a table in a quiet corner of the restaurant.

"I picked up your message," Father Anton said. "I had planned to come in anyway and thank you, Orestes, for driving me home the other night and making sure I was safe." He paused. "I also heard from Father Elias how you came to church the following morning to lend your support." He fell silent and shook his head slowly. "I was in anguish that night, and perhaps I said some things . . ." A whisper of anxiety lingered in his voice.

"You were mumbling, Father," Orestes said quietly. "I was sitting across the room and couldn't make sense of what you were saying."

The priest looked at him intently as if trying to determine whether Orestes was telling him the truth.

"I'm sorry I wasn't at church when you first arrived there yesterday morning," Orestes said. "I understand that Tzangaris and a few council members were there early. Was it very bad?"

"Sam Tzangaris is who he is," the priest said wearily. "After all this time, one knows what to expect." He sighed. "The truth is that I deserved their condemnation." He raised his hand to deflect any objection from Orestes. "I understand your friendship and affection for me, Orestes, makes you want to reassure me. I'm grateful, but I must also live with what I've done."

"Live with it, Father Anton," Orestes said earnestly. "Don't suffer with it."

The priest finished his tea and rose to leave.

"Perhaps it is only when we suffer that we come close to Jesus Christ," the priest said pensively. When Orestes rose, the two men embraced. Orestes felt the meager-fleshed and bony body of the priest in his arms. For a moment their faces were inches apart and the priest looked deeply and keenly into Orestes' eyes.

"God be with you, Orestes," Father Anton said in a low voice. "And may he not be unmindful of me, as well."

As customers began arriving for dinner, Cleon and Orestes alternated greeting and seating them. Many were regular patrons, and the hosts made a special effort to make the guests feel welcome.

At one time or other, many of the city's most prominent politicians, lawyers, and judges came to the Olympia for lunch or dinner. The restaurant was also frequented by journalists, athletes, and entertainers. The wall of the foyer was arrayed with signed photographs of celebrities including the first Mayor Richard Daley, Mayor Harold Washington, and Daley's son, Rich Daley, who was now reigning mayor. There were also photos autographed to Orestes and Cleon from Michael Jordan and Sammy Sosa.

One of their celebrity visitors that evening was Mike Ditka, the former coach who in 1985 had led the Chicago Bears to a Super Bowl victory. When Ditka entered with several friends, Cleon and Orestes went together to greet him.

"I told our chef you were coming in, coach," Orestes said. "He's making your favorite."

"That's great, Orestes," Ditka said. He motioned to the men with him. "Wait till you taste this moussaka!"

"We're delighted to see you, coach!" Cleon said effusively, as he grabbed the man's ham-sized hand. "Any truth to the rumor you're coming back to coach our team?"

"Nothing to it, Cleon," the burly Ditka winked.

"That's the second time you've broken my heart, coach," Cleon lamented as he motioned for them to follow him.

"When was the first time, Cleon?" Ditka asked.

"When you left the team!" Cleon said mournfully as he led them to their table.

From time to time, Orestes walked into the seemingly chaotic kitchen to make sure that integral part of the restaurant was running smoothly. That redolent province of the Olympia was staffed by twenty cooks, bakers, and dishwashers, broiling and frying, baking and grilling, scouring and washing. Kyriakos ruled over them all like an imperious monarch. He seemed to be everywhere in the kitchen at once, scolding and advising, correcting and berating.

If the staff in the kitchen made up one resourceful and well-trained group in the restaurant, another contingent comprised the waiters and busboys who dashed in and out of the kitchen, shouting orders and carrying out the trays bearing heaping platters of food. Many were young men newly arrived from Greece, whom Orestes and Cleon helped by obtaining visas for them and providing the money for their tickets.

Young men who came from the major metropolis of Athens boasted of the marvels of the Acropolis, Constitution Square, and Vassilisas Sophia Avenue, as well as the elegant hotels such as the Grande Bretagne and the King James.

The Athenian youths looked with disdain on the young peasants who had nothing to boast about but their desolate villages, sleepy mountain hamlets with unpaved, dirt streets, windowless stone hovels, and litters of scrawny chickens, cats, and dogs.

If a single element united the waiters from Athens and those youths from the villages, it was their recurring confrontations with the staff in the kitchen. These often-heated exchanges produced an assortment of colorful epithets in Greek and English, sometimes utilizing insults from both languages.

"Lamb chops! I ordered lamb chops! Maybe you should hang one around your neck to remind you what a lamb chop looks like!"

"What's wrong with your ears? I said makaronada! My deaf grandmother hears better than you!"

"Giving birth to a malaka like you must have sent your poor mother into shock!"

"I had a three-legged dog in Greece could move faster than you!"

"Son of a goat!"

"Brother of a pig!"

The flurries of invective being hurled back and forth were muted slightly when Orestes entered the kitchen but never ceased completely. He had abandoned any effort to silence the exchanges because he understood the spirited insults being hurled back and forth were a way for the men working at a frantic pace to energize their emotions and keep their momentum racing.

As Orestes inspected several trays of freshly baked baklava, Kyriakos called to him. The heat and steam of the kitchen had collapsed the chef's high white hat so it drooped awkwardly over one ear. His apron was splattered with butter and flour, his cheeks soaked with sweat.

"Orestes, this spanakopita I made using the recipe I obtained from the chef at the Grande Bretagne in Greece last summer is hot out of the oven," he said. "I'll cut a morsel for you to taste."

Kyriakos deftly cut a piece of the still steaming spanakopita and waited anxiously while Orestes blew on the fragment to cool it. When he tasted the spinach with feta cheese blended in the flaky filo, Orestes was impressed once again at the chef's incomparable skill with food.

"Excellent, Kyriakos!" he said enthusiastically. "Best spanakopita you've ever made!"

Kyriakos looked triumphantly at the assembly of cooks watching around him. In a heartbeat, he returned to his acerbic form.

"What are you standing around for?" the chef cried. "Are you waiting to be decorated? Sotiri, watch the avgolemono! Ares, the sauce is ready for the angenares! God help your sad Anatolian ass if it curdles!"

As Orestes continued past the ovens and freezers to the produce storerooms in back of the kitchen, a waiter named Michali emerged furtively from one of the store rooms. He was a youth of about twenty from a mountain village in Greece who had only been employed for several months. His face was tense with guilt and a faint odor of tobacco lingered about his head. When he saw Orestes, the young man turned pale.

"I've told you before, Michali," Orestes said sternly. "No smoking in the storeroom! If you must smoke, wait until your break and step out into the alley!"

Even as he reprimanded the young waiter, he thought pensively that this was the kind of vigorous, handsome young man the girl in the library deserved as an admirer, not a middle-aged profligate leering at her from the stacks.

"I'm sorry, Mr. Panos," Michali stumbled over the words as he stared woefully at Orestes. "Does this mean you're going to fire me?"

"I'm not going to fire you," Orestes held back a smile which he knew would embarrass the youth. "Just do your smoking outside. Better yet, give up that vice. You know it's bad for your health"

"Yes sir, Mr. Panos!" Michali said earnestly. "Thank you, Mr. Panos. God knows I've tried to quit the filthy weed, but it has a fierce grip on me! My father was just as weak as me, smoked till the day he died! I swear I'll keep trying!"

He hurried past Orestes to return to work.

Orestes left the Olympia at about six to start home. He had momentarily forgotten that his son, Paulie, and his wife, Carmela, and the baby were coming for dinner to celebrate his belated birthday. As he slowly drove the crowded southbound lanes of the Dan Ryan, a restlessness swept over him again. It was as if the routine he had followed for years had become intolerable. He wished suddenly, a feeling tinged with guilt, that he wasn't going home.

In the dreamlike maze of red tail lights blinking on and off in front of him, he thought of the girl in the library again. He struggled to untangle the reason he was unable to get her out of his mind. Certainly, there had been women in the past he had been attracted to and tempted to touch, but nothing ever came of those impulses because he was secure and satisfied in his love for Dessie and his family.

He found it hard to believe that the milestone of fifty could have wreaked such a change. Perhaps he was suffering from some physical or mental ailment that impacted his emotions.

Early in his marriage, during a stressful period when he was having trouble with his business, Orestes visited a psychiatrist half a dozen times. The doctor had helped him understand some contradictory impulses within himself. He considered checking whether the psychiatrist was still practicing and perhaps call for an appointment.

If I do go see him again, what will I tell him, he thought gloomily? I'd say, doctor, there is this young blonde girl in the library who is haunting me with the restless, anguished longings I felt as a young man. Instead of offering him some profound advice on coping with his obsession, the doctor might be tempted to give him a smack across the head to knock some sense into him.

As he turned into the driveway, he recognized his son's Ford Taurus parked outside his house. He climbed from his car and braced himself to offer his family a warm, festive greeting.

"Happy birthday, pa," Paulie said as Orestes entered the kitchen. Carmela, an auburn-haired, pretty girl, came to him holding his granddaughter, Catherine. As he kissed the sweet baby, and hugged her mother, part of him trembled with a sudden surge of love for this beloved grandchild.

"The kids have to get the baby home," Dessie said as she came to kiss him. "We're all ready to sit down to eat."

"Aren't we going to wait for Marika?" Carmela asked.

"She has a meeting at school," Dessie said. "We'll eat now and by the time we've finished she should be here so we can cut the cake." She motioned to Paulie. "You might go and tell mama that dinner is ready."

Let her ride her goddam broom down, Orestes thought with a renewed surge of outrage. Dessie looked at him as if she understood what he was thinking.

Gathered at the table in the dining room set elegantly with Dessie's best china, the family ate a savory dinner of roast lamb and baked potatoes. Paulie ate in silence, but Carmela related, at some length, an experience she'd had in the grocery store.

"I was checking the receipt as I pushed the cart out of the store," she said. "I noticed she'd charged me twice for a pound of bacon. I went back to the cashier, who asked me whether I hadn't bought two pounds of bacon. I asked her if she thought I had taken one pound of bacon to the car and hurried back to cheat her? Can you imagine!"

"What happened?" Dessie asked.

"She gave me the credit, but I'm not sure she believed me. She just wouldn't accept she had made a mistake."

All through Carmela's story, watching Stavroula chew her food doggedly, Orestes found his attention wandering. Suddenly Catherine started squirming in her high chair and began to cry.

"She probably needs changing," Carmela said. She rose and carried the baby from the room.

"That child doesn't look well to me," Stavroula said somberly. "I don't think she's getting enough to eat."

"She's fine, mama!" Dessie said.

At that moment, the back door slammed, and Marika came rushing quickly through the kitchen into the dining room. She brought a cloudburst of energy into the room.

"I'm sorry I couldn't make dinner! We had a student council meeting I didn't dare miss! There's a jerk on the council who keeps spoiling everyone's plans!"

She came to Orestes and bent and hugged him tightly.

"Happy birthday to the best and most special father in the world!"

"I accept that greeting from the finest daughter any man could ever have," Orestes smiled.

"Isn't that stretching it a bit?" Paulie asked, his tone only partially jesting. "The finest daughter would have made it home for her father's birthday dinner."

"Nobody asked for your opinion!" Marika hurled back as she sat down. As Dessie rose to bring her a plate of food, Marika waved it away.

"I'm only going to have a piece of cake, mama."

"Why don't you eat!" Stavroula cried. "You'll get skinny and sick!"

"Some kids brought in a barrel of Kentucky Fried, and I was so angry at the jerk, I ate three pieces plus fries! Ugh! I'm utterly disgusted with myself!"

"Eating food like that will poison you," Stavroula muttered and speared another slice of lamb.

When dinner ended and the dishes had been cleared away, the lights in the room were snapped off, and Marika carried in the birthday cake glowing with candles.

"I couldn't find all the candles I needed," Dessie said. "So just figure each one represents five years."

Carmela carried Catherine to sit beside Orestes as he blew out the candles. Paulie snapped a series of snapshots with his small Canon. Afterwards, they brought him their presents.

"Open mine first, papa!" Marika cried. "I've been waiting impatiently for days now!"

Orestes opened the festively wrapped package from his

daughter to find a bright yellow silk shirt from Calvin Klein, one he knew it highly unlikely he'd ever wear.

"It's wonderful, my darling!" he said heartily. "Just what I needed!"

"Now you can throw some of those dull, horrid shirts you wear away," Marika said. "You're a handsome man, and you need bright colors to bring out your good looks." She turned to Dessie. "Do you like it, mama?"

A wry smile played around Dessie's mouth.

"I think it captures your father's true personality," Dessie said gravely. Only Orestes caught the tinge of irony in her voice, and they exchanged a quick, knowing glance.

Paulie and Carmela had bought him a cashmere robe, a re-gal-looking gown he knew must have cost several hundred dol-lars, a sum they couldn't really afford.

"Do you like it, papouli?" Carmela asked, calling him by the Greek name for grandfather.

"It's beautiful," Orestes said, and it was true the robe was luxurious. He could wear it to breakfast and then thought how chagrined he'd feel the first time he dropped a piece of buttered toast or some preserve on a sleeve.

Paulie and Carmela also gave him a framed photograph of Catherine sitting beneath the glittering Christmas tree, her cherubic face gazing with wonder at the camera.

"It's a beautiful photo," Orestes said. "I'll take it to my office in the restaurant so I'll be able to show it off."

"We'll make you another print so you can keep one at home, as well," Carmela said.

"Now mama has a present for you too," Dessie said, hand-ing Orestes a small, festively wrapped package.

Orestes felt the old woman watching him grimly as he opened the package to find a fine Parker fountain pen in a felt-lined box. He knew that Dessie had bought it for her mother to give to `im.

"Mama picked it out herself," Dessie said. "It's for your office in the Olympia."

"Thank you, Stavroula," Orestes said.

"They give too many presents in this country," the old woman grumbled. "In Greece, we were grateful just to have food on the table."

The final present Orestes opened was from Dessie, a fine new 35mm camera, to replace the old one he had been using for years. He rose and kissed her in thanks for the gift.

"We'll use it on our trip back to Greece next year," Dessie said. She looked quickly to see what response her words elicited from Orestes.

They had been to Greece for the first time five years earlier, a trip that Dessie loved and that Orestes tolerated. He found Dessie's relatives oppressively boring and life in the village without indoor plumbing a hardship. Despite Dessie's eagerness to return, he had used one excuse or another to keep from having to go back.

"Are you really going next year, mom?" Paulie asked.

"I hope we can go," Dessie said. She looked once again at Orestes.

"It's a little hard to get away from the restaurant for a couple of weeks in the summer," Orestes said, "but we'll try to work it out."

Marika left the room to take a call on her cell phone while Carmela and Dessie picked up the dishes. Paulie carried the baby into the living room, and Orestes joined him. He sat in an armchair while Paulie played with the baby on the floor.

Orestes watched father and child, feeling a curious incongruity in the sight of this son, with curly black hair and a face that looked as if he should still be in high school, playing with his child. Even as a boy, Paulie had been brooding and withdrawn. When he became older, alienated from the rituals of the Greek Orthodox Church, he began searching for another faith. That led him from Buddhism to Hare Krishna. Now he was attempting to live a conventional life as a husband and father. Yet, Orestes felt his son was still searching for something beyond his life in the real world.

"How are things at the shop?" Orestes asked about the printing and copying shop where Paulie worked as a manager.

"All right, I suppose," Paulie said. "Some days are busier than others. One of the regular girls quit, and I'm trying to hire another."

"How are things going with Fanaris?" Orestes asked about the owner of the shop, who, as a favor to Orestes, had given Paulie the job.

"He doesn't come in very often," Paulie said. "I'm glad about that because he's a pain in the ass."

"Remember what I told you about our trying to buy the business if you find you like it," Orestes said. "I think Fanaris would be willing to sell. It could be a good business for you."

"I don't mind working there for a while," Paulie said. He crouched over Catherine and lowered himself gently to kiss the soft crown of her head. "But I don't want to spend my life printing and copying other people's letters."

"What else do you want to do?" Orestes couldn't keep his voice free of grievance.

Paulie retreated into a sullen silence that Orestes knew well.

"How are things going at home?" Orestes lowered his voice as he asked the question. For a moment Paulie looked somberly at him and then looked away.

"There are ups and downs," he said quietly.

"You'll get those in any marriage," Orestes said. He waited for his son to continue, perhaps share whatever problems he and

Carmela were experiencing. But Paulie remained withdrawn and silent, raising and lowering his body to accommodate the squirming and wriggling of the baby on the floor.

After everyone had gone, Dessie and Orestes sat in the living room for a while. Marika and Stavroula were both up in their rooms.

"I felt some tension between Paulie and Carmela," Dessie said. "Did he say anything to you?"

Orestes shook his head.

"I hope if they're having problems, they can work things out," Dessie said. "For both their sakes and for the sake of the baby."

She put down the magazine and rose from her chair.

"I'm going upstairs," she said. "Are you coming?"

He recalled their promise to make love, but he felt weary and without desire. He briefly looked up from his paper.

"I'll be up in a little while," he said casually.

Dessie bent to kiss him good-night.

"Don't be too late," she said. He watched her walking from the room with mixed feelings of love and guilt.

He must have dozed in the armchair because something startled him awake. He couldn't be sure whether the sound came from somewhere in the house or whether he carried it from a fitful dream.

He sat tensely listening for a little while but heard nothing. From time to time, a car passed on the street before the house, its rumble trailing away. There was the lonely bark of a dog, the distant wail of a siren, the squeal of a small animal, perhaps a gopher or rabbit caught in the claws of a cat.

The events of the day passed through his mind, Cleon's excited plans for the millennium party, the pride with which Kyriakos offered him the spanakopita, the flustered young waiter he had caught smoking in the storeroom. Then there was the visit of Father Anton, concerned about what he might have revealed to Orestes that night. Finally, there was the birthday dinner at home with his family. He could not rid himself of an uneasy feeling that Paulie and Carmela were having problems. He hoped they would not do anything too drastic without considering the welfare of the child.

He wondered suddenly whether the girl was sleeping alone or with a lover. She might even have a husband. If she lived somewhere in the neighborhood, she might be listening to the same sounds of the night he was hearing now.

Was it restlessness and boredom that set his heart adrift when he first saw her? He had always believed these emotions were luxuries of a society that had too much . . . too much to eat, more clothing than it needed, houses so large they could provide shelter for a dozen poor families in countries overseas.

He had everything a man could want, a loving wife, a loving family, a good business, loyal and devoted friends. Why then should a strange, disquieting attraction to a girl invade his life?

He was suddenly aware of time as if it were a clock inside his body, his organs throbbing and ticking, liver and heart aging with each beat. After a while, he rose and snapped off the lamp. He lowered the thermostat and started up the stairs to bed.

Six

In the morning, Orestes woke to rain falling from a gray and overcast sky. During the night, he had navigated an erotic dream, which he couldn't remember but which left him, upon waking, tense and restless. After he left the house, he drove directly to the library.

He walked into the building and hung his wet raincoat on the rack inside the door. A librarian he didn't know sat behind the desk.

"I hope Mrs. Kohn isn't ill?"

"It's her day off," the librarian said.

Orestes moved into the stacks, idling his way up one aisle and then down another, furtively scanning the chairs and tables for the girl. He was disappointed not to find her there, and thought, unhappily, the rain might have kept her away. Then, as he moved from the shelves of history to the racks of fiction, through one of the gaps in the shelf, he saw her enter the library. She wore a light tan raincoat with a tan beret tugged down over her blonde hair. Just inside the front door, she closed a small plaid umbrella and put it into the rack. As she slipped out of her raincoat, Orestes reached quickly for a book and sat down in one of the reading chairs.

He read and reread the same page without paying any attention to what he was reading. Meanwhile, he remained watchful as a hunter in a quarry for any sign of the girl. Minutes passed, and he had decided to walk into the main area of the library to locate where she might be sitting when she entered his aisle.

He kept his eyes on the book.

"Hello, there," she said, and when he looked up, feigning surprise, he was taken once again by the way her smile brightened her face.

"Hello," he tried to sound casual as he rose. "You're the young lady who loves Kazantzakis."

"I was reading his novel *Saint Francis* last night," she said. "It's a profoundly moving book." She pointed at his book. "What are you reading?"

For a flustered moment, he couldn't recall the book he'd been holding. He only remembered he had taken it from the fiction shelves.

"Just a novel that caught my eye," he said. "I've read a few pages, but it's not very good."

For a moment both of them were silent. The girl smiled again and started to move away. He spoke quickly to avert her departure.

"You know I'm really impressed with your knowledge of Kazantzakis," he said. "And it's remarkable that you spent all that time in Crete. Were you studying there or working overseas for some U.S. company?"

"I was painting."

"You're an artist!" he said, and for some reason, that pleased him, as well.

"I love to paint," she said. "I saved some money from my job back here and decided to take a year and travel. I planned to go into Italy and Spain, but when I got to Crete, the color of the sky and the sea fascinated me. I rented a room in a house in a village some kilometers from Ierapetra and spent the year painting."

"That's wonderful!" he said. "To have such an experience at your age." He paused. "Now that we've spoken several times about Kazantzakis and Crete, I believe we're no longer total strangers. My name is Orestes Panos."

"Orestes is a fine, ancient Greek name," she said. "Mine is Sarah, Sarah Fleming."

"I'm very pleased to meet you."

He found her level gaze disconcerting.

"And I'm pleased to meet you," she smiled.

Anxious not to have her walk away from him again, he mustered his courage.

"I was just getting ready to go across the street to the coffee shop." He braced himself for a rejection. "Perhaps you'd jgin me for a cup of coffee and a doughnut?" He hastily added, "I'd be interested in having you tell me a little more about your stay on Crete." A nervous tremor rippled through his body. "Unless, of course, you've got an appointment or have to be somewhere else."

As he waited for her response, he noted the striking blue of her eyes and the fullness of her lips, bare of any lipstick.

It seemed to him she took an interminable time to answer.

"All right," she said. "There's just some reference information I've got to look up first."

He couldn't believe she had accepted.

"I'll go over and get a table," he said, trying to conceal his excitement. He wondered if she sensed he wished to avoid the two of them walking out of the library together. "You come over whenever you're finished. Take all the time you need."

She nodded and moved away. With his heart beating rapidly, he slipped into his coat and left the library. As he crossed the street, the wind whipping raindrops across his cheeks, he felt himself trembling as though he were bound for some illicit rendezvous in a secluded bedroom.

"You're only going with the girl for coffee and a doughnut, boofo!" he hissed. "Not filet mignon and champagne in a suite at the Ritz!"

Orestes entered the coffee shop, where a solitary patron slouched on a stool, and took a table in a corner. From there he watched the library entrance through the plate glass window.

A thin, dark-haired waitress smoking at the counter put down her cigarette and came to his table. He ordered coffee and then walked into the cramped men's room, which smelled of urine and disinfectant, and relieved himself. He looked nervously at his reflection in the cracked mirror, wondering whether the girl, who had to be in her early to middle twenties, might take him for less than fifty. He resolved sternly that if she asked, he wouldn't lie. When he returned to his table, he started to dial the Olympia on his cell phone to tell them he'd be delayed. As he saw the girl emerge from the library, he put the phone away. She paused on the library steps to open the plaid umbrella and then she started down the stairs and across the street.

He recalled a painting he'd had seen in one of the Impressionist galleries of the Art Institute, a Parisian girl holding an umbrella in the rain. The painting and Sarah crossing the street merged into one enchanting figure. She held the umbrella jauntily above her head and walked with a quick, graceful swing of her body. He rose from the table and walked to meet her at the door.

She carried in the moist smell of rain as she closed her umbrella and set it down by the door. Orestes helped her off with her coat.

As they walked together to the table, he noticed the counterman and waitress watching them, perhaps speculating as to whether the girl might be his young sweetheart. The thought both embarrassed and yet pleased him. They sat down, and the waitress strolled over.

"I'll have tea, please," Sarah said. "With lemon."

"How about a sandwich or a doughnut?" Orestes asked. "I highly recommend their doughnuts."

"Thank you, just tea."

As the waitress walked away, the gird reached for a napkin. For the first time then he noticed with a shock that the index finger of her left hand was missing, in its place a tiny stump over which a cap of skin had healed. That miniature amputation filled him with sympathy.

He looked up to see her watching him.

"It was an accident," she said quietly.

They sat in silence for a moment and Orestes recalled an old myth about a father who fearing the gods would steal his daughter because of her flawless loveliness, severed one finger of her hand. That solitary blemish marred her perfection and made the gods reject her so she could remain among mortals.

"Are you able to read Kazantzakis in Greek?" she asked.

"I speak and read Greek fairly well," Orestes said, "but I find him too difficult in the Greek text. He creates words of his own that I can't really understand."

"That creation of words is part of his power," she said. "I learned some Greek while I was in Crete, but not well enough to understand his Greek. Yet, even in English, he offers so much to his readers. And I feel so fortunate to have read him in the mountains of Crete where the characters in his books lived. That added a new level of meaning to his work for me."

They fell silent again. She raised her hand and brushed a strand of blonde hair away from her cheek, a simple gesture made uncommon because of her missing finger. He looked down at the table, resisting a surge of anxiety that rose to unsettle him.

"You don't need to feel nervous," Sarah said. He looked at her quickly and saw her watching him calmly. "I mean, there's no need to worry that I'll misunderstand why you asked me over here. We both love Kazantzakis, and it makes sense for us to have a cup of tea and coffee and talk about him."

He was grateful for her understanding, yet part of him was not reassured.

"That is the reason you asked me over, isn't it?"

He wondered if she were teasing him.

"Of course," he said firmly.

"Orestes," she said slowly. "I like the name. It suggests journeys and adventures."

And murders and tragedies, he thought bleakly.

"Where did you live in Crete?" he asked.

"In a village called Platina," Sarah said. "About ten kilometers from Ierapetra, which is on the southern coast. I roomed in a house with the village priest, Father Lefteris, and his wife, Papadia Froso. They had two teenaged sons."

"Teenage boys can be an ordeal. Did you have any trouble with them?"

The waitress brought a small pot with Sarah's tea. She idly toyed with the string holding the bag.

"No trouble at all," she said. "The boys were too frightened of their mother and father. They sometimes helped me carry my canvas and brushes to the seashore where I painted."

"What about the villagers? Did any of them resent you because you were a foreigner? Sometimes Greeks, especially villagers, can be suspicious of strangers."

"They were wonderful to me," she said. "You know the Greek word 'filotimo,' which means hospitality? They exercised great filotimo toward me and made me feel as if I belonged." She laughed. "They'd say about me, 'Einai kali kopela . . .' She's a good girl."

A man and woman entered the coffee shop, and Orestes looked up to see if he knew them. When he turned back to the girl, he saw her watching him. He had a disconcerting feeling that she understood his anxiety.

"The only person in Platina I had a problem with"—a slight

smile trembled her lips—"was Father Lefteris, the priest. I'd notice him watching me, and several nights I was sure I heard him lurking outside my bedroom window. Sometimes he even followed me to the seashore where I was painting."

"He should have been ashamed of himself!" Orestes said fervently.

"His wife, Papadia Froso, kept him in line. He never really bothered me, he'd just sit sometimes not far from where I would be painting and watch me. I even did a painting of him once."

Orestes felt a surge of compassion for the poor smitten priest living untroubled in the gray, bleakness of the village until the golden-haired girl moved into his house.

"Do you have to go to work?" she asked.

"I own my own business. I have a partner, too, but the business belongs to me so I can set my hours." He paused, and she seemed to be waiting for him to continue. "I own a restaurant on Halsted Street."

"I've eaten in some of the Halsted Street restaurants," Sarah said. "Which one is yours?"

"The Olympia. It's near Jackson and Halsted."

"I know where the restaurant is," Sarah said. "I've never eaten there, but it looks to be a very nice place."

"We're fortunate to do a good business."

"I'll have to stop by sometime."

He imagined the reaction of the lusty young waiters when they saw the girl. He had seen them whispering and rolling their eyes at the entrance of some attractive girl. And what about Cleon? His canny partner would probably suspect at once that Orestes had a prurient interest in the girl.

"I'd be delighted to have you stop in."

The girl smiled again and then looked toward the window. "It's stopped raining," she said. "I better go."

"It was good of you to come over."

He walked with her to the door. When he took down her coat from the rack, a faint fragrance of some perfume floated from the fabric. She slipped on her beret, pulled it down over her ears, trapping the soft, glowing strands of her hair. She looked up at him, her eyes unwavering and lovely.

"I'll see you again in the library sometime," he said.

For a long moment she didn't speak, and he had the disquieting feeling that she was probing his soul.

"Perhaps we can meet again somewhere else," she said quietly. "If you'd like, maybe we could have dinner together one night. We can talk a little more about Kazantzakis and Crete."

He was startled by her forthrightness. Yet it also bewildered him because he lacked the confidence to believe that she might be drawn to him as he had been drawn to her. He managed to respond that he'd like to have dinner with her.

She fumbled in her purse, brought out a small card.

"Here is my number," she said. "Phone me, and we'll make plans."

He took the card and nodded. He opened the door for her and watched her walking with quick, graceful steps away from the coffee shop.

He returned to the counter to pay for the coffee and tea, trying furiously to bring order to the chaos in his head. There were any number of possible explanations for her willingness to meet him again. He might have reminded her of her father. Perhaps she felt sorry for him and was throwing him a dinner as one might throw a dog a bone. Then again, she might be leading him on so she could make a fool of him. He had heard of women who toyed with men in that way. The possibility of that malicious game being true made him suddenly wary.

He stepped out onto the street, stood for an uncertain moment watching cars passing, their wheels splashing loudly through the rain-filled gutters.

Finally, he allowed himself the luxury of believing that she might simply feel attracted to him as he was attracted to her. That audacious speculation was assailed at once by doubts and misgivings. His mind seething with thoughts that accused one another, he walked brusquely to his car in the library parking lot.

When he arrived at the Olympia, his friends at their table were in the full heat of an argument on the relative merits of the modern Greek poets.

"What is most remarkable," Professor Platon said, "is how a small country the size of Greece, with a population of less than ten million people, could produce two Nobel Prize poets in Gorgios Seferis in 1963 and Odysseus Elytis in 1976."

"They should have had three, at least," Banopoulos said. "Yiannis Ritsos was as great a poet as Seferis or Elytis. He was also an activist and a resistance fighter against the Junta, not merely a poet."

"It would be a mistake to judge poets by their activism," Professor Platon said. "And I cannot agree about Ritsos. Certainly he isn't the equal of Seferis, who in his poetry captured so vividly the relationship of the modern Greek to his hallowed past."

"I'm not denying Seferis," Banopoulos said. "I'm merely saying that Ritsos should have been given a Nobel Prize, as well."

"What about Angelos Sikelianos?" Karvelas said. "He was one of the great lyric poets of Greece, a prophet and master of language in the grand tradition. Don't forget that in 1946, along with Kazantzakis, Sikelianos was also nominated for the Nobel Prize."

"You are all overlooking the finest of the Greek poets," Dr. Savas said. "The old Alexandrian poet Constantine Cavafy."

"Cavafy was a homosexual, a weak, self-obsessed man," Professor Platon said. "He wasn't even in the pure tradition of Greek poetry."

"Are you suggesting that we classify poets by their sexual orientation?" Dr. Savas scoffed. "Cavafy was a poet's poet. His lines were simple and unadorned, without the baggage of adjectives and metaphors so many other poets use."

"He wrote some decent verses," Professor Platon said, "but he isn't in the class of the great Hellenistic poets."

"The hell he isn't!" Dr. Savas snapped. "I've read many of your Greek poets, not only the ones you've mentioned, but Engonopoulos, Kavadias and Gatsos, and I tell you Cavafy may well be the greatest. His theme in poem after poem is that what matters in life is not the goal but the voyages one takes toward that goal, not freedom attained, but the struggle for that freedom. In the poems written near the end of his life, Cavafy proved himself a master poet of old age."

"Seferis also wrote brilliantly of old age and death . . ." Professor Platon interrupted, but Dr. Savas cut him off brusquely.

"Cavafy's poem 'Ithaca' is one of the most magnificent poems ever written in any language," Dr. Savas said. "In that poem, he refers to Ithaca being our ultimate destination."

"Is he talking about the island Odysseus came from?" Lalounis asked.

"He's not writing about the real Ithaca," Dr. Savas said. "He's referring to a mythical Ithaca one might also call Death, Purgatory, Paradise. After we have been through the battle of life, squandered all our energy, our flesh and blood expired, we eventually drop anchor at that island. Listen to the final lines . . ."

In a rasping voice that trembled slightly, Dr. Savas began reciting.

"Always keep Ithaca fixed in your mind.
To arrive there is your ultimate goal.
But do not hurry the voyage at all.
It is better to let it last for long years;

and even to anchor at the isle when you are old,
rich with all that you have gained on the way,
not expecting that Ithaca will offer you riches.

Ithaca has given you the beautiful voyage.
Without her you would never have taken the road.
But she has nothing more to give you.

And if you find her poor, Ithaca has not defrauded you.
With the great wisdom you have gained, with so much
    experience,
you must surely have understood by then what Ithacas
    mean."

"Good for you, our Hippocratic friend!" Professor Platon
said earnestly. "With all the time you spend probing, poking, and
testing, I wouldn't have thought you'd find time to memorize
poetry."

"I make time," Dr. Savas said. "At the end of a day spent staring into the mouths and up the rumps of patients, the poetry
refreshes me."

Orestes was surprised, at times, by how bright and literate
the group of men were and how their dialogue, though often
abrasive and intolerant of the opinions of others, was a pleasure to hear. They were veterans of experience and survivors of
life's battles.

Yet the truth was that with the exception of a few social functions they shared at the church, he knew little of their lives. Each
man was married to a decent, supportive woman except for Dr.
Savas, who had lost his wife to cancer five years earlier.

Orestes didn't know if during their years of marriage any of
them had been unfaithful. Looking at them now, it was hard for
him to imagine the undertaker cavorting with a mistress, or the

coolly lucid Professor Platon writhing in passion. As for Dr. Savas, who was a widower and had the right to seek out female companionship, Orestes couldn't help thinking that when confronted with a naked woman, Dr. Savas would probably whip out his stethoscope.

He was startled from his bawdy reverie.

"What do you think, Orestes?" Professor Platon asked gravely.

"About what?"

"I thought you were listening. About the relative merits of Seferis, Elytis, and Cavafy?"

"I think all three are fine poets," Orestes said. "Each of them has made a contribution to Hellenistic culture. Making comparisons as to which one is better is a waste of time."

"Well spoken!" Banopoulos said. "Sometimes, Orestes, you make me forget you as a dispenser of food and drink. You exhibit a real appreciation for literature!"

"Why do you think I chose him as a partner?" Cleon arrived at the table in time to hear the editor's words. "Did you think I'd let myself be harnessed to a fool?"

"Listen to the man passing judgement on fools," Karvelas sneered. "I'm certain he's never read Seferis or Ritsos!"

"I deal with living people!" Cleon snapped. "If I were an undertaker whose customers could no longer eat, drink, or complain, perhaps I'd have more time to read!"

Orestes left them debating the merits of the poets and retreated to his office.

The balance of the day dragged interminably for him, his thoughts returning inexorably to the girl. He wondered how soon it might be prudent to phone her. Where could he take her to dinner and not be recognized? If he suggested a place too far away, wouldn't she fathom and be hurt by his maneuver?

He had a sudden feeling the whole risky business was preposterous, the fanciful play-acting of a man undergoing a middle-age crisis. He made up his mind he simply wouldn't phone the girl. If he saw her in the library, he'd explain his busy schedule kept him thoroughly occupied.

Yet, even as he sought to put his struggle to rest, an unsettling vision of the girl returned to him, her lovely face and glowing hair, and in her slender, delicate hand, the small stump in place of a finger.

He took her card from his wallet and hid it far back in his desk drawer. He closed the drawer with a sigh of resignation and tried to remember what the Greek poets had written about the frailties of human beings.

In the late afternoon, Dessie phoned him. The moment Orestes heard her shaken voice, he understood some misfortune had taken place. His first thought was that something might have happened to Stavroula. Then Dessie told him Carmela was at the house with Catherine.

His heart skipped a beat as he remembered his premonition about Paulie and Carmela.

"Are they having trouble?" he asked.

"Yes," Dessie said. "I've been talking to her, but it doesn't help. I think she'd like to talk to you."

"All right," he said. "I'll leave now."

The rain had ceased on his drive home, but the pavements remained drenched, the tires of cars around him making loud, splashing sounds. When he arrived at his house and pulled into the driveway toward the garage, the sun had emerged from behind the burdened clouds, reflecting a scarlet light across the wet trees and flowers. He entered the kitchen where Carmela, her eyes swollen and her cheeks wet with tears, sat at the table with the baby on her lap. Dessie sat across from her, her face tense and distraught.

Orestes greeted Carmela with a kiss and gently kissed his

granddaughter. He took a seat at the table beside Dessie. Carmela's pretty face was so wracked by grief, it appeared swollen and unsightly.

"Paulie wants to leave us," Carmela said, her voice trembling with distress and fear. "He says its only for a while, but I think he really wants a divorce."

Because Orestes understood something of Paulie's unstable, restless nature, he didn't tell either Dessie or Carmela that he wasn't surprised.

"What is it, Carmela?" he asked her gently. "Have the two of you been having any particular problem?"

"I swear to God I don't know," Carmela said. Her voice trembled as if she were about to cry again. "Paulie has been unhappy about working at the shop. He complained a lot about it. Last night he told me he wants to leave . . . that he doesn't want to work . . ."

"He's never wanted to work," Orestes sighed. "All he's ever wanted to do was stumble from one religion to another faith."

"I've tried to be a good wife!" Carmela said earnestly. "I really have! I know I'm not a good cook yet, but I try. I clean the house and do the laundry. He wants me to go to school, to take courses, make myself smarter, and I've told him that I don't have the energy or the time."

As Orestes listened, his daughter-in-law's voice seemed to float in and out of his range of hearing. He knew he and Dessie were helpless to avert the separation and even divorce if Paulie was determined to leave his family.

"I'll talk to him," Orestes said, in an effort to console her. "I'll come over a little later this evening and talk to him."

"They're working on a big job for some sales meeting," Carmela said. "He won't be home from the shop until late."

"Then I'll go to the shop to see him first thing in the morning."

"Do you want to stay here tonight?" Dessie asked. "You can sleep in the guest bedroom and we'll put up the travel crib for Catherine?"

"I better go home," Carmela said. "When Paulie finally comes home from work later tonight, he may want to talk again."

As she rose, awkwardly holding the baby tightly in her arms, Orestes felt a surge of pity for mother and child. He was also angry at his son. Then he remembered how hard he and Dessie had pushed for him to marry the girl he had made pregnant.

He carried the baby to the car and helped Carmela strap her into the car seat. He kissed the baby gently and then hugged his grieving daughter-in-law.

"Don't worry, my darling," he said soothingly. "You know how erratic Paulie can be. A single night could change his mind."

He waited until she had driven off. Then he walked slowly and heavy-hearted back into the house. Dessie hadn't moved from the kitchen table, a look of resignation on her cheeks.

"Do you think Paulie means it?" she asked.

"He probably does."

"That poor girl and baby," Dessie sighed. "We'll have to stand by and help them now." She shook her head. "Wait until mama hears."

He saw the pain on Dessie's cheeks and in her eyes, and he understood a man could never feel as a mother did about her child. A woman carried the fetus in her body, nourished and nurtured it, until it was time for the baby to enter the world. That link remained unbroken for as long as mother and child lived.

"What about Mario and Theresa?"

"Carmela hasn't told them yet," Dessie said. "Mario will be furious. You know he's never really liked Paulie."

Orestes started from the kitchen.

"I'll have dinner ready in a little while," Dessie said.

"I had lunch at the restaurant and I'm not really hungry. You eat something with your mother. Is Marika coming home for dinner?"

"She's studying tonight with a friend. They're having pizza."

Later that evening, he phoned Paulie at the shop. His son's voice was tense and wary on the phone as they arranged for Orestes to meet him at the shop in the morning.

He showered and read for a while in bed. Marika came in to kiss him good-night and then went to her room. Dessie emerged from the bathroom in her nightgown and climbed into bed, shifting her body closer to his own. He closed his book.

"Read if you wish," Dessie said. "It won't bother me."

"My eyes are tired," he said. He reached up and switched off the lamp.

They lay together for a few minutes without speaking, the only sound in the shadowed bedroom, the rain lightly pelting their window.

"Do you remember him as a little boy?" Dessie's voice was low and sleepy. "He always wanted to do things by himself."

"He never played well with other children," Orestes said. "He's always been a loner." He paused. "I was that way as a child."

Dessie turned toward him in the bed, reaching out to gently caress his cheek.

"Poor Orestes," she said. "You spent your childhood in an unhappy house."

"That isn't true for Paulie," Orestes said. "We provided him love and attention and care. He can't have a complaint about that."

"No matter how much we want to do for our children, we cannot save them from pain and grief," Dessie said.

They fell silent again, and he felt Dessie's body slowly relaxing, slipping into sleep.

For a long while he could not sleep. He listened to the rain, marked the slow, regular throbbing of his pulse, a faint heartbeat that was all that kept him from death.

In the midst of his love and concern for Carmela, Catherine, and Paulie, his thoughts returned once more to the girl. For a moment, he indulged a fantasy about living with Sarah on some remote Greek island, shielded from cares of business and family, the two of them basking naked on the beach in the sun.

Orestes Crusoe and his young sweetheart, Friday, the sequel, he thought, mocking his daydream. He shifted closer to Dessie, feeling a tremor of compassion when he considered how hard the days ahead would be for her.

Seven

THE FOLLOWING morning, Orestes left the house early and drove to the print shop his son managed in Evergreen Park. He entered the small storefront building with its panoply of copiers, printers, and fax machines. He warmly greeted Nora and Beverly, the two young women who worked for Paulie.

"Paulie's in the back room, Mr. Panos," Nora said.

Orestes walked beneath the sign that read, EMPLOYEES ONLY into a large bare-walled, back room. In the far corner, Paulie stood beside a copy machine that was swiftly spitting out pages,

"This run will be finished in a couple of minutes, dad," Paulie said as Orestes reached him.

"Finish your work," Orestes said. "I'll just sit here and wait."

He sat nearby and watched Paulie removing batches of pages from the tray. For a moment, Orestes was able to observe his son without the distraction of conversation.

Paulie was of average height with a slender, small-boned build. He had played various sports in school without showing aptitude for any of them. He had also been only a fair student in his studies.

But the light, curly hair that framed the pale oval of his face and his blue eyes (an anomaly in their dark-eyed family) had made him a favorite with girls. Orestes remembered how bold some of them had been in their pursuit, sending Paulie flirtatious notes and phoning him late at night. After a while, however, many of them were disillusioned by the aura of gloom that radiated around him.

Ever since his son's adolescence, Orestes had been frustrated because they had difficulty communicating meaningfully. As his son grew older, every effort to bridge the chasm between them bogged down in dispute.

Although Orestes assumed most of the blame for this lack of rapport, it was also true that Paulie's melancholy nature hindered any efforts at accommodation.

The machine flipped out a final page and stopped. Paulie gathered papers from the tray and turned to Orestes.

"I know you and mom heard the news from Carmela last night."

"Is it true, Paulie?"

The youth's blue eyes gazed solemnly at his father.

"Yes," he said in a low voice.

"But why, Paulie!" Orestes said urgently. "After only a little more than a year of marriage and the birth of your baby, why are you talking about separation now? You had told us you loved Carmela and the baby. How can you think of doing this to them now?"

"Loving them isn't enough," Paulie said slowly. "What I can no longer endure is the way one futile day follows another. I'm in this shop for ten hours and then I spend three, four more hopeless hours at home before its time for bed. All that faces me each evening are soiled diapers and the drone of the television set. I feel my life slipping away."

"Millions of young families live that way," Orestes said earnestly. "But you don't have to stay home at night listening to television. Bring in a baby sitter and take Carmela to a play or to a concert. If you wanted to go off on a vacation, just the two of you, your mother and I will manage to look after the baby for you."

Even as he made the offer, a part of him feared the responsibility of having the helpless, tiny baby in their house.

"It'll take more than a week's vacation," Paulie said. "I am weary as hell in my mind and heart. I look forward to bed and when I do lay down, I have trouble sleeping."

"Take a sleeping pill for a while. They have good products for sleep on the market now that are not addictive."

"You always have all the answers," Paulie's tone turned resentful. "If I'm not hungry, I should still eat. If I cannot sleep, I should take a pill. If I'm heart-weary, I should take my wife to a concert. It's not all that simple."

"Nothing has ever been simple with you," Orestes sighed. "In school you daydreamed when others studied. At recess you watched while others played. You've always gone out of your way not to do what others are content to do."

"I am who I am," Paulie said defiantly. "You can't add the ingredients you want me to have. I'll make my own decisions!"

"For once, try not to think only of yourself!"

Their voices had grown louder, and Orestes knew the girls in the front of the shop must have heard them arguing.

"I didn't come here to fight with you, Paulie," Orestes spoke more quietly. "I understand you must make your own decision. But I implore you to think about it carefully. Consider Carmela and the baby. Give yourself and your family a chance. A single year of marriage isn't giving them a chance."

"I won't abandon them," Paulie said. "I'll continue to support her and the baby."

"How?"

"I'll find a way."

Orestes stared helplessly at his son. Were all sons and fathers forever destined to be in conflict? His own relationship with his brutal father, Moustakas, had left its wounds. Despite his yearning to be a more loving and caring father, had he also fostered wounds in his son?

"I've told you before that I could never speak to my father," Orestes said. "I had no rapport with him at all. But I have tried to be a caring father to you . . ."

"You and mom have done your part," Paulie said. "The fault is mine." He paused. "Souls not good enough for heaven and not bad enough for hell must keep journeying."

Orestes felt a surge of compassion for the driven and often bedeviled young man.

"Maybe your mother and I are to blame," he said slowly. "When Carmela became pregnant, we pressed you to marry her. Perhaps you weren't ready to marry."

"It wasn't just your urging that made me decide to marry," Paulie shrugged. "I did love Carmela and part of me wanted to marry her. Then there was her old man, Mario, who let me know he'd shoot me if I hadn't stepped forward to do the right thing. He might have shot me anyway because he was so pissed that I'd gotten her pregnant."

"Mario wouldn't have done anything so foolish."

"He wouldn't have done it himself," Paulie said. "He's Italian, and every Italian is related to another Italian in the Mafia. He'd have gotten someone else to knock me off, or, at the least, broken my legs with a baseball bat."

"If he had tried something like that, I'd have tried to get someone in the Greek Mafia to protect you," Orestes said with a wry smile.

A silence drew out thin between them. In the front of the store, one of the girls laughed, a high-pitched sound that carried clearly to the back room.

"Anyway, I wasn't planning to leave right away," Paulie said quietly. "I just wanted everyone to start thinking about it. I'll stay with Carmela and the baby until the end of the year, until the beginning of the next millennium. Then, I'm going to leave."

"Carmela said she was afraid that this separation would lead to a divorce. She felt that was where this is leading to."

"I'm not really thinking about a divorce now," Paulie said. "All I want to do is get away for a little while."

"Your mother and I and, I'm sure, Carmela's parents will be grateful for the additional time," Orestes said. "It would have been a shame for all of us not to be able to spend Christmas and the beginning of the new millennium together."

"Yeah, that will be great," Paulie said, but there wasn't any joy or anticipation in his voice. "I've got to get back to work now. We've got a big job they'll be picking up soon."

"And I have to get to the Olympia!" Orestes hesitated and then, feeling a need to express the love he felt for his son, he moved impulsively to hug him. Paulie stiffened for a moment and then let his father take him in his arms for a brief and awkward embrace.

As Orestes walked from the shop, he wondered sadly why he and his son were capable of feeling strong emotions and yet not be able to convey them to one another.

In his car, he dialed Dessie on his cell phone. When she answered, the tension and distress she'd felt the evening before lingered in her voice.

"Paulie's going to stay with Carmela until the end of the year," he said.

"Thank God!" Dessie said. "Do you think by then he might change his mind?"

"I don't know," Orestes said. "I honestly don't know."

"Has he told Carmela he's staying until then?"

"He didn't say."

"Maybe I'll phone her. The poor child probably spent a sleepless night." She paused. "Will you be home for dinner?"

"I think so," he said. "I'll phone you later from the Olympia."

He drove from Evergreen Park toward the expressway. For an instant, he considered stopping at the library on the chance he might see Sarah. He decided that pandering so quickly to his own desires would be a betrayal of Paulie. What would his son think if he knew his father were pursuing a girl nearly the same age as he was? He'd be justified in calling him a hypocrite. Orestes wouldn't be able to offer any defense except to say it was in the nature of man to prefer folly and passion to wisdom and calm.

Orestes spent a busy afternoon in the restaurant, ordering from various suppliers on the phone. He also worked on the menu for the following day and on a program for a major fund raiser in the Olympia to benefit a prominent Greek American judge running for reelection.

At about three, a waiter brought him word that Irv Kupcinet was in the restaurant and asking for him. Orestes walked out to greet the newspaper columnist, a beloved figure in the city who had been writing "Kup's Column" for more than fifty years. Orestes was not only fond of Kup but admired him because he had always avoided snide or cruel references to anyone in his column.

"How are you, Orestes?" Kup greeted him with a heartiness that belied his recent surgery. They shook hands warmly and Orestes motioned to a waiter to bring a plate of olives and cheese to the table.

"Anything good for me, Orestes?" Kup asked.

"Nothing much since I saw you last," Orestes said. "Ernie Banks was in with some friends the other evening. He looks as fit as he was when he played at Wrigley. That man is always so courteous and pleasant, the waiters love him."

"I heard a rumor that the Acropolis up the street may be bought by Rich Melman? Any truth to that?"

"I've heard nothing, Kup," Orestes said. "If it's true, Melman better mend his ways. Someone was telling me they ate lamb at that Greek restaurant of his up north and the meat was soaked in a tangy French sauce. Why would anyone want to smother the natural flavor of lamb?"

They visited a little while longer, and the columnist rose to leave.

"Don't stay away so long, Kup," Orestes said.

Later in the afternoon, a minor crisis erupted in the restaurant when two of the young waiters went into the alley to fight. One of the cooks carried the news to Orestes, who hurried to the alley. By the time he got out there, Cleon had managed to separate the antagonists. Both young men had landed some violent blows, and their faces were bleeding.

"What is this madness!" Cleon shouted. "Have you lost your senses? I should fire both you morons on the spot!"

An excited pack of cooks and waiters crowded through the kitchen doorway behind Orestes.

"What is this about?" Orestes asked the battling waiters sternlq. "What caused this quarrel?"

Both stood battered, silent and defiant.

"It's about a girl," one of the cooks sneered. "They're both sniffing around the same piece of tail."

"You shut your goddam mouth, Vrontes!" one of the youths shouted wrathfully.

"You better shut yours!" Cleon cried angrily. "Or by God, pick up your check and get the hell out of here!" He turned to the watching group. "The rest of you get back to work and move your rumps a little faster to make up for the time we've all wasted on this farce!"

The alley cleared quickly, and the battling waiters went inside to wash up. Cleon and Orestes returned to the office.

"There's been bad blood brewing between those two for weeks," Cleon said gloomily. "I should have watched them more carefully. But when a stallion's blood is boiling, there's little anyone can do." He paused and sighed. "We're lucky, Orestes, they were only using their fists. Over at the Macedonia, a waiter and a cook got into a fight with knives."

"Was anyone seriously hurt?"

"No one was killed. But the waiter had half of one ear sliced off. He's lodged a complaint with the police against the restaurant owner, Cardaras, as well as the cook who carved him up."

Cleon looked grimly at Orestes.

"Have you ever fought with another man over a woman?" Cleon asked.

"I'm thankful to say that I never have."

"Well, it almost happened to me once," Cleon said. "I was about twenty, and this big pousti and I were dating the same sweet girl. We arranged to fight for her in a vacant building one Saturday night. Then someone told me this guy was bringing along a gun. If he didn't like the way the fight was going, he planned to use it."

"What did you do?"

"I never showed up for the fight. I figured there would be other girls, but I only had one life to lose." Cleon grinned. "Better a live coward than a dead hero. I hope my old lady and children think I made the right move."

After Cleon had left the office, Orestes thought gloomily of Sarah. What if a jealous boyfriend saw them together and showed up at the restaurant with a gun? If Orestes were killed, what would Dessie and his son and daughter think of him? He'd leave his family a burden of shame they'd have to carry for as long as they lived. He imagined how that bastard, Sam Tzangaris would gloat!

Although Orestes often remained in the restaurant until later in the evening, when Dessie phoned to tell him her brother, Tommy, was coming over for dinner, he left the Olympia around five. When he arrived home, he found Tommy Vradelas in the kitchen with Dessie and Stavroula.

Dessie's brother was a loving, good-hearted man some five years older than his sister. His life had been marked by a sequence of failure in small business ventures and failure in a pair of marriages that ended in bitter divorce.

"My favorite brother-in-law!" Tommy waved a hearty greeting with his can of beer as Orestes walked into the room.

"Hello, Tommy," Orestes said amiably as he shook his brother-in-law's hand. He kissed Dessie who had just taken a tray of pastitsio out of the oven. Stavroula sat rigid as a prison matron on a chair in the corner. "Good evening, Stavroula." Orestes said. Her response was a barely audible grunt.

"Wash up, honey, we're all ready to sit down," Dessie said. Tommy went to help Stavroula to her chair at the dining-room table. She shook him impatiently away.

"Look after yourself!" the old lady snarled. "I can carry my own shanks to the table!"

"How wonderful, mama, each time I visit to find your sweet disposition unchanged!" Tommy cried. He winked at Dessie and Orestes. "I can't tell both of you how much I envy you having mama with you. Every night I pray she'll change her mind and come to live with me!" He turned to his mother. "How about it, mama? Are you ready to make your son a happy man by moving into his house?"

"Live with you?" Stavroula sneered. "In that pigsty with those mangy dogs and stinking cats?"

"You'd have your own room," Tommy said. "And we could arrange the animal's mealtime so they wouldn't interfere with your dinner."

"I always wondered what hell would be like," Stavroula grumbled as she took a seat at the table. "The first time I stepped foot into your manure dump, I knew."

All through dinner, Tommy's rapid-fire and unremitting monologue dominated the table. Orestes didn't mind because it eliminated any need for him to speak. He was genuinely fond of Tommy and admired his ability to tease Stavroula without fearing her biting tongue in reprisal. Tommy played with his mother the way a skilled angler plays with a savage swordfish, thwarting her barbs, deflecting her complaints.

"There's this little stationary-book store on Sheffield near North Avenue," Tommy said. "I've looked it over carefully and examined the accounts. If I double the greeting-card racks and install a small candy counter to sell fresh fudge, I could increase the gross by thirty-percent."

"Whatever you do will end up like the rest," Stavroula said scornfully. "You'll slink off like a dog with its tail between its legs, whining about the unpaid bills. Don't think you'll get any more money from me."

"Don't be so hard on him, mama," Dessie said. "Tommy works hard and tries. You know that."

"The poor fool has wasted more money in these businesses than most men spend in a lifetime," Stavroula said. "Why doesn't he get a regular job like a normal human being?"

"Because I'm not normal, mama," Tommy cried. "I'm an entrepreneur! A visionary! A creator!"

"You're a moron! A failure! A boofo!" Stavroula spit out each word.

"Mama, shame on you!" Dessie said furiously. "How can he succeed if none of us show any faith in him?"

Through all the baleful and heated exchanges, Orestes held his peace, feeling like a member of the audience in the Roman coliseum, watching the lion in the arena feed on the hapless Christians.

After Tommy had gone and with Stavroula ensconced back in

her lair watching a Tom Selleck video, Dessie and Orestes prepared for bed.

"Poor Tommy," Dessie said. "Mama cuts him down, time after time, and he keeps bouncing back. I don't know why he bothers coming over to visit at all."

"He doesn't take anything she says seriously. I wish I could do the same."

Dessie came and sat beside him on the bed, reaching up to gently caress his cheek.

"Putting up with mama is a real ordeal," Dessie said softly. "You're a saint."

"I'm not a saint. I'm just your husband and I love you and I know her being here is important to you. Besides, she's our responsibility. Someday you or I may need Marika or Paulie to take care of us."

"God help us!" Dessie exclaimed, and they both laughed.

Dessie wore a light sleeveless nightgown with a fringe of lace around her throat. Fresh from her shower, she carried a fragrant scent of soap. Her lovely dark hair was moist at the nape and at her temples, and her black eyes glowed in the lamplight.

They hadn't made an effort at lovemaking since the aborted episode on the living-room floor when Stavroula nearly caught Orestes bare-assed and bare-cocked.

As if sensing his thoughts, Dessie moved teasingly closer. Her hand gently stroked his arm, moved slowly and caressingly down to his thigh.

"Do you ever fantasize you're making love to another woman when you make love to me?" Dessie asked.

She didn't wait for him to answer.

"Oprah had a program about it the other morning. I was surprised how many women actually fantasize they're making love to other men during lovemaking with their husbands." She paused. "I've done it a few times."

"You've never told me that before!" Orestes exclaimed.

"You've never asked," Dessie said. "Besides, I've probably felt a little embarrassed about bringing it up."

"Well, who do you imagine you're sleeping with? A handsome young stud like Tom Cruise?"

"No! No!" Dessie scoffed. "That would be like sleeping with a friend of Paulie's. I fantasize much older men, strong, gentle men like Paul Henreid or Ronadd Colman."

"My God, Dessie! Both of them have been dead for years!"

"I know that. But I first saw them in films when I was a girl, and I've never forgotten them. Do you remember Ronald Colman in *Lost Horizon*? He had a voice that came from the screen like a caress. And remember the scene in—I can't remember the movie—when Paul Henreid lit two cigarettes and handed one to Bette Davis."

"You can't abide smoking."

"I know that! It wasn't the cigarette but the intimacy that I remember. The way he looked at her as he lit the two cigarettes and then took one from his lips and put it to her lips."

"It strikes me as dreadfully unhygienic," Orestes teased her. "Like using someone else's toothbrush."

"You're a clod!" Dessie laughed. "Insensitive and unromantic."

"I'm not unromantic!"

"I know you're not," her tone softened. She paused. "What about your fantasies? I know how you feel about Nicole Kidman. I remember how beautiful you thought she was when we saw her nude scene in 'Eyes Wide Shut.' Do you lust after her?"

"She's a very beautiful woman," Orestes said. "So beautiful she belongs to a fantasy, like a statue of a goddess, something to be admired but never touched."

"Is there anyone else?"

"You."

"You know what I mean! I told you about Paul Henreid and Ronald Colman, so now tell me your fantasies!"

"Well, I find an actress like Meg Ryan very attractive. She's very fresh, and very bright with a good sense of humor . . . she makes me feel loving and protective."

"Anyone else?" Dessie moved closer and kissed him gently on the cheek. Beneath the sheer nightgown, he caught a glimpse of her naked breast with its flushed nipple, and he felt the stirring of desire.

For an instant he was tempted to confess to Dessie the erotic scope of his fantasies. In one scenario, making love to a young, feminine woman like Meg Ryan would bring out his masculine side. (That would be true of Sarah, as well.) But he was also attracted to strong, big, and handsome women like Xena, Warrior Princess. He imagined her tying his hands and feet and then whipping his buttocks and thighs, not brutally, but with unquestioned authority.

The kindling of fantasies sparked his ardor. He reached for Dessie, fondled her breasts, pushed her gently back on the bed, her loosened hair spreading like a black fan across the whiteness of the sheet. He kissed her, tasted her breath, felt her tongue. She seemed as aroused as he was.

"Is the door locked?" he asked. "I can just see your beloved mama pounding in to catch me bare-assed again!"

He smothered Dessie's buoyant laugh with a kiss. They rolled over on the bed, and he was swept with love and passion for the beauty he had married. Their caresses grew more amorous, and he crouched above her lovely face, every limb and muscle of his body glowing and alive.

"Yes, Paul . . ." she spoke in a low hoarse voice. "Yes, yes . . . Ronald. Do that again! Touch me there again!"

"Easy, Meg, easy," Orestes whispered. "The damn bed is getting crowded. Easy, my darling! Easy!"

Eight

FOR THE following week, basking in the afterglow of his love for Dessie, Orestes did not visit the library, nor did he phone Sarah. He avoided those possibly compromising actions out of faithfulness to his wife. But he could not conceal from himself there was another compelling reason he avoided contact. He was afraid of what might happen if he pursued the young girl.

As the days moved into late September, his resolve faded, and he found himself rationalizing all the reasons it made sense for him to get in touch with Sarah. What harm could there be in the two of them having dinner? If they were seen, he'd explain that Sarah was the daughter of a friend who had asked Orestes to counsel her about her choice of profession. Something similar had occurred just the year before when Leo Karabatsos asked Orestes to lunch with his daughter, Thalia, and advise her on her choice of occupation. Of course, in that instance, the girl was planning a career in restaurant management. But, since Dessie knew about that luncheon, there was a precedent he could draw upon.

Finally, on an evening in the last week of September, alone in his office, Orestes carefully pulled the scrap of paper with Sarah's phone number from the back of his desk drawer. After he dialed, he counted his heartbeats through the first to third rings. On the fourth ring she answered.

"Sarah?"

"Yes."

"This is Orestes . . . you know, from the library."

"Of course," she said. He tried to read her voice, which was pleasant but impersonal.

"I would have phoned sooner, but we've been very busy here in the Olympia. Several large conventions in town have filled the restaurant every evening. I haven't had time to think about anything else."

He waited for her to acknowledge his explanation for not phoning, but she said nothing.

"How have you been?" He berated himself for the lameness of the question.

"Fine."

He suffered through another painful silence.

"Are you still reading Kazantzakis?" He felt beads of sweat erupting on his forehead and temples.

"Now I'm rereading Dante, the *Divine Comedy*. I told you how much I love it."

He prodded his courage.

"Would you still like us to have dinner together some evening?"

"That would be fine."

"That's great!" He felt himself torn by both anxiety and jubilation. "I'll check on some good restaurants. Do you like French or Italian food? There are some fine places just north of the loop. You could pick any restaurant you wanted."

"I have another suggestion," she said. "Instead of eating out, why don't we plan to have dinner here in my apartment?"

She spoke the words casually, but they echoed like a thunderclap in his head. For a moment he couldn't muster any response and remained stunned and mute on the phone.

"Hello?" she asked.

"Yes," he said quickly. "I'm here. That would be fine, but I wouldn't want you to go to all that trouble. Why should you have to cook?"

"I'm not a very good cook," she said, "but I enjoy cooking. I have only two or three dishes that I do well. Do you like spaghetti and meatballs?"

"I'm crazy about them!" He hadn't eaten them in years.

"I could make spaghetti or a lasagna."

"Either one would be fine."

"What would be a good night for you? This coming Friday or Saturday? I'm free either evening."

"Friday, or Saturday?" His mind raced to untangle which would be the better night to explain to Dessie why he would miss dinner. "I think Friday would be fine." He thought grimly that catastrophe was available either night.

"Let's make it Friday," Sarah said. "At 6:00 p.m., if that's convenient."

"Fine . . ." he uttered weakly.

"I live at 9650 South Hamilton. That's not far from Ninety-fifth and Western. Apartment 206. You can bring a bottle of wine, if you like."

"Of course," he said. He fumbled for a pad, scribbled down her address.

"See you Friday," Sarah said.

After she'd hung up, Orestes held the dead receiver numbly in his hand for several minutes until it began to click and buzz. He set it down and sat there still dazed.

In his wildest dreams, he couldn't have imagined such an invitation. For the following hour, his thoughts scrambling like mice in a maze, he agonized over what it meant. Was the girl so innocent she couldn't imagine what he might think? Was she so sophisticated that she offered such an invitation casually, assuming he was cosmopolitan enough to understand it meant nothing beyond dinner?

He accepted unhappily that two decades of fidelity had left him totally unprepared for a dilemma of this scope!

"In a world of fools the lout is king," he muttered. "Or is it, in a world of louts, the fool is king." He reassured himself he qualified for both titles.

He phoned Dessie that he wouldn't be home for dinner, apprehensive that she'd sense the turbulence of his thoughts. He also feared the probing glare of Stavroula. The old witch with her link to the forces of darkness might be able to read his frantic mind. He seriously considered capsizing the whole insane business.

He'd phone Sarah and tell her he had to leave town on a business trip for a week, perhaps to meet with some investors about opening a restaurant in another city. Then he simply wouldn't phone her again.

That scenario wasn't totally satisfactory because Dessie would never know how honorably he observed their marriage vow of fidelity. As an alternative, he might actually tell Dessie about Sarah, confess to his wife the staunch struggle he had made to resist temptation, how he'd drawn back from the very precipice. She'd have to admire his valor and character.

His thoughts veered from those pious fantasies into more dangerous terrain. After all, the world wouldn't end if he decided to have dinner with Sarah. The whole experience might be totally innocent. They'd pass a pleasant evening, eat spaghetti and meatballs, drink a glass or two of good wine, discuss Kazantzakis, and he'd be on his way.

Then again, what if the evening were not so benign? What if, for reasons incomprehensible to him, the girl had found him attractive? If he wasn't Antonio Banderas, he wasn't a Gorgon either. If that attraction proved true, as a precaution, he'd need to purchase a package of condoms. The prevalence of AIDS made such an action mandatory.

For a lurid instant, he imagined what would happen if he contracted AIDS. The malignant disease would run its devastating course until he died slowly and painfully in the midst of his family. He could see Dessie's tear-stained cheeks and the look of bitter reproach in her eyes. His son, Paulie (if he were still around), and his daughter, Marika, would grieve for him, as well. As for Stavroula, the bellowing of "I tried to warn you!" and "You wouldn't listen to me!" coming out of the old tornado's mouth would deafen him all the way to hell!

Now the truth was that he might be doing Sarah a terrible injustice. The girl gave every indication of being sweet and virginal. At the same time, it was also true that young people in this day and age routinely practiced promiscuity. He hadn't any idea how many sexual partners Sarah might have had in her young life. Perhaps he wasn't the first middle-aged man she had seduced. He definitely needed to get the condoms. He might not need to use them, but it would be wise to be prepared, just in case.

Now what if the evening did become amorous and Sarah and he were consumed by passion? How on earth would he bring up the matter of using a condom? Pull it out casually the way Paul Henreid might light a cigarette? How would the smooth-voiced, debonair Ronald Colman have handled the moment of decision? If he bungled the whole business, Sarah might be outraged and demand he leave at once.

Another even more disabling thought possessed him when he considered the bleak prospect that his intense nervousness might render him impotent. Perhaps, as a precaution, he could get Dr. Savas to write him a prescription for that new miracle drug, Viagra, that everyone was raving about. He'd tell him that he was having some minor problems with impotence when he made love to Dessie. That would be embarrassing but better than trying to tell his old friend the truth. As he slogged on through the quagmire of possibilities, the whole superstructure collapsed.

"My God, the girl has simply invited you to dinner, and you're girding yourself to attack the fortress of Navarone!" he berated himself scornfully. "While you're about it, imbecile, why don't you ask Savas for a prescription to treat dementia!"

He was grateful when there was a knock on his door and Cleon entered.

"You've been locked in here for hours!" Cleon said. "A few of the boys at the table are asking about you. I've been trying to mediate an argument between Karvelas and Banopoulos. But those two gamecocks need at least an archbishop." He paused. "Are you all right, Orestes? You look pale as a ghost . . . if you don't mind my saying so. Did you receive some bad news?"

For an instant Orestes considered taking his partner into his confidence and then decided he couldn't place that burden upon him. Even if Cleon didn't judge him, he'd worry about him.

"There are some serious problems with Paulie and Carmela." He brought that troubling matter up to justify his preoccupation.

"Goddamit, Orestes, that's terrible!" Cleon said. "I knew those kids were on thin ice, but I hoped they'd hang in there. This must be awful for Dessie and you, as well as for them." He shook his head grimly. "To say nothing about Mario. That hot-headed Sicilian isn't likely to take the news with a compassionate heart."

"Paulie is afraid that he might actually harm him," Orestes said. "Maybe beat him up or something like that."

"Then let's you and me talk to Mario first!" Cleon said. "Invite him for dinner here at the Olympia, stuff him with lamb chops and our best rodytis, and try to straighten things out for Paulie."

"We might do that," Orestes said and rose from his desk. "For the moment, let's go make an effort to mediate that dispute between Karvelas and Banopoulos."

As the week passed, the days drawing closer to Friday, his nervousness intensified. All the possible scenarios he had considered for his dinner with Sarah returned like furies to haunt him.

To prepare for his missing dinner on that fateful evening, he told Dessie that some restaurant men from Detroit would be coming to town on Friday and had invited him for dinner some place near their downtown hotel. He was grieved at how effortlessly she accepted his lie. He knew it was because she trusted him, and now he was violating that trust.

On Wednesday afternoon, foraging to purchase some condoms from a store where he wasn't likely to be recognized, he drove the Eisenhower west to Oak Park and located a Walgreen pharmacy. He took a cart and filled it with two cans of shaving cream, two bottles of mouthwash, several tubes of toothpaste, and several packages of soap. In the midst of these products, he dropped a small box of a dozen Trojan condoms. He loitered until the checkout cashier had no other customers at her register and then quickly pushed his cart into place before her counter.

As she swiftly scanned the items, he watched her anxiously for any recognition that she viewed the Trojans critically. When she came to scan them, to his horror she waved the small box briskly in the air.

"These are on sale," she said. "Buy one and get a second box free."

He couldn't believe the way fate had skewered him!

"That's all right," he said casually. "No need to bother."

"No bother," she said. "I can get a clerk to bring you a second box." She pressed a buzzer. "Howie!" Her voice boomed like a cannon shot throughout the store. "Bring up a second package of Trojans."

An old woman pushing her cart nearby raised her ears like a hound catching the scent of prey.

"On second thought, just forget about them," Orestes said quickly. "I'll let my son come in and buy his own."

"They're on sale until Saturday," the cashier said.

Orestes paid thirty-seven dollars for assorted toiletries he didn't need and left the Walgreen's without the condoms.

On Thursday afternoon, he closeted himself in his office and logged onto the Internet. His Hotmail account was replete with sex aids ads, and he entered their Websites, bewildered by the multiplicity of products and services being offered.

Get Larger Today! Where it really counts!
Do you want to give your partner more pleasure?
Do you want to stay Rock Hard longer?

If you answer "yes" to any of these questions, then our Laboratory-Approved pill is guaranteed to enlarge your private part. Lengthen and Expand by more than 50%. And 100% guaranteed.

Orestes sighed and switched to another web site,

BRAND NEW! FIRST TIME ON THE MARKET!

Fast acting version of Viagra! A tiny tablet that works up to 8 times faster and more effectively than Viagra. Compounded by licensed pharmacists.

Originally developed by the German Drug Firm Harnishflegger as a kidney medication, Sildenafil Dexatimine increases blood flow by relaxing arteries. During these studies, the Harnishflegger scientists were astonished to notice a sizeable increase in the size and erectile functions of the male organs in their kidney patients. In some instances the erections were maintained for four to five hours!

Recommended quantity for first order.

10 Sildenafil Dexatimine tablets @ $ 27.00 each. Ten tablets for $260.00. A saving of a dollar per tablet.

*ANNUAL PHYSICIAN FEE FOR PRESCRIBING INITIAL PRESCRIPTIONS
AND UP TO TEN REFILLS OR 100 TABLETS, $85.00 TOTAL $345.00
PLUS SHIPPING AND HANDLING.*

Seeing an on-line ad for Frederick's of Hollywood, he logged on and for a little while floated in a sensual haze of butterfly brassieres, microfiber teddies, lace-heart panties, thigh-high, lacy, webbed stockings. Feeling giddy, he fantasized how Sarah might look in the Vinyl Rosebud, Ribbon-Lacing, black-bikini panties and black silk stockings. If they got to know each other intimately, he might even buy her a few of these provocative items.

He descended from that sphere of orgiastic indulgence to another Website for Apex Miracle Cream.

Men, here is a revolutionary product that will have your woman screaming for more every time you have sex!

Bring your woman to her knees, give her multiple orgasms, make her think you're the most virile stud in the world! Only $89.95 for a four-ounce tube!

With less than thirty-six hours to go, all of these extravagant opportunities were useless to him. Even if he were offered the elixir of Zeus, it wouldn't arrive in time. In despair and resignation, late Thursday afternoon, knowing there was indeed no other way, Orestes brought Dr. Savas into his office.

"First time in a long time I've been granted a private audience into this culinary Vatican," Dr. Savas said. He peered sharply at Orestes. "Is anything wrong? Are you having chest pains or kidney malfunction?"

"Nothing like that, Dr. Solon," Orestes said. "Sit down, please." He motioned to a chair and then seated himself in an armchair facing the old, white-haired doctor he had known for a lifetime.

"My friend," Orestes began. "I need your help." He took a deep breath. "I'm thoroughly ashamed to have to make this confession, but I would be even more ashamed if I lied to an old friend who had delivered both my children."

Dr. Savas stared at him gravely.

"This sounds serious, Orestes," he said. "Are you trying to tell me you've contracted a venereal disease?"

"My God, no!" Orestes exclaimed. "That would be a horror!"

While the doctor waited for him to continue, Orestes struggled for the right words.

"There is a girl . . ." he began. He waited anxiously for the doctor to express quick disapproval, but Dr. Savas said nothing, nor did his expression change.

"I'm not sure it's serious," Orestes started again. "I mean, I met her in the library. We had coffee together. She's invited me to dinner in her apartment."

Once again he waited in vain for the doctor to speak.

"Believe me, Dr. Solon, this dinner could well prove to be totally innocent! She's less than half my age! It might be an act of an unbalanced and perverted mind to even consider anything beyond that!"

He felt his throat dry.

"Can you say something, please?" he asked weakly.

"What do you want me to say, Orestes?" the doctor's voice was casual, and without any tone of censure. "You have entered the Disneyland of Dionysus. In that pleasure arcade, you'll encounter the Lion of Lechery and the Leopard of Lust. Because you're also a decent man married to a lovely woman, you'll also suffer the Tiger of Guilt and the Wolf of Remorse."

"That's quite a menagerie," Orestes sighed. "I knew I could depend on you to describe my dilemma colorfully."

Dr. Savas grinned.

"Why are you telling me this? Are you confessing before the

fact and plan the more lurid confession to your parish priest later? Do you want my opinion? My approval? Just what is it you want from me?"

"Once again, my friend, try to understand," Orestes pleaded. "I may be doing this young girl a terrible injustice! If she knew I were even thinking such a thing, she might be outraged! She is young, sensitive, lovely, and she reads Kazantzakis!"

"Good for her," Dr. Savas said. "But Medea might also have been a well-read lady. I understand your reservations, but good sense and prudence bids you be prepared. I understand that, as well."

"Thank you, my friend!"

"Don't thank me," Dr. Savas said. "Illicit passion is a multi-headed monster. I don't envy you your dinner with this young Persephone." He paused. "So what do you want from me?"

"Perhaps a prescription for a few tablets of that new drug, Viagra!" Orestes blurted out. "I haven't had any problem with Dessie, but I am nervous as hell about this encounter. I tried to buy condoms in Oak Park, and it was a disaster. I'll make another effort at the condoms myself, but I'd like a prescription for Viagra."

"Have you ever taken Viagra?"

Orestes shook his head.

"Some men swear by it, but I must warn you that it has devilishly perverse consequences, as well. A few men for whom I have written Viagra prescriptions return to my office to embrace me and call me brother. But other men using it for the first time suffer adverse effects, heart palpitations, shortness of breath. I have even heard of a few cases where a man suffers renal failure or a fatal heart attack."

"My God!" Orestes cried in a low hoarse voice. "What if I expired in the girl's apartment! What would Dessie say? My children would carry the burden of shame for as long as they lived! My bloody mother-in-law would be so overjoyed at my ignominious end, she'd dance at my funeral! My entire life would go up in smoke!"

"That's the price one pays for sinning," Dr. Savas grinned. "My advice to you is forget about the Viagra. If this girl is as attractive as you say, you'll probably find your libido stimulated enough to produce an adequate erection. As for the condoms, I have some samples in my office that I provide for husbands and wives seeking to avert pregnancy. Stop in tomorrow morning. If I'm busy with a patient, I'll leave a plain, unmarked package for you with Aphrodite. I'll tell her they're antihistamine tablets."

"God bless you, good doctor!" Orestes said gratefully. "You've saved my wretched life!"

"If all it took to save a life was to provide a sheath for one's prick," the doctor laughed, "they'd be passing out condoms like candy on every street corner."

Nine

ON FRIDAY morning, Orestes woke after spending a wretched and sleepless night, his dreams replete with images of hangings and decapitations. He moved quietly from beneath the sheets in order not to wake Dessie, who was still asleep beside him. Slumped for a moment on the edge of his mattress, seeking the energy to rise, he wondered if his lurid dreams were a portent of things to come.

He contemplated his bedraggled countenance in the bathroom mirror.

"Did Don Juan and Casanova go through this agony each morning?" he queried his reflection. The doleful image grimaced in response.

Dressed, and ready to leave, he sat for a moment in the kitchen drinking a hot cup of strong black coffee. Dessie came into the kitchen in her robe. She bent to give him a light, consoling kiss.

"I heard you tossing all night," she said.

"Something I ate must have bothered me."

"You shouldn't just be drinking coffee. Maybe an egg and toast would help settle your stomach."

"I'll have something at the restaurant." He rose from the table to leave. "Don't forget tonight I'm having dinner with the restaurant men from Detroit. I may be late, so don't wait up for me."

"Try to rest a little at the Olympia today," Dessie said. "If you're tired, the evening will become an ordeal."

He accepted that unhappy prediction as true.

When he heard Stavroula on the stairs, grunting and rumbling in a noisy descent, he kissed Dessie quickly good-bye and fled.

On his way to the Olympia, he stopped in the Washington Street office of Dr. Savas. The doctor's nurse, Aphrodite, a dried prune of a woman who had worked with him for nearly thirty years, was just opening the office.

"Doctor had a call to make at the hospital," Aphrodite said. "He shouldn't be long."

Orestes sat and nervously waited, feeling the old nurse's eyes probing and assessing him as if she knew the reason for his visit. He was about to leave and return later when Dr. Savas entered.

The doctor motioned to Orestes to follow him into his office. Once inside, he closed the door. "I thought you'd be sleeping late this morning to conserve your strength."

"I had a terrible night," Orestes sighed.

"The merciless price one pays for the pursuit of passion," Dr. Savas grinned. He rummaged in one of the drawers of his desk and brought out several small packets of condoms.

"Will a dozen be enough?" he asked with a wink.

Orestes lacked the spirit to respond to the banter.

"On second thought, I don't wish to encourage recklessness and excess. For the first encounter, one package of three rubbers should be more than enough."

Orestes buried the small packet in his trouser pocket. He started for the door, offering Dr. Savas a final, plaintive wave of farewell.

When he arrived at the restaurant, he told Cleon he wasn't feeling well and spent the better part of the morning doing paperwork in his office. From time to time, he leaned back in his chair and dozed. In the early afternoon, Kyriakos came to ask his advice on a menu for the dinner party of a city politician that night. Having trouble concentrating, Orestes, distracted by other concerns, made a few random suggestions.

"If that's the best you can do," Kyriakos grumbled, as he left the office, "Next time I won't bother to ask . . ."

At four o'clock, Orestes went into the bathroom behind the office to shave for a second time, and to wash and put on a fresh underwear top.

He had been deliberately vague in providing Cleon any details of the fictitious evening's dinner and he managed to slip out of the Olympia without talking to his partner. On the sidewalk he encountered a longtime friend, Don Stevens, on his way into the Olympia with a small party. The silver-haired trader on the Mercantile Exchange shook hands warmly with Orestes and introduced him to his party, which included an attorney and a judge.

"I hoped you'd join us for a drink, Orestes," Don Stevens said.

"Unfortunately, I cannot, my friend. I have a dinner with some visiting restaurant men from Detroit."

A lie procreates like an amoeba, Orestes thought gloomily as he walked to his auto. He entered and drove into the stream of northbound traffic on Halsted Street.

The Friday evening rush hour had not yet begun, and he made the drive to the South Side quickly. He cruised slowly along Sarah's street until he located her building. After searching vainly for a parking space nearby, he drove to a Ninety-fifth Street parking garage. It was only a little past five, and he had almost an hour before he was expected.

He walked along Ninety-fifth and found a liquor store, where he bought a bottle of vintage Bordeaux. He paid $65 for the wine in cash.

"That's a really fine wine." The liquor store owner handed him the wrapped bottle. "I hope you enjoy it."

"Is there a florist nearby?"

"Right around the corner."

Inside the flower shop with its profusion of colorful blossoms, he finally decided on a dozen red roses that the florist wrapped and tied with a ribbon.

At a quarter to six, he left the florist, laden with the wine and the bouquet of roses. He walked quickly, with his head bent, fearing he might run into someone who knew him. When he did look up warily, the men and women he passed on the street stared at the wine and flowers and then leered knowingly at Orestes, as if it were readily apparent that this middle-aged lecher was on his way to an illicit rendezvous with a younger woman.

When he entered the vestibule of the three-story brick building in which Sarah lived, the mailboxes revealed there were a dozen apartments. He located Sarah Fleming's name and pressed the buzzer. An instant later, he heard her voice.

"It's Orestes."

"I'm on the second floor. After I buzz you in, the stairs are to the right." A moment later the buzzer sounded and he entered.

He walked slowly up the stairs. When he reached the second floor hallway containing four apartments, Sarah opened one of the doors. She greeted him with a smile.

He had forgotten how small and how lovely she was, and, for an enchanted moment, he stared down at the girl. The pale oval of her face, framed by the long, golden strands of her hair falling about her shoulders, glistened in the shadows of the hallway. She wore a pink knit blouse and a light flared skirt.

"How kind of you, Orestes, to bring both flowers and wine." She took the flowers, and he followed her into the apartment.

His first impression was that he had entered a chapel shimmering with candles. There were candles burning on the sideboard and on the mantle above the imitation fireplace. In the middle of the room, a small table had been set for two with a silver candelabra holding six glowing candles as a centerpiece. The apartment also held a pervasive scent of incense.

Sarah unwrapped the roses and put them in a vase. The flowers snared the glitter of the candles, which deepened their color to a blood-red bloom.

"They're beautiful," Sarah said. "They remind me of lines from a poem although I cannot remember the poet.'Dying summer brings the fading day, and the last sweet bloom of roses.'"

Her voice echoed pleasingly through the candlelit room.

"Dinner will be ready in a few minutes. I've made spaghetti and meatballs that I hope you enjoy. If you like, you can open the wine."

Orestes had taken the precaution of slipping a small wine opener into his pocket and he pulled it out and swiftly opened the bottle of Bordeaux. He partially filled each of the wine glasses on the table.

While he waited for Sarah to bring the dinner to the table, he studied the apartment. There was a living-dining area with a couch and armchair, a small kitchen, and two doorways leading to what he presumed were a bedroom and a bathroom. There were several small bookcases full of books and a CD player on a stand in a corner. In another corner, just to the side of the large bay window, stood an easel covered by a cloth.

"I don't see a TV set," he said.

"I had a small black-and-white set, but it took up too much of my time and I gave it away. I prefer to read and paint."

Sarah brought the platter of spaghetti and meatballs to the table. She had also prepared a small green salad and a side dish of creamed carrots and peas.

"It's not a very substantial meal," she said ruefully. "I hope you weren't expecting a big dinner."

"This is just fine," Orestes said. When she was ready to sit

down, he rose and held her chair and was rewarded with a luminous smile.

"You can cut the bread," she said, motioning to a baguette on
a breadboard. He cut several slices.

Orestes had little appetite, and he ate just enough so Sarah
wouldn't feel he didn't like the dinner. He also drank several
glasses of wine and filled Sarah's glass several times, as well.

"The wine is wonderful," she said.

They spoke of Kazantzakis and her stay in Crete. She related
a little more about the people in the village where she'd lived.
She asked him to tell her about the restaurant, and he described
for her something of the day's routine, Cleon managing the restaurant and Kyriakos overseeing the kitchen. He also told her
about the young waiters who came from Greece to seek their
fortunes in America.

"Do many of them return home?"

"Only for short visits to see their families," Orestes said.
"Most of them come from poor villages where its almost impossible to earn a living. If they become successful here, perhaps
acquiring a restaurant of their own or doing well in some other
business, they'll make at least one visit to their village to show
off. They'll drive a big American car with an attractive Athenian woman on their arm, and the entire village will share in
the celebration."

"That sounds sad," Sarah said. "There should be more in life
for them than mere wealth and showing off that wealth."

He was impressed with her good sense.

At the end of dinner, Sarah brought small demitasses of
strong sweet coffee to the table. She also set out a small tray of
grapes and feta cheese.

"I bought the feta from an Italian grocery on Western Avenue. I hope you find it authentic."

Orestes reassured her that it was very good.

Within the multiplicity of flickering candles, the cloying odors of melting wax and incense seeping into his nostrils, the anxiety he had felt in the beginning passed into a curious languor. When he asked if he could see some of her paintings, she told him she'd save the viewing until his next visit. After they'd finished their coffee, she started to clear the table. He rose to help her.

"No, please," she said. "There are just a few plates. You go and sit on the couch."

As he rose from the table, he felt curiously light-headed, his vision slightly out of focus. He blamed it on the profusion of candles and scents of incense as much as the wine. He had a sudden sense of the small apartment as a misted and secluded sanctuary, far removed from the city and its teeming streets.

He walked a little unsteadily into the adjoining living room, a slight current of air induced by his passage fluttering the flames of the candles on the sideboard. He sat down on the small couch. After several minutes, struggling against a yearning to sleep, he couldn't resist closing his eyes.

He wasn't sure how long he dozed, but a rustle of movement caused him to open his eyes, and he glimpsed a misted form in the doorway of the bedroom. He thought at first that it was an apparition fashioned by the candles, and then he saw it was a figure so slim and small that at first he thought it might be a child. As the figure came closer, he was startled to see it was Sarah, changed from her blouse and skirt into an ankle-length dress. As she neared the couch, he saw the dress was really a white robe that clothed her from her throat to her ankles. She also wore a filmy, gossamer veil across her head. Below the hem of the robe, she was barefoot, the toes of her small feet gleaming like tiny pearl shells against the darker carpet.

He sat transfixed, trying to collect his senses, accepting with a quiver of nervousness that her changing into a robe meant they were going to make love. He made an effort to break the spell of languor that left him feeling weak.

She stood for a moment above him and then slowly curled down to sit on the floor, close to his feet. She stared up at him with her face radiant in the candlelight, and then, as if she were a child seeking solace from a parent, she placed her head gently against his knee. For what seemed like a long time, she sat that way without moving, her golden hair cascading from beneath the veil down the calf of his leg. When she finally raised her head to look at him, he saw the moist beauty of her eyes.

"Now, I have a confession, Orestes," she said, the words rising in a whisper from her lips. "You might think it strange, but that first day in the library, the first time I saw you, I was overwhelmed at how much you resembled the wonderful poet Dante Alighieri. I've studied many drawings and paintings of him in old books. I couldn't believe how everything about you, your head, your nose, the slope of your shoulders resembled Dante. I am convinced you are his reincarnation."

He couldn't recall any drawing or painting he had seen of Dante, and he hadn't the slightest idea whether the poet of the *Divine Comedy* was homely or handsome.

"I asked that sweet librarian about you," Sarah said. "She told me you were Greek, and a faithful reader of Kazantzakis. Since I also loved Kazantzakis and had lived for that year in Greece, our coming together seemed destined by fate, as well. You don't know how long I've been waiting for you."

Her suggestion that destiny had brought them together pleased him. The veil she wore had slipped down around her shoulders and released the golden fullness of her hair. He felt the warmth of her body against his knee and leg.

"You cannot imagine what a miracle it is that I should finally have found you, Dante, reincarnated . . ." her voice hung suspended for a moment. "Because, you see, I am the reincarnation of the woman Dante loved all his life, his beloved Beatrice Portinari."

He knew something of role playing, and for a moment he thought she was teasing him as a prelude to love. But there wasn't any playfulness in Sarah's voice nor any frivolity or flirtatiousness in her face.

From the street below the building, a bottle shattered against the pavement, and a man's angry voice rose in a curse. Sarah seemed not to hear.

"Dante loved Beatrice from the first time he saw her at the age of nine," Sarah continued softly. "From that moment on, he wrote his poetry and dedicated his life to her. In his great work, the *Divina Commedia*, Virgil leads him through the Inferno and Purgatorio, and then Dante rediscovers his beloved Beatrice. He is as dazzled by her as he was when he first saw her as a child. He is inspired by her presence, and she becomes his guide through Paradiso."

Orestes did not know what to say, what words to offer in response to the extraordinary vision her words created. His reason told him it was a fantasy, yet it also cast a vivid spell that he had no desire to shatter.

"We were fated to come together, my darling," she whispered. "I have been waiting for so long, my soul suspended between the beautiful stars of Cassiopeia and Orion. I have waited, lonely and forlorn, and now I have found you. I swear to you that I am as chaste as I was when you first saw me."

Her face had been transformed by her recital, her beauty become more ethereal and disembodied. Her lips parted, and he saw her teeth, even, small, and bright.

"Chaste . . . chaste . . . chaste," she repeated the word softly. "From the time when you first saw me as a child, I have tried to flee temptation. Some men, however, more driven by evil than by good, sought to lure me away from my vow of chastity. They thought me beautiful because I was vain and considered myself beautiful. Several times I felt myself weakening, my darling, and almost betrayed you. Then an accident sent to me from God cleansed me of the sin of vanity and temptation."

She slowly held up her hand, her outstretched palm with the small, slender fingers and the missing digit framed against the candlelight.

"While slicing meat one day," she said, "the sharp knife slipped and severed my finger. I bled and wept. But, afterwards, I was glad because the missing finger blemished my beauty. When I looked at my hand, I no longer thought of myself as beautiful. The stump of my finger became a constant reminder that I must remain faithful to that chaste, unsoiled love you hold for me."

There was a sudden clamor of voices in the hallway outside the apartment door. As if to retreat from that reality, Sarah shifted closer to him. The voices faded away, and, as the silence returned, he heard the faint ticking of a clock.

"Now that I have made this confession to you," Sarah said, "you must speak the words Dante offered to Beatrice." She closed her eyes and began to recite softly.

"That sun, which first scalded my breast with love . . ." She opened her eyes, waiting for him. He felt his throat tight and his lips dry.

"That sun, which first scalded my breast with love . . ." he said in a low voice.

". . . has now revealed to me, by proving and disproving . . ."
Slowly, carefully, he repeated the words.

". . . has now revealed to me, by proving and disproving . . ."
". . . the sweet and lovely face of truth."
". . . the sweet and lovely face of truth."

As if the confession and recital had suddenly wearied her, he saw her eyelids flutter. For a long time, they remained sitting that way, her head resting against his knee, her hair tumbled along his leg. He struggled to absorb and make sense of her confession.

For a moment, he considered that she might be insane, and, suddenly fearful, he wondered how he might escape. Then the urge to flee passed into tender compassion for the lovely young girl who had brought him into the haunting, fantasy world she inhabited.

His limbs grew stiff, and he reached down and made a gentle effort to raise Sarah from the floor. He was able to tug her awkwardly upright. For a moment he considered carrying her to bed. He was suddenly apprehensive that if she woke, and saw him looming over her on the bed, she might be frightened.

He slowly and gently lowered her to a reclining position on the couch. He brought a small pillow that he placed carefully beneath her head. From the adjoining bedroom, he drew a quilt from the bed, which he carried back to the couch.

He drew the quilt over her bare feet, pulling it up to her throat. Looking down at her small, slim figure, he was shaken at how much she resembled a sleeping child.

He bent slowly and lightly kissed her forehead, felt her flesh warm and moist. Her lips trembled and parted, and she drew a faint, shaken breath.

"My darling Dante," she whispered, her voice low and sleepy. Orestes snapped on a lamp in the corner. In the lamp's faint glow, he walked around the room and blew out the candles that had not already burned down. Afterwards, he left the apartment, quietly closing the door behind him.

He walked down to the street, stepping outside into the fragrant autumn night. As if he were emerging from a dream, he returned slowly to the rumbling sounds of the city. He stared up into the sky, searching for the beautiful stars of Cassiopeia and Orion. In that moment of heightened perception, he understood a little more about the magical, the revelatory nature of life.

He marveled again at life's potential to provide surprises about which man's mind could never conceive. Driven by the stratagems of lust, girded like a knave for seduction, he had been given a glimpse into the bountiful capacity of the human heart to fashion fantasies beyond the reality of time and the earth.

Walking slowly toward the parking garage, his mind still reeling from Sarah's revelation, he fumbled in his pocket and brought out the package of condoms. Without a tinge of remorse or regret, he hurled them far out into the darkness of the night.

Ten

WHEN ORESTES arrived home after midnight, he entered the dark, silent house alert as a thief for any sound of life. He slipped off his shoes, tiptoed up the stairs, and stripped in the bathroom. He took the precaution of showering, including shampooing his hair, to expunge any traces of the candles and incense in Sarah's apartment. As he tried to slip quietly into bed, Dessie woke and shifted closer to him. She mumbled something that included the word "incense." By the time he'd fashioned an excuse (the restaurant where he'd eaten contained candles and incense), she'd fallen back asleep.

Despite his thoughts navigating the terrain of the evening, he was exhausted and slept heavily for a few hours. Later, a vagrant dream woke him, and he opened his weary eyes to the first tracings of dawn. He longed to sleep longer but feared having Dessie question him about the dinner the night before, so he dragged himself out of bed. He shaved, and as he emerged from the bathroom, Dessie's sleepy voice came from the bed.

"Hgw did it go last night?"

"Fine."

"What time is it?"

"A little past seven," he said. "I have an early appointment at the restaurant." He bent and kissed her gently before leaving the bedroom.

Since it was Saturday morning, there wasn't any need to

wake Marika for school. He made a cup of instant coffee and then left for the Olympia.

During the drive downtown, and throughout the morning in the restaurant, he struggled to reconstruct the dialogue he had shared with Sarah. He plodded back and forth over her confession, trying to recall all the things she had said about Dante and Beatrice.

In the afternoon, greeting customers and speaking to cooks and waiters, his thoughts remained obsessively linked to the previous evening. He marveled at how calmly he had accepted Sarah's confession about her being reincarnated as Beatrice. Had she perhaps laced the spaghetti and meatballs with some exotic potion that distorted reality for him?

"Is something the matter with you, partner?" Cleon asked him in mid-afternoon. "Your body is in the Olympia, but you look as if your head is elsewhere."

"I have some weighty matters on my mind."

"Well, while you're pondering those weighty matters, how about devoting a few brain cells to our millennium party. I'm anxious to let the impresario know our decision on Bakalakis, the lyre artist. Every day we delay may lessen our chances of getting him for the Olympia. The sad truth is we may already be too late."

"You go ahead and make the decision."

Cleon stared at him sharply.

"Are you sure? You know my strong feeling that it would be a great coup for us to get Bakalakis! Are you telling me to go ahead?"

"Go ahead," Orestes said. Since he was struggling with cosmic concerns of fantasy and reality, the matter of the lyre player for the New Year's party no longer seemed of any great significance.

"By God, you're making the right decision, partner!" Cleon cried as he walked away.

A little later, while interviewing a young man newly arrived from Greece for a position as a waiter in the Olympia, Orestes found his attention drifting into speculation as to whether he should phone Sarah. He'd begin, of course, by thanking her for the dinner. Then the scenario became murkier. Would he thank Sarah or Beatrice? Would she expect him to call her Beatrice? Would she call him Dante?

He snapped back to the young waiter's anxious face.

"Yes?" Orestes asked.

"The job, Mr. Panos," the waiter asked nervously. "Are you satisfied with what I've told you about myself? Do I have the job?"

Orestes stared at the young applicant for a moment.

"Yes, you're hired," Orestes said briskly. "Go and speak to my partner, Cleon. Tell him you're starting work for us and he'll assign someone to show you your duties."

The young waiter leaped excitedly to his feet.

"Thank you, Mr. Panos!" he cried. "You won't regret it! I promise you that!"

After the new waiter had left his office, Orestes tried vainly to recall the youth's qualifications. For the life of him he couldn't remember anything about the interview.

"Get a grip on yourself, Dante," he sighed. "You could have just put a serial killer on the payroll."

That evening before leaving the restaurant to drive home, with his heart pounding, he phoned Sarah. He was relieved when there wasn't any answer.

When he arrived home that evening, Orestes was grateful because Dessie had made plans for them to attend a barbecue at a neighbor's house. As they mingled with the small laughing group of men and women, Dessie didn't have a chance to ask him about the previous night's dinner. He was spared the further deceit of having to elaborate on his lie. After a couple of burdensome hours, he was able to tell his hosts that he was tired, and he went home to bed.

The following Sunday morning, Orestes drove Dessie, Marika, and Stavroula to church. When he first entered the outer foyer, Sarkas and Mesaras, two trustees he knew, greeted him from behind the candle counter. As he picked up several candles, he thought gloomily that he'd never be able to look at a candle in church again without thinking of Sarah. He lit the candles, crossed himself, and kissed the icon of the Savior. Inside the nave of the church, Leo Rifakes led them to a pew.

Orestes sat in the crowded church as he had so many times before, feeling strangely disembodied, his thoughts drifting back, once again, to Sarah and the apartment. The intense effort to remember and interpret what had taken place made him feel a little tense and weak, and he began to perspire. Several times, Dessie leaned toward him and clasped his arm.

"Are you all right?" she whispered.

"Fine, fine."

He made a determined effort to concentrate on the liturgy, observing Father Elias and young Father Anton in their brocaded vestments, emerging from and reentering the sanctuary. The robed members of the choir led by the choirmaster, Nestor Limberis, chanted the ancient Byzantine hymns. The somber, white-gowned young acolytes carried the candelabras in and out of the altar. One earnest-faced, auburn-haired boy of about ten resembled Paulie as a child, and for a little while, Orestes worried about his son and his family.

Later in the liturgy, when members of the congregation left their pews to enter the lines moving to take communion, Dessie led Stavroula up to kneel with the others. The old lady took communion every Sunday, walking up and down the aisle in the lopsided, shuffling gait that reminded Orestes of Charles Laughton playing the Hunchback of Notre Dame. He had the unkind thought that even communion on a daily basis would do nothing to mellow the virago's rancorous disposition.

After the last parishioners had taken communion, Father Elias emerged from the sanctuary to deliver the sermon. Despite the distracting wails of children in the rear of the church, Orestes made a resolute effort to concentrate on the priest's words. But the homily on the importance of baptism to a newborn child seemed irrelevant to his more complex problems.

During the coffee hour following the liturgy, Orestes greeted a number of friends, including Nikos Karvelas and Professor Platon. Dessie laughed and visited with other friends. Marika held the center of an animated, giggling circle of other high school girls, festooned in colorful dresses, their short skirts exposing their slender legs. In another corner, Stavroula huddled in a coven of crones, their gestures and expressions suggesting they were dissecting some poor devil who had incited their venom.

In the crowd that milled about him, Orestes encountered Sam Tzangaris. The president of the parish council suffered from a severe eczema problem and, to conceal it, wore a pancake makeup that gave him the pallor of a corpse. Each time Orestes saw the man's pasty face and reptilian eyes, he recoiled with a shudder. In spite of his revulsion, Orestes made an effort to greet him cordially.

"Good morning, Sam."

"Good morning," Tzangaris replied brusquely. He turned back to several of his cronies.

Father Anton appeared at the perimeter of the crowd. Orestes hadn't spoken to the young priest since the evening of the delayed communion, which remained a topic of gossip within the parish. Caught up in his own adventures (or should it more accurately be called his misadventures), Orestes had neglected phoning to once again reassure the priest. He waved, and Father Anton waved back and then made his way through the crowd toward him.

"Good morning, Father Anton," Orestes greeted him warmly.

"Good morning, Orestes," Father Anton said. His face seemed drawn, and there were beads of perspiration across his forehead. "Orestes, if you had a little time for me today, there's something I'd like to talk to you about."

"Certainly, Father. Shall we find a quiet corner."

"No, not here!" the priest said quickly. "I'll come to the Olympia later this afternoon. Will you be there?"

Orestes hadn't planned to go into the restaurant, but he didn't wish to disappoint the priest.

"I'll be there," he said. "Come whenever you wish."

"We have the christening of the Argiris baby at three this afternoon. I'll come by the restaurant as soon as the baptism as finished."

After church, as they drove home, Orestes told Dessie he needed to spend a few hours in the restaurant.

"You don't usually go in on Sunday."

"Father Anton wants to talk to me. I told him I'd see him there."

"Is he all right?" Dessie asked.

"I'll find out when I see him."

He pulled into the driveway alongside the house.

"I'm going over for a while to see Christina," Marika said. "I'll be back in a couple of hours."

"You should have some lunch first," Dessie said.

"I'll have a snack with Christina."

Marika scampered out the rear door. In a moment she had disappeared down the block.

Orestes got out of the car and walked around to help Stavroula. The old lady groaned as she uncoiled her arthritic limbs to extricate herself from the car. Once he'd helped her out, she pushed him away.

"Mama, let Orestes help you!" Dessie said. "Last Sunday you almost fell!"

"There was litter in the driveway!" the old lady snapped. "Everybody in this house is too busy for a simple chore like sweeping up."

"As you wish, Stavroula," Orestes said genially. "I'm sure Jesus Christ would be pleased to see you so sturdy on your feet."

"Don't talk to me about Jesus!" the old lady growled. "I was praying to him when you were still soiling your diapers!"

Orestes drove off leaving the old lady fulminating in the driveway.

When he arrived at the restaurant, Orestes found a number of parishioners who had come over after church for lunch. He moved from table to table, greeting families, and then sat down at the corner table with Banopoulos, the editor, and the realtor, Lalounis. Shortly afterwards, Karvelas and Professor Platon joined them. Almost at once, the undertaker launched into a harangue about his travail in having to deal with the grave- diggers union that was threatening to strike.

"They're grave-diggers, in the name of God, not neurosurgeons!" Karvelas cried. "Any lout with a strong back can stick a spade and shovel in the ground! They should be grateful they're working at all let alone striking for a higher wage!"

"I personally endorse cremation," Banopoulos said. "That would eliminate all this nonsense of vaults and caskets, gravediggers and hearses."

"That would also eliminate our friend, Karvelas," Professor Platon said gravely.

"Then the corpse-snatcher might be forced to find an honest profession," Dr. Savas said as he approached the table.

"Here comes the master of malpractice!" Karvelas cried. "How many of your poor patients have you lost since we last spoke?"

"At least a dozen," Dr. Savas grinned, "but I'm referring their families to undertaking establishments on the North Side."

Dr. Savas turned to Orestes, peering at him intently as if he were searching for evidence of unusual wear and tear.

Karvelas appealed to Banopoulos. "I think you should write an editorial about the greed of grave-diggers."

Banopoulos shrugged. "I doubt if any grave-diggers read my paper."

"You just compose the editorial and print it!" Karvelas said. "I'll make sure copies are sent to the union and to the Association of Morticians!"

Orestes left the table and, with a quick glance at Dr. Savas, started for the bar. The doctor rose and followed him.

They sat on stools at the deserted end of the bar, and when Stellios, the bartender, walked over, they ordered coffee and brandy.

"I don't normally pry into a man's sex life," Dr. Savas said in a low voice. "But since you've made me an unofficial co-conspirator, I can't help being curious. Tell me, my friend, what happened that fateful Friday night?"

"Nothing and everything."

"Don't play coy with me," Dr. Savas said. "Speak to me as candidly as you would in confessing to your parish priest. I'll be much less puritanical."

"She was Beatrice, and she wanted to guide me through Paradise."

"We used to call that taking a trip around the world," the doctor smirked. "I must say that Paradise sounds more colorful."

"Not that kind of Paradise. I'm speaking about the Paradise that devout Christians aspire to achieve after they die."

"You mean she's a religious fanatic?" Dr. Savas asked indignantly. "Did she try to convert you?"

They fell silent as Stellios brought them their coffee and brandy.

"Anything else, boss?" Stellios asked.

"Nothing, thanks," Orestes said. The bartender moved away, and Orestes turned back to Dr. Savas.

"It had nothing to do with religious conversion. After we'd had dinner, she informed me that she was Beatrice, the beauty Dante loved from the first time he saw her at age nine."

"Are you telling me this girl is underage?" Dr. Savas asked sternly. "Be careful, Orestes. The law is merciless about older men contributing to the delinquency of a minor."

"She's not a minor," Orestes sighed. "She's a young woman who has somehow gotten it into her head that she's the reincarnation of Beatrice, the great love that inspired the poetry and life of Dante." He paused. "She says that when she first saw me, she was astounded at my resemblance to Dante. She believes I am also reincarnated, and that is the reason we have been brought together."

The doctor stared at him in shock.

"My God," he said finally. "Are you serious?"

"Of course."

Dr. Savas threw up his arms.

"I can't believe it, Orestes! Other men slip into a girl's apartment for a quick tumble. You slip in and find a hallucinating woman who takes you on a literary tour of the Inferno! My God, now I've heard everything!" He shook his white-haired head in disbelief. "When she revealed this astounding phantasmagoria to you, what did you say?"

"I didn't say anything. I just listened. She fell asleep, and I left."

"What's the next step? What will you do now?"

"I haven't the faintest idea," Orestes said. "Part of me wants to run like hell away from her. Another part of me is reluctant to suddenly shatter her fantasy. But is it wise to perpetuate it? Is this whole business hazardous for her? What will happen if I try to bring her back to reality?"

For the first time in all the years they had known one another, the articulate doctor sat there mute.

"Dr. Savas, what should I do?"

"I haven't the slightest idea," the doctor replied somberly. "I deal daily with problems of mortality. But this . . . this goes beyond life and death." He paused. "If she's lived with this fantasy for a long time, I'm not even sure you'd be able to shatter it."

"Is it dangerous? I mean is there a chance the fantasy world will replace the real one for her?"

"Some people are able to shuttle back and forth between the real world and their fantasy," Dr. Savas said. "I had a patient once who was normal in every other respect except that he was convinced he was the reincarnation of General George Patton. He held a job as a pizza delivery man during the day, but in the seclusion of his apartment, he dressed up as that feisty World War II general, including boots, a riding crop, and twin ivory-handled six-guns."

"What happened to him?"

"I treated his high blood pressure for years, but he also had other related medical problems. I lost track of him and then heard about five years ago that he'd died."

For a moment the two men sat in silence.

"All I wanted from you was a package of condoms to fortify my first foray into infidelity since I took my marriage vows." Orestes sighed. "Now I'm embroiled in a fantasy of such staggering proportions that even my wise and experienced family physician has no counsel to offer. How do you account for that?"

"Look on the bright side," Dr. Savas said. "If I cannot advise you, then you won't receive a bill." He stared at Orestes and couldn't suppress a roguish grin. "Tell me, my friend, from now on will it be necessary for your friends to call you Dante?"

Later in the afternoon, while Orestes was chatting with several customers at one of the tables, he saw Father Anton enter the Olympia. Orestes went to greet him, and as they shook hands, he felt the priest's fingers moist and trembling.

"How about a bite to eat, Father? Kyriakos has made one of his delicious spanakopitas. Have a piece with a small village salad . . ."

"Nothing, Orestes, thank you." Father Anton paused. "Can we speak somewhere in private?"

"Let's go back to my office," Orestes said. He led the priest into the office and closed the door. Father Anton sank wearily into a chair, and Orestes took a seat facing him.

For a moment, the priest stared at him silently, as if he were having difficulty knowing how to begin.

"I have a good friend in the parish," the priest said slowly. "He told me in confidence that there is a plan to cause me trouble."

"Whatever trouble they cause you, Father," Orestes said firmly, "you know you have my full support. Your other friends will support you, as well."

"This trouble may be serious enough so you will not be able to help me," Father Anton said in a low voice. He looked down at his pale fingers clasping his knees. "There may even be some of my friends who might not wish to help me." His voice fell to a hoarse whisper. "I am to be accused of molesting young girls."

Orestes stared at the priest in shock.

"I can't believe it, Father! Who would dare accuse you of something like that? Is it Sam Tzangaris?"

"I'm not sure who will make the accusation," the priest said.

"If Sam were behind it, he would never make the accusation himself. He'll use one of those craven men who attach themselves to him like leeches because of his wealth and power."

For a moment, Orestes stared at the priest, struggling to find words to reassure him. He was outraged that some malevolent individuals might make the good young priest suffer this humiliation.

"Father Anton, you mustn't agonize over this slander! Those who know you and care for you would never believe it! I'm sure Father Elias will support you, as well!"

The priest stared at him in silence. For a shaken instant Orestes remembered the night in the priest's apartment when he'd confessed to feeling erotic impulses toward young boys and girls. As if Father Anton had surmised his thoughts, the priest shook his head.

"I pledge to you, Orestes, that to my knowledge, I've done nothing wrong," he said fervently. "But the truth is that there have been times when I've been affectionate. You know? Perhaps my hand lingering around the shoulders of a young girl a little too long. Perhaps standing in the gym locker room when the boys were changing clothes. I swear to you I've done nothing! But others may not make so lenient an assessment."

"We'll fight them, Father!" Orestes said. "We'll get a group of your friends who care for and respect you, and we'll fight them!"

"Thank you, Orestes," Father Anton said. "I'm grateful to God that I have friends like you in the parish." He raised one hand and rubbed weakly at his cheek. "When I was a youth, I dreamed of being a priest in the service of God," he said slowly. "All through divinity school, I studied with fervor and waited eagerly for my ordainment. I decided not to marry because I wished to give myself wholeheartedly to my God."

A boisterous party passed the office door, the clamor of their laughter fading slowly. The priest's soft, pensive voice filled the silence again.

"It's true there have been times I've glimpsed the beauty of this life I've chosen. I've had this feeling during the grace of the liturgy, and while celebrating the glory of Holy Week. Then there have been those fulfilling moments when I have been able to provide help to someone bereaved or troubled."

The phone on the office desk rang, its strident clatter filling the office. Father Anton waited for the ringing to cease.

"But there are also other times when I'm forced to bear witness to cruelty, selfishness, and intolerance," the priest said. "In the confessional I hear the hatred of a wife for an unfaithful husband, the maligning of a wayward son by his father, the bitterness of an old woman whose children have forsaken her. And for many of their laments and grievances, I can do nothing besides offer them my prayers."

For the first time in all the years Orestes had known Father Anton, he understood something of the burdens the young priest confronted each day.

"Then there are those evenings when I am in the midst of jubilant, loving families, parents with loving children, husbands with loving wives, and I go home to my apartment, so silent I can hear water dripping from a faucet, a clock ticking on the wall, the scurry of mice feet in a corner. In those moments, I feel loneliness feed like an animal on my heart."

He paused, smiled faintly as if to reassure Orestes.

"Forgive my self-pity, Orestes," he said. "Please believe me when I say I'm not envious of those loving families, I'm grateful to be able to share their happiness. Their pleasure in life nourishes me. And as for the loneliness, if that is part of the life I have chosen, I can endure it. What I desire above all else, my friend, is peace, the peace to do God's work, the peace to be free of earthly temptation, the peace to sleep without being stricken by dreams."

After he'd walked the young priest to the door and seen him depart, Orestes stood for a few moments by the restaurant window. Twilight had fallen across Halsted Street, the neon lights of the restaurants and shops casting multicolored banners across the descending night. The sidewalks outside the window teemed with men and women on their way to the various restaurants for dinner. A trio of laughing, white-aproned young waiters hurried by on their way to work. An old woman plodded by with a slow, heavy step, and a slim young girl passed, quick and light-footed as a dancer. Antonis Ladas and his wife, Minerva, laden with shopping bags from the Athens Grocery, waved buoyantly at Orestes, who waved back.

In a short while he'd be home for dinner with Dessie and Marika. Later in the week, he'd see Paulie, Carmela, and his granddaughter. In addition to the joy they brought to his life now, they also provided him a storehouse of loving memories that began with his marriage and those miraculous moments when his son, daughter, and grandchild were born. He could not conceive of his life without them, and he grieved for the young priest who would never experience such joy.

"What are you thinking about, partner?" Cleon had come up behind Orestes and gripped his shoulder.

"How much I love my partner, Cleon Frangakis," Orestes said. Although he hadn't been thinking about Cleon, the expression of affection came from his heart.

Cleon stared at him for a moment in silence, and then he quickly wiped a vagrant tear from his eye.

"I love you too, partner," he said, his voice low and hoarse with emotion. "How fortunate we are to have converted that love into a partnership in this good business that keeps us both employed and off the street."

Eleven

THE STORM that Father Anton had spoken about to
Orestes burst within the parish a few days later. On
Wednesday evening, after finishing dinner at home,
Orestes received a phone call from Karvelas. The undertaker's
voice trembled with agitation.

"They've done it now! Tzangaris and the others have been
after that young priest like wolves after a sheep for a long time.
Now they've pounced!"

"Who has accused him?"

"Stathis Brakas."

"The butcher?"

"Yes, the butcher! Everyone knows he is close as a wart to
Tzangaris. He claims Father Anton fondled his fourteen-year-
old daughter, Eugenia."

"The bastards!" Orestes felt his own outrage kindled. "Have
you spoken to Father Anton yet?"

"I phoned his apartment as soon as I heard the news, but
there wasn't any answer. I'll try him again later this evening."

"I think we should start contacting as many friends as we can
to build support," Orestes said. "In the morning, I'll go see Father Elias. His backing will be important, and after I consult
with him, we can plan our course of action."

Orestes hung up the phone and walked into the kitchen to
tell Dessie the unhappy news. She was as distraught as he
had been.

"Poor Father Anton!" Dessie said.

"The bastards wouldn't leave the poor man alone, wouldn't let him do his work in peace!"

"You really believe Sam Tzangaris is behind this?"

"Who else could it be? Sam has led earlier efforts to drive Father Anton from the parish. Besides, Brakas wouldn't have come forward in a matter as serious as this on his own!"

Dessie stared at Orestes for a moment in silence.

"Orestes, is there any chance . . . ?" her voice faltered.

"That the accusation might be true?" He shook his head. "Father Anton assured me he's done nothing. And I believe him, Dessie. But he's also concerned that his gestures of affection when he's around young girls and boys, this affection might be misunderstood."

"What are you going to do?"

"I spoke to Karvelas, and we're going to organize support for Father Anton. If this becomes a legal matter, I'll ask George Cotsirilos to help us. He's one of the best defense attorneys in the country. Don't worry, my darling, we'll do everything we can to defend that good young priest."

Later that night, he and Dessie sat before the television set, watching the nightly news. She slipped her hand into his and he felt the chill in her fingers.

"I can't get Father Anton out of my thoughts," she said pensively. "Perhaps we should have made a greater effort to include him in our holiday celebrations. We forget he hasn't any family of his own and spends so much time alone. I can't help feeling that we're all somehow responsible . . ."

"There's no reason to blame yourself," Orestes said. "He had other friends who invited him for dinners and to share the holidays. At the same time I'm sure people also respected his need for some privacy."

"When I told mama about it tonight, she said that Father

Anton wasn't mean and selfish enough to be a priest. She predicted Tzangaris and the others would eat him, bones and all."

She stood up and then bent to kiss him good-night. "I'm going to bed. Are you coming up soon?"

"I'll just watch Nightline for a while."

He tried to watch the program about the various Republican candidates vying to challenge Vice President Gore in the following year's election, but his attention wavered. He surfed the channels and on one of the shows, a slim, attractive blonde girl reminded him of Sarah.

He gloomily recapped the absurdity of his frenzied preparations for her seduction, his drive to the Walgreen's in Oak Park for condoms, his pleas to Dr. Savas for Viagra. He had floundered like a moron through the whole business.

And what about Sarah? Almost a week had passed since he'd had that fateful dinner in her apartment, and he kept putting off phoning her. Had she now irrevocably accepted him as Dante?

What effect would his reincarnation have on her life? Should he consult a psychiatrist for help in how to treat her fantasy? Perhaps he should urge her to go to a psychiatrist herself. What further bond or vow would she expect of him? Might it not be wise for him to break off any further relationship and never see her again?

Yet, for all his dilemma about Sarah, in view of what was happening to Father Anton, the fantasy of Dante and Beatrice seemed a game played by children in a merciless and unfeeling world.

He snapped off Ted Koppel interviewing John McCain and started wearily up the stairs for bed.

Orestes spent most of the following morning at the Olympia on the phone. He spoke to parish members who he knew respected and liked Father Anton, appealing for their support. He also phoned the bishop's office at the Chicago diocese and spoke to the chancellor, Father Constantine, who assured him that his grace was reviewing the situation.

"Father Constantine, in my opinion and in the opinion of many other parishioners, this accusation is false!" Orestes said urgently. "At the worst it's a blatant lie. Please let his grace know how we feel about this outrage."

"I will, Orestes," the chancellor said gravely, "but you have to understand that the accusation cannot simply be brushed aside. If it is perceived that the diocese is trying to cover this up, it could cause us great harm. Look at what's happening with the Roman Catholics. When it comes to priests abusing minors, every faith is being scrutinized relentlessly."

When he'd first arrived at the restaurant that morning, Orestes had phoned Father Anton at his apartment and also at the church but had no answer at either place. He left encouraging messages on the priest's answering machines.

After lunch, he drove from the Olympia to St. Sophia's church. The secretary, Helen Vranas, told him Father Anton was making sick calls to parishioners in the hospital. When Orestes asked about Father Elias, she told him the priest was in his office.

"He's been on the phone ever since he arrived this morning," she told him. "If you want to talk to him, I suggest you wait outside his office and as soon as he hangs up, go right in."

Standing outside the priest's door, Orestes couldn't help overhearing Father Elias on his office phone.

"We'll do everything we can, Mathon, to get to the truth in this matter, be assured of that," Father Elias said. "Yes . . . yes, I will. Give my best to Caliope, and don't worry."

When he heard the priest hang up, Orestes knocked on the door. As the priest called to him to enter, the phone rang again.

Father Elias motioned Orestes to a chair. The priest listened in silence on the phone for a moment and then spoke.

"Telis, don't do anything so foolish. Your daughters are perfectly safe here at school in the classrooms with teachers and other students. If you withdraw them, all you'll accomplish is to have them fall behind in their studies. We're looking into the matter, and I promise you it will be resolved soon."

When he hung up, Father Elias buzzed Helen Vranas to hold his calls. He looked at Orestes and sighed.

"My phone started ringing at home at midnight last night," he said wearily. "And the calls haven't stopped for a minute since I first arrived here this morning. The callers range all the way from imbeciles who want Father Anton lynched from the church bell tower, to partisans so effusive in their praise that they urge his elevation to sainthood. I wonder where all these ardent champions of his were last year when we failed to get him an 8 percent raise in his salary?" He gazed across his desk at Orestes. "So now, what is it you want from me, Orestes?"

"First of all, Father Elias, I'd like to know whether you agree with me that this accusation is false?"

The priest took a moment to answer.

"I cannot speak for what is in another man's heart," he said slowly, "but if you ask my opinion, I do not think the accusation is true. Has Father Anton perhaps been guilty of being overly familiar with some of our young people? Possibly. He is popular with them and they might well have encouraged his gestures of affection. But you know Tzangaris. He will take any ambiguous conduct on Father Anton's part and build a case based on smear and a distortion of the facts. He wants Father Anton out of the parish, and I'm not sure that anything we do can prevent him accomplishing that end."

"The man's a devil, Father! You know that as well as I do!"

Orestes said heatedly. "But if you do believe Father Anton to be innocent, can we count on your support?"

The priest stared somberly at Orestes.

"I'll offer Father Anton what personal support I can," he said quietly. "But, I'll be candid with you, Orestes, if it appears his cause is lost, I will recommend to him that he voluntarily resign from his position here. Whatever happens, I will have to continue to work with Sam Tzangaris and the parish council. Fighting against them to the bitter end, only to lose anyway, won't do the parish any good."

A special meeting of the parish council to discuss the accusation against Father Anton was called for the following Saturday morning at the church. Although Orestes had resigned from the council, he was eligible to attend the meeting as a past member. He was joined there by Karvelas, a current council member, and Banopoulos, whose credentials as a journalist gained him entry.

On Saturday morning before leaving the house for the meeting, Orestes sat at the breakfast table with Dessie and Stavroula.

"Try not to become too upset and angry, Orestes," Dessie said. "It won't help Father Anton if you have a stroke or a heart attack."

Stavroula chewed robustly on a piece of toast.

"It won't make any difference what you or any of the others do," she said somberly. "Tzangaris will get his way in the end. When that rot-faced pit bull gets his teeth in a piece of live meat, he won't let go until its dead."

"I think you could handle Tzangaris, Stavroula," Orestes said. "Why don't you come with me to the council meeting and speak in Father Anton's defense?"

"I wouldn't waste my time defending any man!" Stavroula made a spitting sound with her lips. "They're all animals seek-

ing any excuse to fight, to cheat, to kill! All the priest and
Tzangaris will get from me is a curse on both their houses!"

"Mama, you like Father Anton." Dessie said. "You've told me
so yourself."

"What's there not to like?" Stavroula sneered. "He's harmless
enough. His most important duty is to stand before the altar
on Sundays in his costume robe and chant his prayers. The
heaviest labor he's called upon to perform is to raise the chalice
for communion."

"If you feel that way about the priests," Orestes asked, "then
why bother taking communion every Sunday?"

Stavroula raked him with a look of contempt.

"Communion is between my God and me!" she said harshly.
"It has nothing to do with those pompous fools who carry the
spoon and chalice!"

"Mama, you're really something," Dessie sighed. She rose to
kiss Orestes good-bye. "Remember what I said. You're not
Jimmy Stewart playing *Mr. Smith Goes to Washington*."

"Of course I'm not Jimmy Stewart," Orestes said wryly. "I'd
rather be someone more militant, like John Wayne riding to the
rescue of a wagon train surrounded by bloodthirsty savages."

"Jimmy Stewart and John Wayne!" Marika had entered the
kitchen. "They were old time actors, weren't they?"

"They were real actors, honey," Orestes said. "Not simply
entertainment personalities like Brad Pott and Johnny Dipp!"

"You mean Brad Pitt and Johnny Depp!" Marika giggled.
"Daddy, they're not just actors, they're heartthrobs!"

"Those beardless schoolboys are about as manly as stale
beans!" Stavroula said scornfully. Then a quiver of warmth and
tenderness laced her voice. "Thomas Selleck, he's the one . . . that
palikari . . . he's a real man!"

"He's your boyfriend, isn't he, Yiayia?" Marika teased her.

"Don't worry about my boyfriends!" Stavroula said. "You try

to find one who doesn't have dirty hair hanging to his backside and rings in his nose and ears so he resembles some heathen cannibal . . ." Stavroula paused for breath. "When you're older, you'll be a lucky girl if you find someone like Thomas Selleck! He's the kind of man any woman would be glad to marry!" She looked scathingly at Orestes, as if to let him know she included Dessie among those women. Orestes sighed and left the house.

When he arrived at the church, there were thirty-five to forty men assembled in the church hall. Most of them were current parish council members with a half dozen former members like Orestes present, as well. Karvelas and Banopoulos arrived soon after him. As they took seats beside Orestes, Banopoulos pointed out a reporter from the *Hellenic Tribune*, a Greek language paper in which Tzangaris had a financial stake, who was busy scribbling copious notes.

"The damn fool is writing his story before the meeting has begun!" Banopoulos said scornfully.

In a corner of the hall, huddled within a group of men, Orestes saw the burly, black-browed butcher, Brakas.

"Will Father Elias be attending the meeting?" Banopoulos asked.

"I saw him a little while ago," Karvelas said. "He told me he may stop in near the end of the meeting. He didn't want to be seen as interfering with the vote of the council."

"That monk would have made a nice fit in Neville Chamberlain's delegation to Munich," Banopoulos said glumly.

Tzangaris, as president of the parish council, struck his gavel on the table for silence. The council secretary sat at the table beside him, to record the minutes of the meeting.

"This meeting is called to order," Tzangaris said briskly. "Let everyone be seated." He paused. "I'd like to remind those attending who are not currently members of the council that our bylaws prohibit them from speaking, nor will they be allowed to vote."

"Shame!" Banopoulos said loudly. "Shame!"

Tzangaris glared at the editor.

"We're going to hear now from a longtime and well-respected member of our parish, Mr. Stathis Brakas. He has brought us this accusation on behalf of his daughter, who is fourteen. Now I have spoken to Eugenia myself. She is a sensible, trustworthy young woman, and I, for one, haven't any doubt that she is telling the truth. But I will allow her aggrieved father to provide the details. Stathis, would you tell us please just what your daughter told you?"

Not accustomed to speaking or to having his opinion sought after, the butcher rose and stiffly faced the gathering.

"My daughter, Eugenia," he began in a slightly hoarse voice. "She told her mother . . . her mother and me . . . she said that several times Father Anton put his hand on her . . . on her knee, and, one time, on her leg." He fell silent and Tzangaris prodded him.

"These episodes took place more than once?"

"That's right!" Brakas said, his voice raspy with outrage. "More than one time! My daughter didn't want to say nothing about it, but it scared her. A few times my wife heard her crying in bed. A few days ago, we made her tell us what was bothering her. I swear to God, if he wasn't a priest, I'd go after the beast with a cleaver!"

"That man's a lout," Banopoulos said in disgust. "I wouldn't trust what he says any more than I'd buy that third-grade meat he sells!"

Orestes looked around at the men in the hall, a perverse excitement glittering in their faces. He thought grimly that they resembled bloodhounds who had sniffed the scent of blood.

"Have any of your daughter's friends confided to her of similar experiences they had with Father Anton?"

"That's right!" Brakas said. "Another girl told Eugenia he done the same with her!"

"One girl or more?" Tzangaris pressed him.

"Two girls, that's right!" the butcher said. "He done the same thing to two girls!

Tzangaris turned from Brakas to address the gathering.

"I know who these other young women are," he said gravely. "They are reluctant to come forward themselves now because of personal embarrassment. When the time comes I have been assured by their parents that they will speak." He paused. "There is also a possibility, we cannot yet be certain, that a boy will also come forward with an accusation against Father Anton."

A hissing of shock and outrage swept the gathering.

"Rumor and innuendo!" Banopoulos exclaimed. "He has the gall to present it as if it were sworn truth!"

Tzangaris struck his gavel sharply on the table. When the crowd fell silent, he continued. "Now these are serious charges, but it's also important that no one complain we are not being fair. When the time comes, we will put these questions directly to Father Anton so he will have an opportunity to respond. Meanwhile, the parish council, as the highest lay body within the parish, has a responsibility to go on record with a preliminary finding. However, before we vote, we'll hear a few comments from some of the members assembled here. If you're called upon to speak, I ask that you keep your comments brief."

A score of men including Orestes, Karvelas, and Banopoulos raised their hands. Tzangaris called on one of his friends, who spoke of his distrust of the priest.

"He never seemed to be a part of the community," he said. "There was always a standoffishness about him, like he was better than the rest of us. I felt that arrogance about him from the very beginning. When I heard recently that he was too busy drinking with some of his friends to go and give poor Andreas

Placouras communion before he died, I told my wife that I'd been right about him all along."

This was the same man that Orestes had heard several Sundays before urging Father Anton to drop by his house for his son's birthday party.

The following three speakers Tzangaris called upon also criticized the priest. One referred to Father Anton as "lazy," and another spoke of him as "unfriendly."

"Isn't the son-of-a-goat going to allow any of Father Anton's supporters a chance to speak?" Banopoulos said indignantly.

Once again, Orestes, Karvelas, and the editor vigorously waved their hands.

"Nikos Karvelas," Tzangaris said, to recognize the undertaker.

Karvelas rose and confronted the gathering.

"I'm going to relinquish my time to Orestes Panos who is better qualified to speak about Father Anton than I am."

Tzangaris pounded his gavel furiously on the table.

"This cannot be permitted!" he cried. "Mr. Panos is no longer a member of the parish council! Only current members are eligible to speak!"

"Shame!" Banopoulos cried. "What kind of kangaroo court are you running, Sam? Give the man a chance to speak."

The room erupted into a chorus of shouts and jeers, many supporting Tzangaris, but there were also voices urging that Orestes be allowed to speak.

Feeling angry and frustrated, Orestes waited for the tumult to quiet down. Karvelas and Banopoulos were both on their feet, waving their arms for silence. Tzangaris kept pounding his gavel.

Suddenly the shouts faltered and the room fell silent as men twisted in their chairs and stared toward the entrance of the hall. Orestes turned around and saw Father Elias standing in the doorway.

"Give the man a chance to speak, Sam," Father Elias said quietly.

For a moment, Tzangaris glared daggers at the priest. T`en he motioned brusquely to the council secretary.

"Let the minutes show that in the interest of fairness we allowed Orestes Panos, a former council member, to speak."

Karvelas nudged Orestes.

"Don't wait!" he whispered. "Go ahead!"

As Orestes stood up, he felt the blood pounding in his temples and a dryness in his throat.

"I know almost all the men in this room, and I believe you wish to be fair," Orestes said. "But it isn't fair if we rush to judge Father Anton before we've heard what he has to say. I, for one, believe him to be a devoted and compassionate priest who is innocent of these charges."

"My daughter is not a liar!" Brakas broke in harshly. "Anyone who says so has got to deal with me!"

Tzangaris brusquely motioned the butcher to silence.

"How many of you has Father Anton visited when you or someone in your family has been ill?" Orestes continued. "How many times has he offered assistance when you or someone in your family needed counsel and support?" He pointed at a man in the audience. "Panayoti, you told me when you were in the hospital last year, Father Anton visited you every day." He pointed out a second man. "Thanasi, when your son was in trouble, wasn't Father Anton in court with you every day?" He pointed at a third man. "Leftheris, when your wife was ill, who came to pray with you at her bedside? You told me afterwards you felt Father Anton helped pull her through."

Orestes wanted to turn and see if Father Elias was still standing in the doorway, but he resisted the impulse.

"Now, because an accusation has been leveled against him, why are we in such a frenzy to condemn him?" He felt his voice gaining strength. "Let's give him a chance to prove he's innocent before we judge him. To do any less for someone who has served us as well as Father Anton has served us would be to our everlasting shame!"

Orestes finished and sat down to a strong surge of applause. He felt his knees trembling and his heart flailing in his chest.

Karvelas pressed his arm jubilantly.

"Wonderful, Orestes!" he said fervently. "You had Tzangaris choking on his bile."

"That's giving these cretins a dose of truth!" Banopoulos said. "I'm going to quote your words in my editorial!"

Tzangaris pounded his gavel for silence.

"Father Anton will have ample opportunity to present his defense," Tzangaris said. "Meanwhile, the parish council has a responsibility to state our position on this issue. What we decide here isn't a conviction, just a statement of our position."

"Condemn the man first and then let him go to trial," Banopoulos said scornfully.

"We will vote by a show of hands," Tzangaris said.

"So many people hate the bastard," Banopoulos said scornfully, "he'd lose if it were a secret ballot."

"Secret ballot!" Orestes and Karvelas raised their voices. Several other men took up the cry. Tzangaris ignored them.

"All those in favor of condemning Father Anton for his immoral conduct," Tzangaris cried, "raise your hands and say aye."

"Can you believe the unscrupulous bastard!" Banopoulos said indignantly.

"He controls this council," Karvelas said gloomily. "They're afraid to defy him."

Under the baleful power of Tzangaris, a nervous fluttering up of arms and hands filled the air. A count was taken several times to reveal a total of twenty-nine votes against Father Anton.

"All those in favor of sanctioning Father Anton's immoral conduct, raise your hands," Tzangaris said loudly.

Orestes, Karvelas, and Banopoulos raised their hands. They were joined by about a half dozen others.

"Shame!" Banopoulos shouted again. "Shame!"

The final count had ten votes in support of the priest. A dozen others had abstained from voting.

"Cowards!" Banapoulos glared at several men near them who had not voted. He turned to Orestes and Karvelas. "Wait until you read my editorial about this fiasco."

"And Sam's lackey from the *Hellenic Tribune* will write his story supporting this judicious and impartial decision," Karvelas said.

After the meeting, Orestes returned to the Olympia. Cleon met him inside the door and greeted him with an embrace.

"I just had a call from Lambo Stavrides!" he said excitedly. "He compared you to that ancient Greek orator, Demosthenes!"

"The man is exaggerating," Orestes said. "All I did was express the feelings many of us have about Father Anton and this whole shabby business. I didn't speak more than two to three minutes. Tzangaris even tried to stop that much."

"Well, partner, however you downplay what you said, Stavrides was impressed as hell!" He paused. "I've got some more good news! We've hired the premier artist, Bakalakis, for our millennium celebration!"

"How much is that costing us again?"

"Only $10,000 plus expenses!" Cleon said. "Believe me, we're lucky as hell to get him. People will come from as far north as Milwaukee and as far south as St. Louis to hear him!" He paused. "Are you having second thoughts about him?" he asked with concern.

"Not at all!" Orestes smiled. "I'm delighted! I'll just slip into my office and compute how many lamb chops we have to sell to make up the $10,000!"

Shortly after he'd entered his office, Dessie phoned to tell him she'd had calls from several wives of men who had been present at the meeting.

"I'm proud of you, my darling!" Dessie said excitedly. "Bessie Volatis said her husband changed his vote because of you!"

"After what Father Anton has done for him, Plato Volatis should have been ashamed to vote any other way."

"Mama's friend Mrs. Davlantis also phoned. Her son-in-law, Lenny Karkazis, was at the meeting. After speaking to Mrs. Davlantis, even Mama seemed impressed. She said she didn't think you had it in you."

"God be praised!" Orestes sighed. "That's the closest to a compliment that blessed woman has offered me in all the years since you and I married!"

Twelve

IN THE weeks following the public accusation against Father Anton, St. Sophia's parish split into hostile factions divided between those who thought the priest guilty and those who felt he had been unjustly accused. The disagreements grew more heated and bitter, conflicts developing within families, between wives and husbands, brothers and sisters, as well as pitting friend against friend. During the services on Sundays, the tension and antagonism in the church produced glares and heated whispers. In several instances, the simmering hostility turned violent, and fights broke out in the parking lot after church.

Orestes had heard of other parishes scourged by such periods of internecine battle. There had been a church in the south where a group wishing to drive the priest away had padlocked the church doors to prevent him entering to perform the liturgy. His supporters complained to the police, and the matter ended up in court with legal bills running into tens of thousands of dollars. In another instance, in a California parish, the priest and his family had been threatened with assault unless they left the parish. Conditions became so acrimonious that the priest and a hundred families that supported him abandoned the church to form another parish.

"I hope to God that doesn't happen at St. Sophia's," Orestes told his friends in the Olympia. "But I don't know what else we can do but fight. We cannot simply stand by passively and accept the unjust dismissal of Father Anton."

Meanwhile, Father Elias went about his duties grim-faced and short-tempered, while, in conversation with parishioners, Father Anton appeared melancholy and withdrawn.

Feeling it would hearten the young priest and show him he had staunch support within the parish, Orestes urged Father Anton to attend several of the fund-raisers he and other friends were holding to cover the cost of mailing flyers on Father Anton's behalf.

"It should reassure you and also motivate your friends to have you present, Father Anton," Orestes said. "You could offer them a few words of encouragement."

"I am grateful, Orestes, to all those who support me," Father Anton said quietly. "But I'm sorry, I cannot come and plead my innocence. Nor will I speak a word against those who feel I am guilty. If it is the will of the parish that I go, then I will leave."

The two girls who were supposed to confirm the butcher's daughter's story with their own complaints against Father Anton had never come forward. Neither was the insidious reference Sam Tzangaris made during the parish council meeting about a boy also coming forward to accuse the priest of molesting him ever substantiated. In spite of these individuals remaining anonymous (raising questions as to whether they existed at all), there were people in the parish who swore they knew of at least four girls and two boys who had been molested by the priest and were too ashamed to go public with their revelations.

For a while, a rumor circulated in church that if the butcher, Brakas, wasn't satisfied with the way the parish handled his accusation, he planned to go to the police with his charges. The general feeling was that Sam Tzangaris was behind the rumor and that he wanted it held as a threat over the parish.

Meanwhile, the bishop of the diocese sent a formal letter to St. Sophia's, which was printed in the church bulletin on the last

Sunday in October, in which his grace stated that "it is our desire that this matter be brought to a swift resolution. Furthermore, if an investigation of these grave charges confirms proof of guilt, we pledge to move swiftly to punish the guilty party."

"As usual, the letter demonstrates the man's reprehensible timidity," Banopoulos complained to Orestes and Karvelas. "Instead of supporting one of his priests until he is proven guilty, his royal eminence seeks to protect himself from any criticism."

A number of meetings in the parish were held to work out some kind of compromise, but they quickly eroded into violent quarrels, a dozen people shouting at the same time. In the end, all these meetings accomplished was to increase the level of hostility and anger within the parish.

"In a time of crisis," Dr. Savas said in disgust at the table in the Olympia, "you can always be sure Christians will act in defiance of moral clarity and reason."

Meanwhile, at the beginning of November, after receiving letters from both sides in the dispute, the ecumenical patriarch of the Eastern Orthodox Church in Istanbul, Turkey, sent a stern encyclical to the bishop of the diocese demanding that the matter of Father Anton's retention or dismissal from the parish be decided quickly.

In response to the patriarch's letter, plans were made for a vote on the second Sunday in November by the entire church membership to determine whether Father Anton should be allowed to remain or be asked to resign. Sample ballots were sent to each parish family that stated:

I VOTE FOR FATHER ANTON STEPHANOS TO BE RETAINED AT ST. SOPHIA'S PARISH ( )

or

I VOTE FOR FATHER ANTON STEPHANOS TO BE DISMISSED FROM ST. SOPHIA'S PARISH ( )

In preparatiof for the voting, Orestes and Dessie joined by other friends of the priest, intensified their efforts to phone and visit parish families, reinforcing those who supported Father Anton and trying energetically to persuade those who opposed him.

"The ladies of the Philoptochos took a sample vote at our meeting last night," Dessie told Orestes, "and two thirds of them voted to support Father Anton. Don't you think that's a good omen?"

"Was Father Elias's wife, Presbytera Anastasia, there?"

"Yes."

"Perhaps the ladies were ashamed to vote against Father Anton in front of her. We'll have to wait to see how they vote later on."

Meanwhile, Banopoulos published a series of passionate editorials in his newspaper, placing Father Anton in the tradition of church martyrs who through the centuries had been sacrificed because of intolerance and zealotry.

At the same time, the *Hellenic Tribune*, the Greek paper in which Tzangaris had an interest, printed a series of lurid stories about the evils of child molestation and how any trace of it had to be purged from the church. The paper quoted a prominent and unnamed psychiatrist who asserted that "what begins as fondling usually ends up in attempted rape."

A week before the vote, Orestes held still another fund-raiser at the Olympia that was attended by almost a hundred people and that raised about $4,000 for flyers, letters and postage. Paulie's print shop, along with the neighborhood Kinko's, became a beehive of photocopying activity.

During these weeks of intense activity on behalf of retaining Father Anton at the church, Orestes still hadn't phoned Sarah. Each day that passed made it harder for him to find a valid excuse for his delay in contacting her. Unless, he thought grimly, his cowardice might be justified as a reason.

Then, on a morning in early November, when the last blooms of autumn flowers had withered overnight in the first sting of frost, as Orestes left his house for his trip to the restaurant, on an impulse he drove to the library. He felt that if by a slim chance Sarah was there, he'd be able to apologize in person for the extended delay in contacting her.

He parked in the parking lot of the library and then sat in the car for the following ten minutes, immobilized by anxiety about what he would do if Sarah were in the library and called him "Dante." Should he respond by calling her Beatrice? What if, however, in an effort to abort the whole fantasy, he tried patiently to explain to her that he wasn't Dante and that she could not possibly be Beatrice? What if that led to a confrontation and she became hysterical and the police had to be called. He could imagine the shocked expression on Mrs. Kohn's kindly face if the police led him out wearing handcuffs. He also envisioned the editorial the *Hellenic Tribune* would print under the heading LEADING SUPPORTER OF FATHER ANTON STEPHANOS OF ST. SOPHIA'S GREEK ORTHODOX CHURCH ARRESTED IN MEDIEVAL SEX FANTASY WITH UNBALANCED YOUNG WOMAN.

Despite all the threatening scenarios, he mustered his courage and entered the library.

"Good morning, Mr. Panos," Mrs. Kohn said. "I haven't seen you in weeks."

"I've been very busy with parish business, Mrs. Kohn."

He walked into the central reading room of the library, where the old men slumped in chairs, reading or dozing over newspapers. He entered the stacks and, after searching a while, felt an unquestioned relief because Sarah wasn't there. His relief was short-lived when, a moment later, he came upon her sitting in the alcove, under the same window where she had been sitting the first time he saw her. While he remembered her head crowned in sunlight and the day now was overcast, the golden strands of her hair were so fine and glossy that they still sparkled in the dim light.

Seeing her intent on her book, unaware that he was standing a few feet away, he had an impulse to turn and flee. Then, he scourged his faint heart and walked toward her. When he reached her chair, she looked up, and he was struck again by her pale, translucent beauty.

"Hello," he said. He waited tensely for her to call him Dante.

But she only said, "Hello," and smiled. Then she closed the book and rose from her chair.

"I'm so sorry." He looked nervously around to make sure no one was within earshot. "I owe you an apology."

"Why?"

"Because I never phoned to thank you for that wonderful dinner, or for the entire evening. We have some problems in our parish church that have kept me very busy. But that's no excuse for my rudeness."

He waited to see if she'd accept his apology as Beatrice or Sarah.

She stared at him, an enigmatic smile on her cheeks. Then she slowly raised her hand and placed her finger gently against his lips.

"No apology is necessary," she said softly. "That night you came to visit was one of the happiest of my life."

He was shaken by her words and wondered whether to ask her to have coffee with him again. Before he could extend an invitation, she reached down for her purse. As she turned to leave the stacks, she spoke to him in a whisper.

"I'll count the days until you can visit once more," she said in a low voice. "You will come and see me again, won't you?"

He stared down at her, his throat dry, and his knees trembling.

"Yes," he said, his voice low and unsteady. "I will come and see you."

He stood there numbly watching her walk through the library and out the door.

On the second Sunday in November, when the balloting was to take place, St. Sophia's was packed with parishioners. In addition to the crowded pews, additional chairs were set up along the walls. A crowd milled in the rear of the church, and another group waited on the stone steps outside.

When it was time for his sermon that day, Father Elias took his place before the podium and for a moment gazed silently down at the crowded church.

"For weeks now our parish has been a battleground," he said, and there was both bitterness and censure in his voice. "Hostile and opposing forces surge back and forth in our church like armies in the field. Whatever vestige of Christian love and charity that existed here in the past has vanished. We are become a parish of adversaries, a community of combatants."

The echoes of his voice, broken only by the shrill wails of a few babies, rang stridently throughout the church. Sitting in the midst of somber parishioners, Dessie reached over to tightly clasp Orestes' hand.

"I tell you now, my brethren, this dissension must end today!" Father Elias said, his voice gaining in strength and in anger. "This snarling and biting that makes a travesty of faith, that mocks the message of love Jesus Christ gave his life for on the cross. By our hatred we prove we are not Christians but idolaters, not worshipers in these sacred surroundings, but blasphemers and vilifiers. In all my years as a priest, I have never been so filled with revulsion as I am now."

As if feeling themselves singed by the fire of his castigation, a murmur of unrest swept the congregation. Men and women looked nervously at one another and then turned back to the priest

"Therefore listen to me now, my brethren. Whatever the balloting produces today, I say to you this conflict must come to a close. Whether Father Anton remains here as a priest or leaves, this ugly, fratricidal war must end! If it does not, I swear before God that whatever happens, I will also leave this parish, leave it to sting itself to death like a nest full of vipers!"

At the end of the church service, people gathered in small groups, whispering about the priest's angry sermon. Then the crowd moved down the stairs toward the hall where the balloting was to take place. Orestes was joined by Karvelas and Banopoulos as well as Professor Platon and George Lalounis with their wives.

In the hall, members of the parish council and ladies of the Philoptochos were seated at tables with membership lists to check off those eligible to vote.

With people still feeling sullen and chastened by Father Elias's angry sermon, the balloting took place in an eerie quiet, few people speaking, and then only in guarded, muted voices.

After he had voted, Orestes joined the ballot watchers, observing the counting as a precaution against any irregularities.

"We can't be too careful because this is Chicago," Banopoulos said grimly. "Voting violations have always abounded in this city. I remember a mayoral election where certain wards brought in twice the number of votes as there were registered voters, and when more votes were needed, they added the votes of those dwelling in the city cemeteries."

Tzangaris was everywhere, moving quickly from one group to another, his face flushed and dark.

"I bet he's angry as hell at Father Elias for his sermon," George Lalounis said. "He doesn't care to be reminded that he's a damn pathetic example of a Christian."

"How I'd love to have that stepson of Satan avail himself of my services!" Karvelas said passionately. "I'd lay him in his coffin with a pair of horns on his crooked head and a tail shoved into his ass!"

"Before he'd let himself fall into your vengeful hands," Banopoulos laughed, "Sam would become an atheist and have himself cremated!"

While the ballots were being counted, the crowd in the hall waited expectantly for the results. Peter Vasilakos, the vice president of the parish, ascended the stage.

"The results of the voting are as follows," he said. "For Father Anton Stephanos to leave, 153 votes. For Father Stephanos to remain, 193 votes."

Orestes joined the other supporters of the priest in a rousing cheer. He saw Tzangaris beat his fist on the table in disgust. The room was clamorous with demonstrations of delight and noisy with expressions of disappointment. Vasilakos tried to calm and reassure the gathering that the balloting should end the controversy, but no one paid any attention.

Before leaving the hall, Orestes, joined by Karvelas and Banopoulos, stopped in the church to see Father Elias. They found the priest in his office.

"Have you heard yet, Father Elias?" Karvelas said jubilantly. "We have beaten back the slanderers and defilers. Tzangaris is licking his wounds like a clawed and whipped cat."

A grinning Banopoulos echoed his words.

"Wait until you see the editorial I compose, Father Elias, proclaiming this to be one of the most glorious days in the history of St. Sophia's!"

The priest stared at them in silence.

"I know how distressed you have been about all this business, Father Elias," Orestes said quietly, "Now I hope the vote pleases you. I believe that justice has prevailed, and, as you indicated in your sermon, perhaps now the parish can begin to heal."

The priest stared at them for a long, somber moment.

"Have we won?" he said, and there was a weariness and futility in his voice and in his face. "Are the three of you really so foolish and naive to think anyone really won?"

Later, as he drove Dessie and Stavroula home from church, Orestes said he planned to spend the afternoon in the Olympia.

"There will be people from our parish there, I'm sure," he said, "Losers as well as winners among them. I think we must try to do what Father Elias said and begin the process of healing."

"The losers may not be as willing to accept healing as the winners," Dessie said. She twisted in her seat to look back at Stavroula.

"What did you think of the sermon Father Elias gave today, mama?"

Stavroula cleared her throat hoarsely before responding.

"In all the years I have been coming to this church, this is the first time I heard that man's sermon make any sense."

Dessie and Orestes looked at each other in disbelief.

"This is indeed a day for miracles," Orestes said in a low voice. Dessie suppressed a smile and nodded.

When Orestes arrived at the Olympia later in the day, the restaurant was crowded with parishioners from St. Sophia's. The partisans of Father Anton made no effort to conceal their jubilation, and those who had opposed him were ill-tempered and disgruntled.

There was talk among the priest's antagonists about continuing the battle, searching out other girls and boys who might reactivate the accusations. But both sides were somewhat subdued by recalling Father Elias's angry sermon and his threat that he might himself leave the parish.

Not long after he'd arrived at the Olympia, Orestes received a phone call from Father Anton, asking if he might come to the priest's apartment.

Orestes hadn't set foot in the priest's apartment since the night at the beginning of September when he'd driven the priest home. After he rang the bell, Father Anton, wearing shirt sleeves and a faded sweater, let him in. The apartment was dimly lit with only a small lamp burning in the corner. When Father Anton entered the beam of light, Orestes saw how his ordeal had burdened the young priest, his face as emaciated as if he'd been on a long, arduous fast.

"We were looking for you after the balloting, Father Anton!" Orestes said. "All your friends were eager to congratulate you."

"I am thankful to everyone who worked so hard for me, Orestes," Father Anton said quietly. "And I am grateful for the results of the ballot. But there is little reason for celebrating. Winning or losing comes to the same end."

"What do you mean, Father?"

"However the final vote turned out, Orestes," Father Anton spoke in a low weary voice, "did you really think I could remain in the parish? Did you think the bitterness Father Elias spoke about, God help us, even the hatreds which these last weeks have produced, did you think it would all go away just like that?" He sighed. "This division will take months, perhaps years to heal. And if I stayed, it would never heal."

"Father," Orestes said in dismay. "Don't tell me now that we've won, you're going to leave! I beg you, don't give Sam Tzangaris and the others that satisfaction! We've beaten them! The parish has voted they want you to remain! We've won!"

"What have we won, Orestes?" the priest asked, his words echoing those spoken earlier by Father Elias. "A narrow margin of numbers cannot erase the deep antagonisms that exist within the hearts of our parishioners. Every time I am seen by one of the people who voted against me, it will rub salt into their wounds. And what about my work with the young people in the Sons of Pericles and the Daughters of Penelope? How will they regard me now? How careful must I be about saying anything or doing anything which might suggest that the accusations against me were true? The suspicion would always be there. Every word I spoke and any gesture I made would become suspect."

With a heavy spirit, Orestes accepted the harsh truth in the priest's words.

"Where will you go, Father?" he asked quietly. "Will you ask the Bishop to transfer you to another parish?"

"Moving me to another parish will simply rekindle the scandal and suspicion I faced here," Father Anton said. "As soon as I am appointed, the rumors will begin and the animosities will spread." He shook his head pensively. "I have become a pariah, as virulent as a disease, so wherever I go, I will infect the people around me."

The shadows of twilight had further darkened the room. Father Anton walked slowly to the corner and lit a second lamp. The beam cast his long shadow across the wall.

"I think I'll travel to Greece for a while to spend time in my father's village in the Peloponnesus. Then, there is a lovely, old monastery in the mountains above Tripoli. Years ago while I was studying for the priesthood, I spent a few months there in meditation and prayer. I've written them and they've granted me permission to join them in the cloisters, a time I will use to pray, and renew my struggle to purify my soul and strengthen my spirit."

"A dedicated, loving priest like you would be a blessing in any parish," Orestes said. "Some time in the future, Father Anton, would you consider assignment to a church again?"

"Who knows, Orestes," the priest said. "At this point I cannot see my future clearly. I may decide to remain in the monastery or serve somewhere in the world as a missionary. Someday I might also feel that I could serve in a parish once again. With time and prayer, I may come to understand what it is God wishes me to do."

"How soon will you leave, Father?"

"Tomorrow."

"So soon! That won't allow time for your friends to tell you good-bye! At least stay long enough for me to arrange a farewell dinner for you at the Olympia. People will want to show their appreciation for all you've done for us."

"Forgive me, Orestes, but I don't wish any farewell dinner. The sooner I leave, the sooner the healing of the parish can begin." Father Anton paused. "I've spoken to Father Elias, and he agrees."

The priest fell silent, and after a moment, he stretched out his arms toward Orestes in a poignant gesture of affection. When they embraced, Orestes felt the lean flesh and bone of the young priest's body, and he couldn't hold back tears.

"God bless you, Orestes," Father Anton said, and there were also tears in his eyes. "I will never forget how you fought for me and championed me. For as long as I live, I will keep you and your beloved family in my prayers."

The priest paused and, for the first time since Orestes entered the apartment, a faint smile lightened his cheeks. "I can't bear to see you look so mournful, my dear friend. Remember that my leaving the environs of this vigorous city doesn't begin to equal the trauma of Ernie Banks leaving the Cubs or Michael Jordan leaving the Bulls. I haven't any doubt that our parish as well as the city of Chicago will quite easily survive my departure."

Thirteen

WITHIN A few days of Father Anton's departure, winter came to the city, the sky turning dark and the weather cold. For a week, the sun remained hidden behind a dense cluster of clouds. At night, a frigid wind blew any autumn petals that still retained color into dry, withered stalks.

Between the onslaught of winter and Father Anton's leaving the city for Greece, Orestes felt irritable and depressed. For several Sundays, he avoided going to church so he would not have to see the gloating face of Sam Tzangaris. At home, he was short-tempered with Dessie, and, in the Olympia, he bickered on petty matters with Kyriakos and several of the cooks and waiters. Even the usually amiable Cleon lost patience with him.

"Get a grip on yourself, partner!" Cleon cried at him one afternoon after a disagreement on a minor matter. "Why don't you get a dog so you can release your bad temper by kicking the poor animal in the ass!"

One evening when he was delayed at the restaurant and arrived home after dinner, Dessie told him that Marika had gotten a tattoo. Orestes was grateful for a chance to vent his frustration.

"For God's sake, Dessie, that's just crazy! Are you telling me that because her current boyfriend has a tattoo, she felt she had to have one too?"

"She wanted to bond with him."

"If she wanted to bond, why didn't they get twin bracelets or twin sweat shirts? Why did she have to mutilate her body?"

"Orestes, lower your voice, please. If mama learns about this, she'll make us all suffer. The tattoo is only an inch or two inches wide at most. And its not ugly. It's really a quite attractive gray, star-winged moth."

Orestes had a distressing image of a gray, star-winged moth engraved on his young daughter's breasts or buttocks. Dessie sensed his anxiety.

"You don't need to worry that its on some intimate part of her body," she said. "It's on her navel, just above her belly button, so its only visible when she wears a two-piece bathing suit or cut-off jeans." She paused. "After all, there's just a single moth."

"In the name of God, isn't one enough?"

"She might have wanted to give the moth a mate." Dessie smiled faintly.

He ignored his wife's feeble effort at humor.

"Is Marika upstairs?" he asked sharply.

"She's in her room. Now, I've already scolded her, Orestes, so try to stay patient."

"I'm going to make it clear to her that it was a foolish, selfish action that showed a complete lack of respect for how we feel! I'll also insist that she have the damn blemish erased!"

"I've heard trying to erase a tattoo can lead to a dangerous infection," Dessie said. "It might also leave a bad scar."

"I won't have my daughter engraved like a freak in a circus sideshow!"

He walked resolutely upstairs to his daughter's room, rehearsing the stern phrases he'd use to censure her. When he knocked briskly on her door, she answered, and he entered.

Marika was sitting cross-legged and barefooted on her bed,

an open notebook across her knees. Perhaps, in an effort to show remorse, she wasn't playing one of her rock music CDs, and the room hung suspended in an unnatural silence.

His daughter looked at him anxiously from the dark, lovely eyes she had inherited from Dessie.

"Marika, I want to talk to you," he said sternly.

"I've been expecting you, daddy," she said in a low, timorous voice.

When he sat on the edge of her bed, his daughter reached out and gently touched his arm. Her small, slender-fingered hand seeking reconciliation and forgiveness nibbled at his resolve.

"Oh daddy, don't be angry with me! I couldn't bear it if you were angry with me!"

He made an effort to keep his voice stern.

"Marika, why would you do something like this without first asking your mother or me?"

"I knew you'd both say no. And I really wanted to do it, daddy, for Lenny's sake and for my own."

Her face was so filled with repentance that he felt his anger dissipating. After all, he had to be grateful because a tattoo wasn't a peril to her health as, God forbid, smoking or drugs would have been.

"Do you want to see the tattoo?" she asked meekly.

"I suppose I better," he sighed.

She tugged the hem of her blouse out of her jeans and raised it slightly over her lean stomach. He couldn't resist a shudder when he saw the gray, star-winged moth tattooed on her flesh.

Dessie had told him it wasn't any more than an inch or two, but the ugly moth was grossly larger, at least three to four inches wide, blemishing the smooth flesh of Marika's navel and distorting the tiny hollow of her belly button.

"Do you really think its so terrible, daddy?" Marika seemed on the verge of tears.

"Well, I suppose it could have been worse," his voice came out quieter and more forgiving than he'd planned. "But, my darling, if you add a tattoo for every boyfriend you'll have before you reach twenty-one or until you marry, there won't be an inch of your body left unmarked."

"Then I'll get a job as a Tattooed Woman in the circus," she giggled.

He was aggravated at her flippancy.

"Marika, it's nothing to joke about!"

Her face quickly turned remorseful once again.

"I know it isn't," she said contritely. "Will you forgive me, daddy?"

He tried vainly to maintain a demeanor of disapproval. Then his resolve collapsed like air from a blown tire.

"I forgive you, my darling," he said gently, "but in the future, will you be a good girl and speak to us first about things you consider doing? Will you do that?"

"I will, daddy! I promise that I will!"

He started from the room and paused at the door.

"And don't let your Yiayia Stavroula see you in a bikini or cut-off jeans," he warned her. "She'll swear you're on the road to hell and drag you to church for confession and communion."

As he descended the stairs, like the detonation of a victory celebration, the noisy tumult of a rock group shook the house. He imagined his triumphant daughter bouncing jubilantly on her bed, the wings of the gray, star-winged moth tattooed on her navel fluttering to the sound of the brass and the drums.

Dessie waited anxiously for him in the kitchen.

"How did it go?"

"I told her how unhappy we were about the whole wretched business!" Orestes frowned. "I said it was thoughtless and disrespectful for her not to ask us first!"

"Did she seem sorry?"

"No question about it," Orestes said. "When I finished tongue-lashing her, she seemed on the verge of tears."

"Poor darling," Dessie said. "She can't stand to have you angry at her. She'll probably cry herself to sleep."

"It's just too bad if she does break down and cry," Orestes said, his voice stern and unyielding, "but I wasn't going to hold back telling her exactly how I felt."

With the echoes of his daughter's abominable music resonating through the house, Orestes beat a retreat to the living room. For a while then, taking refuge behind his newspaper, he gloomily pondered the enigma of why fathers were so helpless when dealing with young daughters.

On the following Friday afternoon in the Olympia, Orestes entered the kitchen to confer with Kyriakos.

"I want a really special dinner for my son's in-laws, Mario and Theresa Barzini, tomorrow evening," Orestes said to the head chef. "I want to put them in a better mood to discuss certain family problems."

"I'm a chef, not a witch doctor," Kyriakos said brusquely. "My menus are to please palates, not to soothe ruptured tempers."

For an instant, Orestes considered how satisfying it would be to give the cantankerous chef a smack across his arrogant head.

"This is important to me, Kyriakos," he said quietly.

The chef must have sensed his agitation.

"Fish or meat?" he asked.

"How about sea bass the way you prepared it the other evening for Joe Hannon and his party?"

"That was sea bass carpaccio marinated with mint and lemon."

"Joe told me everyone in his party thought it was delicious. Let's use that as our entree. What about the soup?"

"I suggest roasted egg plant soup with a dollop of cheddar. That's always received very well."

"Fine."

"And then a chilled endive salad garnished with a sauce made of prosciutto, nuts, and olives. That too is a favorite."

"That sounds just right, Kyriakos. I knew I could count on you."

Orestes turned to leave, and the chef called him back.

"Cleon told me this man, Barzini, is Italian and that he's probably a member of the Mafia."

"Cleon is wrong," Orestes said firmly. "Mario is a florist, a very reputable businessman."

"Remember the Spike O'Donnell gang from the 1930s?" Kyriakos said somberly. "Spike owned a flower shop too."

"Because the man's Italian doesn't mean all Italians belong to the Mafia," Orestes said impatiently.

"He better not come into the kitchen waving a gun if he doesn't like the dinner," Kyriakos grumbled and turned away.

On the following day, Dessie came to the Olympia in the afternoon, bringing fresh flowers as a centerpiece for the dinner. Cleon escorted her to the elegantly appointed table set for four in the alcove, where Orestes joined her.

"The table looks lovely, Cleon," Dessie said warmly.

"I set it myself!" Cleon said. "Our best crystal and china. And for the dinner, Kyriakos has selected a menu for royalty!" He laughed. "You two don't have to worry. We'll have them purring like kittens!"

"Or scratching like tomcats," Orestes said gloomily after Cleon had left. "Even after a fine dinner, Mario may still want to shoot Paulie for deserting his family."

"Before I let him harm my son, I'd shoot him first," Dessie said emphatically.

"We should let Stavroula take care of him," Orestes sighed. "If she set her sights on him, he'd probably sell his flower shop and move back to Italy."

Later that evening, when Mario and Theresa Barzini entered the restaurant, Dessie and Orestes hurried forward to greet them. At the door, Cleon took their coats with the gallantry and effusiveness he reserved for celebrities.

"Your dear relatives have arrived!" Cleon cried to Dessie and Orestes, who shot him a warning look.

Mario Barzini was a bulky-bodied, dark-complected, and dour man. His wife, Theresa, was an overweight matron with large jeweled earrings dangling from her ear lobes, and her fingers adorned with several glittering rings.

Hard as he tried, Orestes had never been able to muster any fondness for either husband or wife. He found Theresa petty and spiteful and Mario dull and sour tempered. When they had first met the Barzinis prior to Paulie and Carmela's wedding, Orestes had made an unkind comment to Dessie that the less they saw of Paulie's in-laws, the better.

But that evening, masking his antipathy, he kissed Theresa fondly and shook hands warmly with Mario. Dessie kissed Mario and hugged Theresa.

"Orestes and I are so pleased you could join us on such short notice," she said.

They led the Barzinis to the table in the alcove.

"Aren't Paulie and Carmela coming?" Mario asked.

"I thought we'd keep tonight's dinner for just the four of us," Dessie said. "Give us a chance to talk over things without the kids present."

"I don't think there's anything to talk over," Mario scowled. "A man either accepts his responsibilities as a husband and father, or he doesn't."

Orestes cast a quick, despairing look at Dessie.

One of the quickest and most courteous of the Olympia's young waiters, Christos, had been assigned to serve them, and after they were seated, he brought the tureens of steaming soup. At the same time, Cleon brought them a bottle of wine and a tray of succulent appetizers.

"I hope you'll enjoy the wine, Mr. Barzini." Cleon extracted the cork with a flourish and poured a little into Mario's glass. "It's from our private reserve."

Mario frowned and raised the glass to his lips. He paused as if he were assessing the vintage and then nodded somberly.

"I told Orestes that we had to be sure to serve only the best for a wine connoisseur such as you!" Cleon beamed.

Orestes shot him another warning look as Cleon finished filling the glasses.

"Are those little sausages spicy?" Theresa asked. "If I eat anything spicy, it gives me a terrible heartburn."

"I told that to Orestes," Dessie said, "and he instructed the chef that nothing in our dinner tonight was to be spicy."

"It isn't spicy food that gives her heartburn," Mario said. "She just eats too much."

Theresa glared at him.

"What kind of salad dressing is this?" Mario asked when Christos brought their salads.

"It's a special dressing our chef made with prosciutto, nuts, and olives," Orestes said.

"I don't care much for these fancy dressings," Mario said. "I prefer regular Italian."

"I think the dressing tastes delicious!" Theresa said. "How much do you have to pay a chef like you got here? I bet he gets a bundle."

"We pay him a substantial salary," Orestes said. "And there are restaurants on the street that would probably pay him much more."

A short while later, Cleon uncorked a second bottle of wine. In spite of his good intentions and a series of beseeching looks from Dessie, Orestes drank a little recklessly to anesthetize himself against the drudgery of the dinner. For all their concerns about salad dressings and spicy food, he noted that the Barzinis ate like a pair of tiger sharks.

He was jerked from his reverie by Mario's aggravated voice.

"I told Carmela that she should put her foot down. She's too easy on your son. He needs to be reminded that a man looks after his responsibilities."

"I'm sure they truly love each other, Mario," Dessie said. "But from time to time young people have their ups and downs. We've got to allow them to work out their own problems."

"My poor daughter and that poor baby." Theresa took a long swallow of wine. "I don't know what I'd do if I saw them unhappy."

"Anybody who makes my daughter unhappy has got to deal with me," Mario said somberly.

"I'm sure they love each other," Dessie repeated. She looked desperately at Orestes for help.

"They love each other, I'm sure," Orestes said. He closed his eyes for a moment and when he reopened them, he saw a grinning Cleon bring still a third bottle of wine to the table. Cleon popped the cork and moved quick as a fox to Mario's empty glass.

"Don't mind if I do," Mario said. He raised the full glass and took several noisy sips. "Like I said, anybody makes my little girl unhappy has got to deal with me."

"We've just got to give them a chance to solve their problems," Dessie said. "Remember what it was like when we first married."

"That's so true." Theresa wiped a vagrant tear from her eye. "In our first year of marriage I was so unhappy, I almost went home to my mother three times."

"Who you kidding!" Mario snickered loudly. "She couldn't wait to get you out of the house." He gestured at Orestes and Dessie. "On our first date, her old man asked me if my intentions were serious. They were crazy to get her off their hands."

"My father had heard about your reputation," Theresa snapped. "He wanted to be sure you weren't just fooling around."

"He didn't have to worry about me," Mario said. "I'm the kind of man who meets his responsibilities." He looked grimly at Orestes. "Anybody don't meet his responsibilities to his wife and family isn't a man but a bum!"

Dessie looked entreatingly at Orestes, a plea for him to make a final effort to salvage the dinner.

"I'm sure Paulie understands that and wants to do the right thing," Orestes said. "In the loose moral climate that exists in society today, young people sometimes have a hard time stabilizing their gwn lives . . ."

He gave Dessie a resigned look and signaled Christos to pour everyone more wine.

"If we owned an elegant restaurant like this instead of a flower shop—" Theresa sighed—"I wouldn't be able to lose a pound."

Orestes felt light-headed, his vision blurred. There was a tightness in his chest, and he wondered if he might be having a heart attack. He had to get away from the table, and he pushed himself awkwardly to his feet.

"I just thought of a matter I need to discuss with our chef," he said. "Please excuse me. I'll be back as soon as I can."

"Don't be long." Dessie's voice held a fervent plea.

Orestes started for the kitchen and then turned and walked into his office. He locked the door and slumped in the chair at his desk. He felt trapped and frustrated, angry at his son for having chosen the daughter of such a family, angry at Dessie for having suggested the dinner in the first place. With his courage emboldened by the quantity of wine he'd drunk, he felt an urge to return to the table and order the Barzinis to get the hell out of his restaurant.

Realizing that imprudent action would shatter Dessie, he foraged for some other means to allay his frustration. On an impulse, he decided to phone Sarah.

He fumbled in the back of his drawer for her number and dialed it. Her soft voice answered on the third ring.

"Beatrice?" As soon as the name popped out of his mouth, he shuddered at what he had done.

There was a moment of silence.

"My beloved Dante," she said. "I've been waiting for you to call."

He stared at his fingers clenched around the phone, his wine-soaked tongue struggling for the words to speak next.

"How have you been?" he asked weakly.

"I've been fine, my dearest. How have you been?"

"Fine," he grimaced at the ceiling. "Fine."

There was another pause.

"Would you like to come to dinner again?"

He was taken back at how swiftly she offered the invitation.

"Just a minute now," he said, his voice slightly slurred. "I mean last time you went to all that trouble. Why don't we go to some restaurant instead?"

"Don't you want to come here?" Her voice held a tremor.

"Of course I'd like to come," he said weakly. "I just didn't want to put you to all that trouble."

"It's no trouble," she said. "Can you come next Saturday evening."

A premonition of danger penetrated his stupor.

"I'm very sorry, but I can't," he said quickly. "We have conventions in town all week and Saturday is very busy. I just can't get away."

"How about Friday of that week then?"

He stared helplessly at the phone.

"Let me check my calendar," he said. He fumbled at his desk calendar, considering telling her he was busy the following weekend, as well. But he couldn't muster a coherent excuse to explain any further delay.

"All right," he said weakly. "The following Friday is all right."

"Six o'clock?"

"Fine."

"You can bring the wine again, if you like."

"I'll bring the wine," he said grimly.

"I look forward to our evening," she said. "Good-bye, my dearest Dante."

"Good-bye," he said and hesitated. "Good-bye, Beatrice."

After hanging up, he sat for several moments pondering what he had done. Instead of breaking free from the girl and her fantasy, he had blithely encouraged her, proving himself as emotionally unbalanced as she was.

"It's those goddam Barzinis!" he cried. "I wouldn't be in this mess now if it weren't for them!"

A knock on his office door made him jump.

"Yes?" he cried.

"Mr. Panos, it's Christos," the waiter's voice carried through the door. "Mrs. Panos wants to know how much longer you'll be."

"Tell her I'll be right there," he said. He went into the bathroom to relieve himself and to splash cold water on his face. His reflection frowned back at him.

"Weak and dim-witted," his reflection sneered. "You and the Barzinis deserve each other."

Before leaving the office, he made a small enigmatic sign on his calendar to fix the date of his dinner with Sarah. When he could think about the matter soberly, he might find a way to get out of it.

He returned to the table as the Barzinis were finishing a desert of marinated fruit and raspberry ice cream tarts covered with fragrant powdered sugar. Husband and wife looked as stuffed as Thanksgiving turkeys.

Dessie gave Orestes a bitter look.

"I'm sorry," he mumbled. "Some pressing restaurant business in the kitchen."

He collapsed into his chair.

"This was certainly a fine dinner," Theresa said.

"I'll tell our head chef you said so," Dessie said. "I know it will please him."

A while later, after the Barzinis had left, snapping at each other all the way to the street, Dessie and Orestes sat morosely silent in the shambles of the table.

"It was painful enough with them when you were here," Dessie said wearily. "But how could you leave me alone with them like that? You were gone almost forty-five minutes that seemed to me like three hours!"

"I'm sorry, honey," Orestes mumbled. "I couldn't help myself. If I hadn't gotten away from the table for a little while, I'd have become sick to my stomach, or said something to them that we'd all regret. For the life of me I can't understand how those two could have had a daughter as sweet as Carmela!"

They stared gloomily at one another.

"In my worst nightmare, I couldn't imagine it would be this bad!" Dessie's voice was singed with futility. "The whole evening was a total disaster. Instead of helping them understand something about Paulie, we poured oil on the fire."

Kyriakos chose that moment to come from the kitchen to their table, his white chef's hat crumpled slightly on his head, and his apron soiled with stains of butter and flour.

"Did the gangster like the dinner?" he asked brusquely.

Orestes stared resentfully at his chef, who made a satisfying scapegoat for the calamity of the evening.

"They thought the food was too spicy," Orestes snarled. "Mrs. Barzini got a terrible heartburn and Mr. Barzini got sick to his stomach. He went to the toilet twice to vomit. He told me if he ever sees you on the street, he's going to shoot you!"

"Orestes!" Dessie cried. She gestured in apology to the chef. "He's just joking, Kyriakos," she said. "Everybody loved the dinner. Mrs. Barzini said it was one of the finest meals she'd ever eaten!"

Kyriakos scowled at Orestes.

"Anybody who jokes about food would spit on his mother's grave!" he said in disgust and stalked away.

Fourteen

B Y T H E start of December, anticipation about the arrival
of the new millennium became frenzied. Newspapers
and radio and television programs harped obsessively on
the auspicious event. Utopians spoke of the new century heralding an era of prosperity and harmony among countries and
peoples. Then there were the Y2K doomsayers who predicted
that the millennium would bring total chaos. All monitoring
systems would break down. Nuclear missiles might accidently
be launched from their silos, sanitation systems would over-
flow and flood raw sewage into the streets, and power trans-
formers would fail. In the worst scenario, the millennium would
herald Armageddon.

Even the leaders of other nations succumbed to a general
panic. Orestes read that Japan's prime minister, Keizo Obuchim,
planned to declare a three-day emergency holiday over the New
Year so his citizens might be ready to meet any catastrophe.

Meanwhile, a microcosm in all the worldwide planning, in
the Olympia, preparations continued for the elaborate New
Year's Eve party. Orestes carefully reviewed the menu for the
party with Kyriakos. Reciting the litany of the exotic dishes he
would create filled the master chef with passion, and his eyes
glowed with the flame of a culinary messiah.

"Green peppers stuffed with anthotiro," Kyriakos said, "and
a sauce made of dill and black-eyed beans."

"Excellent!" Orestes responded.

"Sweet and sour chicken, basted in honey and vinegar, and filled with Cypriot haloumi cheese."

"Wonderful!"

"Tender pork fillets filled with myzithra cheese in a bitter-sweet fig and yogurt salsa."

"Superb, Kyriakos!"

Lost as the chef was in his creative rapture, Orestes wasn't sure he even heard his congratulations.

Meanwhile, Cleon supervised the training of the restaurant's cooks, waiters, and busboys in the proper ways to service the large party. Workmen were brought in after the restaurant closed at night to wash and repaint the walls. The ladies' and gentlemen's toilets were renovated. All the dishware was inspected for cracks, and additional china, crystal, and silverware was ordered from a major supply house. New copper pots were ordered for the kitchen, and the copper carafes for retsina and rodytis wines were polished to a high luster. Cleon even made arrangements for an emergency generator to be connected in the restaurant utility room in case power failed during the celebration. He also took charge of travel and lodging arrangements for the famed player, Bakalakis.

"A suite at the Ritz Carlton?" Orestes exclaimed when Cleon told him of the plans. "Isn't that a little rich for a lyre player from a poor village in Laconia? He probably didn't own a pair of shoes until he was twelve. There's a fine Days Inn just up the street. That way the artist won't have to worry about traffic jams getting here to perform."

"Partner," Cleon said, his voice dripping with pity, "I'm sorry to say you've got the soul of a myopic bookkeeper. Bakalakis is, without a doubt, the finest lyre player in the world! Is a Days Inn on Halsted Street all the wretched hospitality you're proposing we offer him?"

"How much is the Ritz Carlton suite costing us?"

"A thousand a night for three nights." Cleon shrugged. "That's for three bedrooms. After all, you know an artist like Bakalakis travels with an entourage."

"Why doesn't his entourage stay at the Days Inn?" Orestes took perverse pleasure in provoking his partner.

"Nonsense!" Cleon cried. "What if he needs something in the middle of the night? Is he supposed to phone the Days Inn and tell his people to jump in a cab and hurry over to the Ritz Carlton?" He shook his head. "All I can say, my friend, is that you're fortunate to have me as a partner. Without me you'd gain a reputation for being the most niggardly, and tight-fisted restaurant owner on Halsted Street!"

Several days after the dinner with the Barzinis, Orestes phoned Sarah to tell her he couldn't make the Friday night dinner in her apartment.

"We're getting ready for a huge millennium celebration here in the restaurant, you know, and there is a lot of work to be done."

While he waited anxiously for her response, he had the uneasy feeling that his voice betrayed the lie.

"I understand," she said finally. "What about the following Friday?"

He started to tell her that the entire month of December would be frantic and it would be prudent to wait on their dinner until after the first of the year.

"I'm so looking forward to seeing you again," she said, her voice so pensive, he felt his resolve wavering.

"All right," he said cravenly. "A week from this coming Friday will be fine."

After he'd hung up, he consoled himself that the phone call had bought him an additional reprieve so he could reflect on the problem the girl presented in his life.

During this hectic time, Orestes tried to avoid having dinner at home with his somber mother-in-law at the table, which caused him indigestion. He knew that his absence meant that Dessie would have to eat dinner alone with her mother. By the time he arrived home, dinner was over and Stavroula had retreated to her burrow to watch a Tom Selleck movie on her video player. The fact that Dessie never complained about his absence further prodded his guilt.

Orestes also began having trouble sleeping, and, during the day, he fought the lethargy that came from sleeplessness. He grew concerned there might be something seriously wrong with him, and he checked his pulse a number of times a day to determine if it were beating erratically.

Finally, he made an appointment to see Dr. Savas. The old general practitioner examined him thoroughly.

"I can't hear or see anything," Dr. Savas said, "but it won't hurt for you to take some additional tests. I'll make arrangements over at Rush Hospital for you."

"If you think it best," Orestes sighed, premonitions of heart disease or an incurable cancer roiling his mind.

The following Monday, he spent most of the day at the hospital undergoing a series of tests. In the radiology department, he waited in a bleak corridor among silent, anxious men clad in those absurd hospital gowns, displaying their knobby knees and a bizarre assortment of shoes and stockings. When it came his turn, a technician took x-rays of his chest and his abdomen, and another technician took enough of his blood to satisfy a vampire's hunger. A cardiologist checked his heart, and a urologist probed his prostate.

Three days later, he sat with Dr. Savas in his office to review the results of the tests.

"Heart checks out all right, cholesterol looks good, blood pressure slightly elevated but still within a normal range. Your triglycerides are good, your prostate a little larger than it should be, but it shouldn't cause you any trouble for a few years yet." He paused. "All in all, Orestes, you're in fairly good shape for a man your age."

"I feel this heaviness of spirit," Orestes said gloomily. "I can't seem to shake it."

"I think you're under severe stress," Dr. Savas said. "This lingering business with the girl who thinks she is Beatrice, the unhappy departure of Father Anton, your son's marriage problems and his possible flight from his family, and then, reaching the milestone of fifty . . . all of these are wreaking havoc on you." The doctor shrugged. "These emotional concerns are endemic to our affluent society. That's a luxury denied the ethnic Albanians of Kosovo who have been driven from their homes, tens of thousands of men, women, and children become wretched refugees fleeing into Albania and Montenegro. The primary concern of those poor wretches is survival."

"I know what you're saying is true," Orestes sighed. "And I do try to be grateful for my good fortune."

"When you feel yourself becoming depressed, get a grip on yourself," Dr. Savas said brusquely. "Self-pity is acceptable in the dying and in the desperate, but a healthy man who whines is a disgrace." He pointed a stern finger at Orestes. "You need some interest beyond that goddam restaurant. When did you and Dessie last go out together?"

"I'm trying to remember," Orestes said. "I know last week we attended a Philoptochos dinner at the church."

"I'm not talking about one of those spirit-numbing church functions," Dr. Savas said sharply. "I'm talking about an evening in the city outside the parish with your wife. Take her to dinner and a show. One of my patients told me he'd enjoyed a film fantasy called *Shakespeare in Love*. Make a date with your wife to go to dinner and then see the film. It will do you both good."

Orestes started for the office door.

"How fortunate I am," he said pensively. "I have a physician who not only provides me excellent medical care but psychological counseling and cultural recommendations."

"Keep praising me like that," Dr. Savas laughed, "and I'll double the next bill I send you."

That week, the first letter from Father Anton since the priest had left the parish arrived for Orestes at the Olympia. When he saw the envelope postmarked from Greece on his desk, he closed his office door so he might read the letter undisturbed.

My dear Orestes:

I had meant to write you sooner, but when I first arrived in Greece there was so much to do. I had forgotten how frantic and crowded Athens is, and, at first, I was anxious to leave the city. But I had also forgotten how lovely the illuminated Parthenon is at night and the marvels that are displayed in the Archeological Museum so I remained a few days longer.

Two weeks ago I rode a bus crowded with humans, chickens, and rabbits to my father's village. When I first stepped into the small house my father was born in, I was overtaken with emotion. I've been visiting with a few old relatives I still have here, and then, next week, I'll begin my pilgrimage to the monastery. I am leaving most of my clothing and a few personal possessions I brought from America behind me here in the village.

Part of me is looking forward to the experience of the monastery, and part of me dreads it. Alas, that dread comes because my weak, spoiled flesh knows it will be an austere life, without many of the conveniences I had grown used to in America.

But I am girding my spirit and there are even moments I contemplate my journey with joy and anticipation. I will be experiencing the world's passage into the third millennium after Christ among good men who are unconcerned with worldly things and who will help me focus on my relationship to God without distractions. I begin to think, friend Orestes, that all this is part of a greater plan than I can understand. Perhaps Sam Tzangaris was God's instrument to bring me here. If it were not for him I would still be at the church, performing my daily tasks, a young priest with a good heart and with limited talent.

So, in my prayers now I thank the Lord for the zealous enmity of Tzangaris as I thank him, as well, for your friendship and love. Give Despina my love, as well.

Your devoted friend,
Fr. Anton Stephanos.

Orestes took the letter home and read it to Dessie. By the time he finished, she had tears in her eyes.

"Poor, lonely man," she said pensively. "I hope he finds his peace." She paused. "Do you ever think, Orestes, how much he and Paulie resemble one another?"

"I hadn't thought of it," Orestes said.

"I don't mean any physical resemblance," she said, "but a gentleness in each of them, a basic goodness that isolates them from others. I could imagine Paulie going to live in the cloisters of a monastery."

His wife's melancholy voice and tear-stained cheeks filled Orestes with love.

"How about a date this weekend, my darling?"

Dessie looked at him in surprise.

"Don't look so startled," Orestes said. ""You're my wife and its only natural that we should, from time to time, go out to dinner and a show."

"Do you know how long it has been since we have spent a night out together?" Dessie asked quietly. "I don't mean a church dinner with two hundred other people, but just the two of us?"

"I can't honestly remember," he said ruefully.

"It was August 17," she said. "More than three months ago. We had dinner at Pheasant Run and saw *Man of La Mancha*.

He sighed.

"Then we'll do it for sure this Friday evening!" he said firmly. "And I promise you, Dessie, that after the first of the year, we'll go out together much more often!"

Almost at once he remembered his Friday night dinner with Sarah. Having committed to that night, he was reluctant to phone her and cancel the dinner once again. "On second thought, my darling," he said to Dessie, "We can't do it Friday. I have some suppliers to see about the millennium party. Let's do it Saturday evening instead. We'll go to one of the fancy downtown restaurants like Ambria, and then plan to see a new film people are talking about . . . *Shakespeare in Love*."

"I accept your invitation," Dessie said. "I'll break the news to mama that on Saturday evening she'll have to eat alone. Unless," she smiled teasingly at Orestes, "you'd like to perform the Christian act of taking her with us."

"That would be a Christian act that might earn me sainthood," Orestes sighed, "but I'll be candid with you, my dearest, and confess that the prospect of dinner and a show with your blessed mother tagging along chills me to the bone."

As Friday evening and his dinner with Sarah came closer, Orestes vowed he'd make a resolute effort to break off their relationship. He'd try to do it in a way that left her fantasy intact, but, one way or other, he couldn't keep seeing the girl and risk Dessie finding out. Innocent as the whole business was, it would be difficult to convince his wife—or anyone else—that a middle-aged man having dinner alone in a young girl's candlelit apartment was pure and harmless.

Perhaps he could somehow convince Sarah that Dante had to resume his spiritual journey.

"I'll tell her I had a fax from Virgil," he muttered, "about a special Olympic Airways flight and hotel package for a one-way trip to Purgatory."

On Friday afternoon, growing more nervous as the hour approached for his dinner with Sarah, he waited until Cleon was occupied in the kitchen and then slipped out of the Olympia. On his way to the young woman's apartment, he bought another bottle of wine, but, in place of flowers, he purchased a box of chocolates.

When he rang Sarah's bell and she answered, he ascended the stairs and entered the apartment with its myriad candles and the small table set for two. Sarah wore a light white blouse and darker skirt, and as she took his coat to hang on a clothes rack, he was struck once again by her pale, sensitive beauty. He couldn't resist a vagrant flutter of lechery imagining how her small, slender body would look naked. The erotic image made him feel lightheaded before he'd even had a glass of wine. Then, glancing at her chaste, innocent face, he felt a stab of shame.

"I've been waiting anxiously for you to return," she said. "I've looked for you in the library a number of times but haven't seen you there."

"As I explained on the phone," he said, "we're very busy at the restaurant planning a very big New Year's Eve party."

He uncorked the wine and poured them each a glass.

"If you're hungry, dinner is ready," Sarah said. "Otherwise we can wait a little while to eat."

"I'm famished," he said. The sooner they ate, the sooner he'd be able to bring up the ending of their relationship.

Sarah brought him a bowl of steaming celery soup, and a small green salad. He sipped the first spoonful.

"Delicious!" he said. "As good as anything our master chef at the Olympia could make!"

After they'd finished the soup, she brought the main dish from the kitchen.

"I hope you enjoy the lasagna," she said. "I prepared it the way I saw Martha Stewart make it once on television."

"I told you after our last dinner that you were a fine cook," Orestes said earnestly, "and I know this dinner will be just as good."

During dinner they spoke a little more of her stay on Crete and about Kazantzakis. She told him she'd been rereading *Freedom or Death* and enjoying it.

When she asked what he'd been reading, he offered the excuse once again that he was busy in the restaurant. Meanwhile, as their conversation meandered back and forth, he sought an opportune moment to bring up the matter of ending their relationship.

He remembered that he'd become drunk during their last dinner and fallen asleep on the couch, so he was careful how much he drank. Sarah seemed to be drinking more than she had on his previous visit, and several times she asked him to refill her glass. When he bent closer to her to pour the wine, he inhaled a delicate fragrance about her he found pleasing.

"This is wonderful wine," she said.

He didn't see any reason to tell her the bottle cost considerably less than the wine he had brought to their last dinner.

She must have sensed his nervousness.

"You seem tense tonight, my darling."

He found the steadiness of her gaze disconcerting.

"The pressures at the restaurant . . ." he offered that shopworn excuse once more.

"I can't do anything to help you with the restaurant," she said quietly, "but you mustn't be troubled about us. I understand there is a world outside where you have your business and your family and where you must deal with other people. But when we are together here, we can confide in one another, share with one another who we truly are. This will be our sanctuary."

He couldn't think of anything to say and he shook his head in somber agreement.

When she rose to bring them small cups of coffee, he decided that perhaps it might be better to break off their relationship in a more neutral environment such as the library.

After they'd finished the coffee and a small chocolate mousse dessert, they moved to the living room.

"Now you make yourself comfortable," she said, "and I'll be back in a few minutes."

He waited on the couch while she walked into the bedroom. A small bowl of fruit caught his eye, the candlelight reflecting across scarlet plums and a cluster of yellow grapes. In the silence, he heard the ticking of a clock, watched the flickering flame of the candles.

If he did ever decide to explain this strange relationship to Dessie, he wondered whether she'd understand. As pristine and immaculate as the whole business had turned out to be, Dessie might ask what he had hoped would happen at the time of his first visit. He concluded gloomily that it might be better if he never mentioned the whole bizarre relationship to his wife, at all.

Sarah emerged from the bedroom, once again barefooted, and wearing the white robe and veil he recalled from his last visit. She carried a book and came to curl up on the floor at his knees, her hair shining in the soft sheen of the candles. She opened the book, which he saw was the *Divine Comedy*, to a page somewhere in the middle, and in a soft, tremulous voice, she began to read.

"I saw a ladder of the color of gold,
From which the rays of light rebounded, rising,
Up so high that my eye could not follow it.
I also saw many splendors coming
Down the steps, that I thought every light
Shining in the sky had come pouring down it."

She moved the open book to his knee and motioned to a
marked passage.

"These next lines are for you to read," she said. Orestes bent
closer to the book and, a little self-consciously, began to read,

"Whoever wishes to understand clearly
What I now saw, let him picture—and retain
The picture, while I speak, like a solid stone—
Fifteen stars that in many different places
Enliven heaven with a light so brilliant
That it shines through any texture of the air."

Once again she drew the book to her and read.

"Look down and see what a universe I have
Already contrived to put beneath your feet,
So that your heart may confront so joyfully
As it can the triumphant multitude."

She motioned for him to pick up the verse, and he bent du-
tifully over the book.

"For all winter long I have seen the thorn
Look very vicious and unyielding.
And later seen it with a rose on top.
And I have seen a ship sweeping fast ahead

Across the sea along its given course,
And perish at the end on entering port."

A strand of her hair had fallen free, cutting across her cheek.
She brushed it aside and resumed reading.

"The power of loving kindness, my brother,
Pacifies our will and makes us desire
Only what we have and thirst for nothing more.
    If we were to desire to be higher,
Our wishes would be in disharmony
With the will of him who has arrayed us here."

He felt himself relaxing, drifting in the rhythm of the words,
reminded suddenly of the many nights he had read stories to
his own children. He looked down at Sarah fondly and thought
how much she was like a child.

She smiled up at him and handed him the book. He bent
his head and read.

"I turned my eyes to Beatrice, and she heard
Even before I spoke and gave me sign
That made the wings of my desire grow . . ."

He was conscious suddenly that the candles had burned
down, draining the room of color, the furniture slipping deeper
into the shadows. As he finished the passage, Sarah looked up
at him, an enigmatic expression in her eyes.

Instead of continuing the reading, Sarah closed the book and
put it down on the floor beside her. She leaned her head gently
against his knee, the warmth of her cheek radiating into his
thigh. A moist loose strand of her golden hair lay matted against
her temple.

As the silence stretched out between them, she reached up and clasped his hand. He felt the warmth of her palms, noticed once again with a twinge of sadness, the missing finger. She held his hand gently for a moment and then raised it to her lips and kissed his fingers. He felt a tingling at the touch of her lips on his flesh. Then she lowered his hand slowly, bringing it to rest gently over the small high mound of her breast.

His first startled reaction was that her gesture was made in innocence, her breast by chance in the way. But when he made an effort to withdraw his hand, she held it tightly, pressing it harder against her breast until, trembling like a sparrow through his fingers, he felt the pulsing of her heart.

"My darling," she whispered. She spoke the endearment differently than any way she had spoken the word before. She gazed up at him again, and he saw her lips, still moist from the wine. She seemed to be waiting, and, drawn to the glow of her eyes, he bent awkwardly and kissed her lightly, the casual kiss a brother might offer his sister.

She resisted his move to end the kiss, her lips curling urgently under his mouth, the contact sweeping a flash like an electric current through his body. While he struggled to catch his breath, she stroked his thigh, her palm permeating an erotic tremor through the cloth to his flesh.

His lips burning from the kiss, he was suddenly fractured with shock. Lulled into a chaste fantasy of platonic love, he felt helpless to come to grips with what was happening.

"My darling," she whispered again, her voice low, throaty with unmistakable desire. "Oh my darling . . . hold me . . . love me."

For a frantic moment he tried to recast himself in the role of a gentle, manly lover, suavely accepting the bounty of young beauty he was being offered. But shock and bewilderment eviscerated his passion, his phallus limp and numb, only a faint, futile quiver proving it was alive. He resisted an impulse to grasp the wayward organ and shake it into action. Perhaps it too was in shock, or perhaps it was haunted by the specter of lethal disease or an unwanted pregnancy.

Wary of pushing her away, trying to collect his shattered senses, he made a weak effort to rise from the couch.

"This isn't right, Sarah . . . Beatrice," he mumbled, making another half-hearted effort to rise with her still clinging to his leg. "Dear girl, we've drunk too much wine. This isn't right . . ."

Somehow, awkwardly, his thigh bumping the side of the couch, he broke free and lurched to his feet. She remained on her knees, staring up at him, her cheeks pale and her eyes luminous.

"I better go," he said, the words falling shrilly from his lips. "You're so lovely and I'm tempted, believe me, Beatrice, I am so tempted, but, my darling, I think it best for both of us that I go!"

Without waiting for her to respond, he hurried to the hallway and tugged his coat from the rack. He turned back and offered a final flustered flap of his fingers in a mute farewell to the girl still on her knees. Then he left the apartment, stumbling slightly on the stairs in his hasty descent.

When he emerged from the building onto the street, a draft of damp, cold air struck his face like a slap. At the same time, he was assaulted by the sights and sounds of the city, the rumble of traffic, the lights of passing cars.

With a dazzling clarity he recaptured her young, stunning beauty inviting his caresses. Perhaps under the stimulant of the wine, the fantasy Beatrice had succumbed to the flesh-and-blood Sarah! His inexcusable, confounding response to this amorous transformation had been to flee! What kind of dunce was he? If he had stayed and made love to her, his passion might well have resuscitated his organ! Impaled on a spear of indecision, he considered rushing back upstairs. Of course, she'd think him a total knucklehead and fool! She might not even let him back into the apartment! He understood, suddenly, that the charmed, erotically charged opportunity was forever lost!

A groan of anguish fell from his lips. He couldn't even console himself thinking he had fled because it was the decent, moral thing to do. The disabling truth was that sheer panic and wretched impotence had driven him away from the nest of love.

He staggered along the street, reeling with a riot of emotions—remorse, regret, disbelief.

An older couple, a man and woman, passing him on the street, perhaps thinking him a slobbering drunk, swept him with a scathing look of disapproval. He turned around to glare angrily after them. With all the bravado and confidence he'd lacked in Sarah's apartment, he loudly cried out for all within earshot to hear, "Son-of-a-bitch!" he bellowed. "Goddam son-of-a-bitch!"

Fifteen

FOR SEVERAL days following his visit to Sarah's apartment, Orestes painfully recalled the frantic flight and humiliation that ended the evening. He imagined how contemptuous Sarah had to feel about his totally demoralized departure. He had been offered a feast (about which he'd fantasized a number of times) that his panic had rejected. The whole deplorable affair added one more remorse to the multitude he had accumulated in his life.

He tried to console himself by rationalizing that the evening's fiasco had at least achieved the end of the bizarre relationship. Sarah would never want to see him again, and for a prudent period of time he'd stay away from the library. If he needed some reference material or wanted to take out a book, he'd visit the libraries in Oak Lawn or in Evergreen Park.

Remorsefully, he also postponed the Saturday evening he had planned with Dessie. Still reeling with shock from the interlude with Sarah, and fearing that Dessie might sense his agitation, he feigned a digestive problem and promised his wife they'd have the dinner and a show the following weekend.

Then, on the afternoon of the fourth day following his visit to Sarah, while consulting in the kitchen with Kyriakos, Cleon came to tell him he had a phone call.

"It's probably a supplier," Orestes said. "Tell him I'll call back."

"It's not a supplier." Cleon gestured urgently that he should take the call. Orestes returned to his office and picked up the phone.

"Orestes Panos speaking," he said crisply.

"Have I called you at a bad time?" Sarah's soft voice froze his blood.

"Not at all," he managed to respond. He wondered if she had phoned to taunt him.

"I won't keep you, my darling," she said. "I've been waiting anxiously for you to call, and I just couldn't wait any longer to tell you how much I admire you and how grateful I am. I'm ashamed of myself . . . I drank too much . . . my spirit weakened, but your strength saved us. You confirmed you have Dante's pure soul!" She paused. "Now, I won't keep you from your work any longer. Oh my darling! Please call me soon because I can't wait until I see you again!"

After hanging up the phone, Orestes sat numbly for a long time, contemplating the vagaries of fate. Instead of being branded a craven milksop, he was being hailed as a stalwart hero. Instead of the evening ending the relationship, his precipitous flight had reinforced the fantasy. He uttered a long, heartfelt sigh.

As he walked back into the restaurant, Cleon greeted him with a leer.

"Who was the call from, partner?"

"A friend."

"I never heard such a soft, silky voice," Cleon said fervently. "It floated right out of the phone and massaged me!"

"Get your mind off massages and onto getting us ready for the party!" Orestes snapped. "The reservations aren't coming in as we projected. Your hero, Bakalakis, will be playing to an empty restaurant."

"This is the millennium, my friend. People need time to make up their minds. I'm confident there will be a last minute rush that will pack the house."

As Orestes started away, Cleon called after him.

"Why don't you invite your friend here to dinner? I'd love to see the goddess who belongs to that voice."

The following morning, not long after he'd arrived at the Olympia, his concerns about Sarah and the millennium party were swept aside by a phone call from Dessie who told him Stavroula had fallen down the stairs.

"When I reached her at the bottom, she was still conscious, but I wasn't able to get her on her feet," Dessie said, her voice tense and distraught. "I called 911, and the ambulance just arrived. We're going to the emergency room of Little Company of Mary."

"I'll leave for the hospital right now," Orestes said.

He told Cleon about Stavroula's accident and that he was leaving for the hospital.

"I hope the old Medusa is all right," Cleon said somberly as he waved Orestes good-bye.

Orestes parked near the emergency room entrance. Above the great looming structure of the hospital, the sky was overcast, the cold air carrying a scent of snow.

The cavernous emergency room was crowded with people and smelled of sweat, grief, and pain. A mother holding a crying baby sat across from a man with a blood soaked bandage around his head. In a corner, two frightened children clung to their mother's arms, while a nurse attended a third child who was crying shrilly.

Orestes was directed to Dessie inside a curtained enclosure where Stavroula lay prone on a gurney. The old woman's eyes seethed with anger, as always, but now held terror, as well.

"How are you feeling, Stavroula?" Orestes asked gently.

"I'm in the emergency room!" Stavroula said hoarsely. "How do you think I'm feeling?"

"You'll be fine," Orestes reassured her.

"You wouldn't know how to check my pulse so stop babbling about how fine I'll be!"

"I was just getting ready to phone Tommy." Dessie's face was drawn, her voice tense.

"I'll call him." Orestes hugged her in reassurance. He turned back to Stavroula. "Can I bring you anything?"

She didn't bother to respond, and he left the enclosure.

He phoned Tommy from a phone in the corridor, and when his brother-in-law answered, Orestes told him what had happened.

"Oh my God!" Tommy's shaken voice came shrilly over the line. "I've been dreading this moment! Poor mama! Oh my God!"

"She only took a fall, Tommy," Orestes said quietly. "She's probably just had the wind knocked out of her. You know how tough she is."

Tommy had already hung up, leaving Orestes unable to tell him to be careful driving to the hospital

In the next hour, the hospital staff drew blood and took x-rays of Stavroula. Each time they wheeled her gurney in and out of the emergency room, she railed and snarled at the nurses, technicians, and orderlies, warning them to keep away from her, and that she wanted to go home.

Tommy arrived not long after Orestes had phoned him. He appeared haggard and near hysteria as he came rushing into the enclosure where Dessie and Orestes waited.

"How is mama?" he cried. "Where is she? How is she doing?"

"They've taken her in for a second x-ray," Dessie said. "I don't think it's anything serious."

"Poor mama." Tommy shook his head. "I've been waiting for her luck to run out! Once you hit eighty, all hell breaks loose!"

A little while later when an orderly wheeled Stavroula's gurney back into the enclosure, Tommy hurried to her. His anguished words of solicitude were throttled by Stavroula's loud, impatient response.

"Stop your blubbering! There's nothing wrong with me and I'll be going home soon!"

As the day wore on, Orestes felt his own nerves assaulted. The emergency room served an unending sequence of frightened, injured, or ill men, women, and children. Parents brought in a child with a broken arm, a great-bellied woman entered in the first pangs of childbirth and was hurried upstairs, an old man who appeared to have suffered a stroke was helped in by a neighbor. Meanwhile, the ambulance paramedics continued to carry in patients on stretchers.

Throughout the long afternoon of testing and x-rays, Orestes was appalled at the merciless constancy of Stavroula's snarl and bite. Even the nurses and interns who treated her seemed stunned by her ferocity.

Orestes mentioned to Dessie and Tommy that he thought the staff exhibited remarkable patience with Stavroula.

"This is a hospital and they must get all kinds of people," Tommy defended his mother. "They're used to dealing with difficult patients."

Not like Stavroula, Orestes thought grimly. The old barracuda would exhaust the patience of Mother Teresa.

Later in the afternoon, a handsome, olive-complexioned doctor brought them the results of Stavroula's x-rays and tests.

"I am Dr. Farzad Najafi." he spoke in clipped, precise English. "I'm the doctor in charge of your mother's case." He approached Stavroula on the gurney. She stared suspiciously up at him.

"How are you, mama?" he asked with exaggerated politeness.

"I'm not your mama!" Stavroula spit the words between her teeth. "Why don't you go back to India and ask your own mama how she feels! I'm fine, and I want to go home!"

"I'm not from India, mama," Dr. Najafi said cheerfully. "I'm from Iran, and I'm pleased to say my mama lives here in this country with me. She's home right now cooking dinner."

He turned from the gurney and motioned for Dessie, Orestes, and Tommy to follow him outside the enclosure.

"I'm sorry for my mother's rudeness, doctor," Dessie apologized. "She has an unhappy disposition anyway, and the fall she took hasn't improved it."

"That's quite all right," Dr. Najafi smiled, revealing a concourse of sparkling white teeth. "My own mama is tough too. I'm used to the abuse."

He studied his clipboard.

"Has she fallen before?" Dr. Najafi asked.

"Not that I know about," Dessie said. "But she might have fallen and not told us."

"The x-rays of her head show scar tissue that suggests she's taken other falls. But this fall today is the most serious. She has a subdural hematoma, a large blood clot in her head that appears to be pressing against her brain. I think we should plan to admit her and then operate as soon as we can."

"Are you sure that's necessary, doctor?" Tommy asked. "She seems strong and alert to me and she really wants to go home."

"The clot is very large and any kind of a fall or even a minor bump might cause it to move," Dr. Najafi said. "If it didn't kill her, it might well leave her paralyzed. If we can drain the clot, she should come out of this all right."

"We'll have to talk to her, doctor," Dessie said. "You've seen how stubborn she is. It's going to be a real battle to get her to agree to have an operation."

"I understand," Dr. Najafi said. "I suggest we take this one step at a time. Right now, if you agree, I'll make arrangements to admit her. We'll tell her we need to take additional tests and once she's settled in the hospital, you can talk to her about the operation. Since her condition is critical, even if she doesn't consent, you can authorize the surgery. But I don't think the operation should be delayed more than a day or so. It's too dangerous to wait."

The doctor flashed them a final smile and then turned and walked briskly away.

"We have to tell her she can't go home," Dessie said, her voice forlorn.

"I can't do it!" Tommy said, a plea in his voice. "Don't ask me to do it!"

"I'll tell her," Dessie said.

"We'll go in together," Orestes said. "That will provide her two of us as targets."

He took Dessie's hand and braced himself for Stavroula's reaction. As soon as she saw them entering, she grasped their mission.

"When I first saw that Indian voodoo doctor, I knew he was trouble!" she cried. "I've told you that I'm fine! I want to go home!"

"Mama, you're not fine," Dessie said. "You have a dangerous blood clot in your head from the fall. It could paralyze or kill you . . ."

Stavroula waved her warning aside.

"Are you deaf?" she cried. "I'm fine, and I want to go home!"

"Shut your mouth for once and listen to me!" Dessie's voice rose with stinging and uncommon anger. "All day long, you've tormented every person here who has tried to help you! Now you just make up your mind you're going into the hospital! That clot in your head could move at any time, and if it didn't kill you, you could be paralyzed! If you end up in a wheelchair, I swear to God I'll have you in a nursing home in twenty-four hours!"

Stavroula and Orestes were both shocked by Dessie's outburst. Tommy came hurrying into the enclosure.

"Dessie, for God's sake!"

Dessie waved him sternly to silence and confronted her mother.

"Do you understand what I'm saying?"

Her words were less a question than an emphatic declaration.

"All right," Stavroula said, her voice suddenly low and subdued. "You don't need to carry on like a crazy woman. Let the voodoo doctor do what he wants with me."

The hospital admitted Stavroula later that afternoon, and the following day, despite a resurgence of her objections, Dessie and Tommy signed the authorization for her operation. Before Stavroula underwent the surgery, Orestes consulted with Dr. Savas, who concurred in the diagnosis.

On the morning of her surgery, Stavroula retreated into a stolid, resigned silence. Dessie, Tommy, and Orestes spent time sitting with her, making an effort to cheer her up. She stubbornly resisted all their efforts. The only time she showed a spark of animation was when Marika joined them for a little while before Orestes drove her to school. Paulie also came by to see his yiayia before they took her into the operating room.

"She motioned me to come close to her, and I thought she wanted to hug me," Paulie said. "But she slipped me a ten dollar bill and asked me to call her a taxi."

Dessie and Orestes looked at each other and couldn't suppress their smiles. Tommy lowered his head and stared at the floor.

"Poor mama," Tommy said, and he hung on the verge of tears. "Poor mama . . ."

When Stavroula was wheeled into surgery, Orestes, Dessie, and Tommy waited in an alcove in a tense silence. Orestes found it hard to sit with them and restlessly walked the hospital corridors. Several times he went into the cafeteria and brought back small cartons of coffee for Dessie and Tommy, who maintained their vigil.

The wait reminded Orestes of hospital vigils he had endured in the past when his mother had been hospitalized several times before her death. He also thought bleakly of his father's last days.

Several hours after Stavroula had been taken upstairs to surgery, Dr. Najafi brought them news about her condition.

"She came through the surgery fine," he said with a reassuring smile. "She's one tough lady."

"Thank God!" Tommy exclaimed gratefully. "When can we see her, doctor?"

"Because of her age we're taking the precaution of keeping her in post-operative intensive care," Dr. Najafi said. "Wait a little while, and then you can visit her for just a few minutes after they've cleaned her up. I'll see her again later in the day."

"I never had any doubt that mama would make it," Tommy said jubilantly after Dr. Najafi had left. "It will take more than a blood clot to kill someone as strong as she is!"

A short while later, they walked to the intensive care unit to visit Stavroula. At the last minute, Tommy decided he'd rather not see his mother.

"I know I'll break down," he apologized in a low voice.

Orestes could see that Dessie wasn't any more eager than Tommy to enter the IC unit.

"I feel terrible for hollering at her that way," Dessie said pensively. "I might start crying, as well."

"She probably won't be conscious anyway and won't know you're there," Orestes said, "so why don't you two just wait out here. I'll take a quick look in on her and let you know how she is."

Dessie nodded gratefully while Tommy murmured a fervent "thank you!"

Orestes walked to the nurse in charge of the IC unit and was directed to Stavroula. He pushed aside the curtain and entered the enclosure.

For a startled moment, he thought he had the wrong patient. He had forgotten they had shaved her head for the surgery, and Stavroula now lay on the pillow with her skull fully bandaged, only the narrow oval of her face visible. There were tubes into her nose and intravenous cords running from bottles hanging above the bed to both her wrists. Her breathing came in low and hoarse, mingling with the hissing of the oxygen. Her only movement was a slight trembling of her lips.

Orestes stood for several moments beside the bed looking down at the battered old lady struggling for life. He remembered all the years she had tormented him and bullied everyone else. He wanted her to get well for Dessie and Tommy's sake, but as for his own feelings, he felt drained of any capacity for pity.

After a moment, he walked back to the waiting room to tell Dessie and Tommy that Stavroula was sleeping soundly.

A few days after Stavroula's surgery, a heavy snowstorm struck the city. The snow clogged alleys and streets, and Orestes wasn't able to get his car out of the garage. The following morning the city plows had cleared the boulevards and expressways. Paulie came over to help him dig out his snow- barricaded car. Orestes dropped Marika off at school then took Dessie to the hospital. Afterwards, he drove downtown to the Olympia.

Meanwhile, after some initial improvement, Stavroula's condition worsened. While she appeared to have recovered from her surgery, she contracted a staph infection. In addition, she developed problems with her kidneys. Even the normally cheerful Dr. Najafi appeared concerned.

Dessie and Tommy had been alternating hours in the hospital with Stavroula, spending most of the day and part of the night with her. Orestes dropped by on his way home from the restaurant to pick Dessie up after Tommy relieved her.

Between the inclement weather and her exhaustion, Dessie

came down with a severe cold and decided against visiting her mother. Since Tommy wouldn't be going to the hospital until evening, Orestes left the Olympia in mid-afternoon to spend a few hours with Stavroula.

As he walked from the parking lot into the hospital, the snow-covered trees made wet, murmuring sounds. He entered the lobby and took the elevator to Stavroula's floor.

He found Stavroula alone in her room, the adjoining bed empty. The old woman was sleeping, and for a little while Orestes sat quietly beside her bed, listening to her slow, fitful breathing. The hospital room held nearly a dozen baskets and vases of flowers. Orestes had sent one from Dessie, Marika, and himself. There was a large, ostentatious basket from Cleon and the staff at the Olympia. There were also smaller flowered plants from Paulie and Carmela and from Mario and Theresa, and several from other friends at church.

Orestes had never observed Stavroula as closely as he did in those moments he sat beside her bed. Her head was still bandaged, her normally ruddy cheeks pale. She had lost weight, and her arms resting limply above the covers seemed fragile poles of parchment stretched tightly over bone.

Yet, despite all the signs of her serious illness, he saw, as if for the first time, what a lovely woman she must have been as a girl, delicate featured, with small, shapely ears and a small, well-formed nose.

As if she finally sensed his presence, she opened her eyes. He braced himself for one of her vitriolic attacks, but she just gazed at him for a moment in silence. Finally, she spoke.

"Where's Despina?"

"She has a bad cold and decided she better not come."

She nodded slowly. Her tongue emerged from her mouth, and she weakly licked her dry, crusted lips.

"Water," she said in a low, hoarse voice.

He held the glass with water and a straw to her lips. She sucked the fluid through the straw in small, jerky spurts, from time to time pausing to draw a labored pinch of breath. Standing close beside her, he inhaled a smell of decay that rose like a sour vapor from her body.

He placed the glass back on the table and sat down again beside the bed. Several minutes passed while she continued to stare at him in silence.

"Before you leave today, take some of these flowers and give them to the nurses for other patients," she said. "There are enough here to open a florist shop."

She twisted her head slightly to stare out the window at the solemn grayness of the sky.

"Each morning I think for once it would be nice to see the sun," she said quietly.

"The weather is supposed to get better before Christmas," Orestes said.

They fell silent again. From one of the adjoining rooms, a woman's plaintive voice rose in a plea for a nurse.

Stavroula looked back at him.

"I've been hard on you," she said in a weary voice. "All those times you drove me to the dentist and to the doctor. You did a lot for me."

"You were a part of our family, Stavroula," he said. "I never minded doing it."

She shook her head slowly.

"I should have thanked you," she said. "I should have let you know I was grateful instead of always barking at you."

"I understood why you've always resented me, Stavroula," Orestes said. "I know you wanted a professional man for Dessie, a doctor or a lawyer, not just a restaurant man."

"It wasn't about who I wanted her to marry," Stavroula said. "I just didn't want her to marry you." She paused for breath. "It was your father, Moustakas. I knew the mad brute he was, with no woman ever safe around him. He even tried pawing me a few times until I warned him I'd slit his throat. I felt you had to have his bad blood. That was the reason I never wanted Despina to marry you."

She had never confessed that to him before. He nodded slowly.

"I don't mind telling you now that I was wrong," Stavroula sighed. "You've been a good husband and a good father."

He was grateful for the first words of praise he had ever heard from her lips.

"Thank you, Stavroula."

"Don't thank me," she said. "I'm glad I didn't die on the table before I had a chance to tell you." She stared at him grimly. "You know I'm going to die now, don't you?"

"You're not going to die, Stavroula!" Orestes exclaimed. "You came through the surgery with flying colors! Dr. Najafi says you're a strong woman and will be fine. In a few more days we'll take you home for Christmas."

"Don't talk nonsense," the old woman said, a trace of the old harshness returned to her voice. "I expect it from Tommy and even from Despina, but I thought better of you. I know what I'm talking about. I've lived in this old body for too long not to know when it's ready to go. I can feel death breathing in my lungs, blowing like a dark wind through my veins."

He felt chilled at the certainty with which she spoke.

"You've been a good husband, and I know that you'll look after Despina," Stavroula said, "but after I'm gone, I ask you, for my sake, to watch out for Tommy too. He's always lived somewhere in the clouds, not a part of this world. In some ways he's remained a child. I'll be grateful if you kept an eye on him."

"I promise I will, Stavroula."

"I know Paulie has been having trouble in his marriage," she said. "I think Despina hasn't told me how bad that trouble really is. I know you will want to help him, but remember, he's a man now and must pay for his own mistakes."

Orestes nodded once more.

Speaking had wearied Stavroula and she shifted her head against her pillow and closed her eyes. After a moment she opened them again.

"You better watch Marika too," she said. "She's a good girl but wild like young people today are wild. I'll tell you now what I never told you and Despina before. I came downstairs one evening and she was in the living room on the couch with a boy. I don't know what they were doing but he had his pants around his ankles. You know what I'm saying?"

"I'll keep an eye on her, Stavroula," Orestes said. "You can be sure of that."

A nurse entered the room, crisp and antiseptic in her white uniform, to take Stavroula's temperature. All the while Stavroula lay with the thermometer between her lips, she stared at Orestes with a curious intensity.

The nurse checked the thermometer.

"You're doing fine," she said. She smiled at Orestes and walked briskly from the room.

"That's all they ever say," Stavroula sighed. "Like a flock of parrots who've learned only one line. 'You're doing fine'."

She focused on Orestes again.

"Don't spend a fortune on my funeral because it'll be a waste," she said. "That scoundrel, Karvelas, is a thief. He makes 500 to 600 percent profit over what those coffins cost him. And I'm sure the cemetery gives him a kickback for every grave they open. His father was the same, a skinflint without a heart. He nearly went to jail for selling the same cemetery plot to several families. The old swindler figured by the time the last ones got around to needing the graves, he'd be dead and safe."

Orestes made an effort to break her melancholy litany.

"Listen, Stavroula," he said. "I really believe that in a few more days when you get a little stronger we'll have you out of here!"

She ignored his words.

"There's something else I'll ask you to do for me," she said slowly. "The photograph of the palikari Thomas Selleck I have in my room, the one Marika gave me. When no one is looking, you slip that photo under the pillow in my coffin. Don't trust it to Karvelas or anyone else. You do it." For the first time since he'd entered her room, the old lady managed a wry smile. "Who knows? If that beauty goes to hell too someday, the devil may tell him I've got his photo and I might get a chance to meet him."

Once again she asked for water, and he held the straw and glass to her lips. Above the neck of her nightgown, he saw the dry and shriveled ridges of flesh at her throat.

At that moment Tommy swept into the room, his cheeks red from the cold and snowflakes sprinkled across his stocking cap and coat. One of his shoelaces was loose and dangled around his wet shoe.

"Hi, ma!" he said heartily. "Hello, Orestes!" He tugged off his cap and briskly shook it free of snow. "It's starting to snow real heavy again."

"You're an idiot," his mother sighed. "Why would you come out on a night like this? First thing you know you'll have an accident and lose your insurance."

Tommy winked at Orestes.

"I lost it two years ago, mama," he said. "But whether I have insurance or not doesn't make any difference because my driver's license is expired anyway."

Stavroula looked at him sadly.

"You've got a good heart, my son," she said quietly, "but God gave a squirrel a bigger brain than he gave you."

She motioned to Orestes.

"You don't have to stay any longer now that Tommy is here," she said. "Despina is probably waiting for you."

"You wanted me to take out some of the flowers," he said.

"Tommy can do that," Stavroula said. "You go home now to your wife."

Orestes walked to stand for a moment beside her bed. She looked at him for a long pensive moment and then gestured weakly for him to bend down. He bent closer to her, and with her fingers trembling, she gently tugged his face close to her cheek, so close he could see every pore in her withered flesh. In a whisper that only he could hear, she said softly, "Forgive Despina," her voice trembling slightly. "That is my final plea to you. Forgive Despina."

Her eyes resembled shrunken olives in the small oval of her face. Even as he looked intently into them, he saw them moisten with tears. She reached out and tenderly stroked his cheek.

"Good-bye, my son," she whispered.

Two days later, on the twentieth of December, during a bitter cold spell that followed the heavy snowfall, Stavroula died. The hospital called that morning at dawn, and even as Orestes reached for the phone, he knew what the message would be. When he hung up the phone, he looked at Dessie who lay staring at him and nodded slowly. She turned her head on the pillow and began to cry softly.

Because it was so close to Christmas, they had Stavroula's wake the next evening and the funeral at the church the following morning. As Stavroula had requested, without telling anyone, Orestes secretly placed the photograph of Thomas Selleck under the pillow in her coffin.

Those few acquaintances who had been Stavroula's age were dead, so it was mostly friends of Dessie, Orestes, and Tommy who attended the wake and the funeral.

On the trip from the church to the cemetery, snow began to

fall again. By the time the funeral procession led by the hearse entered the cemetery, the tombstones and markers they passed were mantled with snow. When they parked beside the open grave where Stavroula would be interred, the funeral attendants had to brush snow off the casket as the pall bearers carried it to the grave. In a few moments, the casket was once again coated thickly with snow.

Father Elias read a few final words while people huddled and brushed the snow from their faces. Afterwards, as the grave-diggers waited to lower the platform into the grave people plucked flowers from the wreaths and tossed them onto the casket.

As people dispersed to return to their cars, Tommy, Dessie, and Orestes lingered a moment beside the grave.

"It's too bad she couldn't have lasted a few more days," Tommy said in a low, choked voice. "We could have had one more Christmas together."

"She never liked Christmas anyway," Dessie said quietly. "Remember when we were children how she'd holler while we were setting up the Christmas tree? We were putting the lights on wrong or the ornaments were crooked. Nothing we did pleased her."

Tommy looked at her in sharp rebuke.

"For God's sale, Dessie, forget those bad memories now!" he cried. "Let's try to remember the good times!"

He stared down at his mother's flower-strewn coffin and crossed himself a final time.

"I'll make you proud of me, someday, ma," he said in a low, choked voice. "I swear to God I will."

Cleon had been the first to leave the cemetery to return to the Olympia to prepare the funeral luncheon. The fifty people who attended ate codfish and salad and drank the tiny tumblers of ouzo and glasses of wine. As it always did at the luncheon following a funeral, the atmosphere lightened and the voices of people swirled in small, shrill bursts of laughter.

At the end of the luncheon, Orestes pulled Tommy aside and gave him a check for $1000.

"This is your mother's money, Tommy," he said. "She worried because you said you didn't have insurance and that your driver's license had expired. She wanted me to give you this money so you could renew your license and take out some insurance on your car."

Tommy stared at Orestes for a long, shaken moment and then nodded.

"And one more thing," Orestes said. "Right after the holidays, let's talk about that stationary shop you wanted to buy. I'm confident that you can make it a paying proposition so it makes good business sense for me to help you finance the purchase. Let me know how much you're going to need to pull it off."

Tommy continued to stare intently at Orestes, his lips trembling in an effort to hold back his tears.

"I don't think this money comes from ma," he said earnestly. "But I'll take it, Orestes, so I can do what ma wanted, renew my license and get some insurance." He paused. "As for your offer to help me buy the business, I'll take that help too. I know you're doing it because of ma and you won't be sorry. I swear to God you won't be sorry!"

Sixteen

S NOW FELL on Christmas Eve and continued falling Christmas Day. The sounds of shovels and snowblowers clattered and rumbled through the crisp, cold air.

Standing at the window, Orestes watched the jubilant neighbor children bundled in gloves and scarves build a rotund-bellied snow man, using a carrot for a nose and an old, black derby propped on its head. He recalled with nostalgia the snowmen he had built with Marika and Paulie when they were children.

The Christmas tree in their living room had been decorated before Stavroula's accident, and its multicolored lights and glittering ornaments stood now in stark contrast to the melancholy mood that existed within the house.

On Christmas Day, Dessie customarily cooked dinner for the family and a few friends. The evening before, Orestes had suggested they cancel the event.

"With your mother's death, everyone will understand. We'll phone them this evening not to come, and you, Marika, and I can just spend tomorrow quietly."

"What will Paulie, Carmela, and the baby do?" Dessie asked. "And I don't want Tommy to be alone so soon after mama died. I have the lamb already bought, so let's just go ahead with the dinner."

On Christmas Day, Paulie, Carmela, and the baby were the first to arrive, and Tommy came shortly afterwards. In addition, Dr. Savas came and Cleon and his wife, Aspasia, a stocky, comely woman with an ebullient laugh. Orestes and Dessie had also invited Carmela's parents, Mario and Theresa, for the Christmas dinner, but they were still furious at Paulie and declined the invitation.

Stavroula's death dampened all their spirits. Aspasia was somber and Cleon restrained while the normally talkative Tommy sat at the table in gloomy silence.

Everyone praised Dessie's dinner of roast leg of lamb, seasoned with clove and garlic. There were also oven-browned potatoes sprinkled with oregano and a green salad with chunks of feta cheese and black kalamata olives in dark-green virgin olive oil.

"I've told you before, Dessie, and I'll tell you again," Cleon said. "Anytime you want to come to the Olympia as head chef, I'll fire Kyriakos in a flash!"

"Then who will cook for Orestes and Marika?" Dessie laughed.

"Your talent should be shared with the city of Chicago and not just two people," Cleon said. "Let Orestes and Marika eat their meals at the restaurant."

"I'd like that," Marika said. "Could I bring my friends?"

"The Olympia isn't a food kitchen," Paulie said. Orestes tapped his knife against his wine glass. When he had everyone's attention, he raised his glass.

"I offer a toast now to a remarkable lady who is missing from this table," he said quietly. "If she were here and heard me say anything too sentimental, I know she'd snap at me to shut my mouth. So, on this first Christmas without Stavroula, I'll only say that she kept our heads on straight and our feet on the ground. So, Merry Christmas to you, Stavroula, where ever you are."

Marika rose and walked around the table to kiss her father.

"That was lovely, daddy," she whispered.

At the other end of the table, Dessie's cheeks were moist and she blew Orestes a kiss.

"Thanks, Orestes," Tommy spoke with a tremor in his voice. "Ma would have liked that toast."

"It's true Stavroula was one of a kind," Cleon said gravely. "I recall once when she came into the kitchen at the Olympia and tasted a morsel of pastitsio Kyriakos had baked. She told him it was a disaster. I got between them quickly because I was sure there would be a murder!"

"If that cook laid a hand on ma, she'd have put him in the hospital!" Tommy said earnestly. "She was strong as a bull! I was about fourteen or fifteen when I did something that made her mad and she slapped me. It wasn't a hard slap, but I'll never forget how my teeth rattled."

"A few years ago she came in to see me about some medical problem," Dr. Savas said. "She didn't like my diagnosis, called me a quack, told me to confine my practice to gypsies, and stormed out of my office."

"I can't believe she really said that," Dessie said in dismay.

"It's the truth," Dr. Savas grinned. "I think a few of my patients in the reception room who heard her got up and left without waiting for their appointments."

"Stavroula was very perceptive," Orestes smiled. "I've had similar feelings after you've finished poking and probing me."

"However much I abuse you, you still keep coming back," Dr. Savas said with a wink. "I think its probably because no other doctor would tolerate your endless complaints."

Orestes noticed that everyone at the table laughed at the recollections of Stavroula except Paulie and Carmela. His young daughter-in-law sat somber and silent, picking at her food and eating very little. Paulie kept watching her, his expression balancing futility and remorse. Settled in a high chair between them, bright-eyed Catherine sat unaware of the friction between her parents.

Orestes felt sorry for Carmela and the baby, and yet there wasn't any way he could prevent Paulie from leaving. In the hospital before she died, Stavroula had told him that Paulie would have to pay for his mistakes. What was even more grievous was that Carmela and the baby would have to pay for Paulie's restlessness, as well. Orestes knew how much their grief also saddened Dessie.

As soon as they had finished the dessert of cheese and fruit, Cleon rose to leave.

"Forgive Aspasia and me for eating and running," he said earnestly, "but I must get back to the Olympia. There are a hundred final details for the millennium party. These last few weeks I have felt like a general planning a major campaign in a war!"

"Can you imagine any army with this man as general?" his wife, Aspasia scoffed, as she rose from the table. "He cannot organize his socks and underwear in the dresser drawer."

Cleon flashed her a smile.

"I leave those humdrum tasks, to you, my beloved first sergeant!" he said crisply as he took her arm and led her to the hallway. Orestes and Dessie walked them to the door. Orestes helped Aspasia with her coat and kissed her good-bye.

"I'll be glad to come in to the Olympia if you think I can help," Orestes said to Cleon.

"Better stay home with your family today," Cleon replied in a low voice.

Aspasia and Cleon walked gingerly across the snow-covered walk to their car parked at the end of the driveway.

Paulie and Carmela prepared to leave shortly afterwards, as well. While Dessie helped Carmela dress the baby in her snowsuit, Orestes waited with Paulie in the hallway.

"Have you made plans to leave?" Orestes asked.

Paulie looked at him unhappily.

"No special day," he said. "Sometime next month. I'll make sure everything here is in place before I go. Then I'll just get in the car and drive."

A silence drew out tensely between them.

"What are your plans for New Year's Eve?" Orestes asked.

"A neighbor of ours is throwing a small party," Paulie said. "Carmela said she doesn't want to go, but if she changes her mind, we might stop over for a while."

"Remember the big millennium party at the restaurant," Orestes said. "A lot of our friends will be there including your godparents, John and Ann Graven. They were asking about you the other day. Jimmy Damon will be singing, and I know Carmela enjoys his songs. Maybe she'd like to come."

"I doubt it," Paulie said. "But if I can, I'll stop in earlier in the evening myself for a little while."

He looked pensively at Orestes.

"I know what you and mom would want for the millennium," Paulie said in a low voice. "If I could grant you that wish, I would. For Carmela and the baby too. It may seem selfish, but I've got to have some time away to breath on my own."

"Do what you have to do," Orestes said quietly, and he turned away from his son to bid Carmela and his granddaughter good-bye.

Shortly afterwards, Dr. Savas rose to leave.

"I've got to make a hospital call," he told them. "Eleni Buzanis is about ready to have her baby. I promised I'd look in on her."

A few minutes later when Tommy also rose to leave, Dessie objected.

"I watched you dozing at the table," she said firmly. "You've drunk too much wine. Just stay here a while longer now."

"I'm fine!" Tommy protested. "Sober as a judge!"

"You're not fine! You just go into the study and nap a while on the couch. After you wake, I'll make you some black coffee and you can be on your way."

"If ma were here she'd have told me the same thing," Tommy said pensively. He walked slowly and unsteadily into the study and closed the door.

Orestes cleared the last of the soiled dishes and silverware from the table and carried them into the kitchen where Marika and Dessie were cleaning up.

"When we're through here, is it all right if I go over to Callie's for the afternoon?" Marika asked. "She's having a few of the kids in for a Christmas party."

"All right, but I don't want you driving out of the neighborhood," Orestes said. "The streets are much too slick." Marika agreed and a few minutes later went for her coat. She returned to the kitchen, clad in wool hat and scarf, to kiss them goodbye.

"Tell Uncle Tommy I said good-bye," she said, with a final, hasty flutter of her fingers.

Not long after Marika left, Tommy rose from his nap.

"You didn't sleep very long," Dessie said.

"Believe me, I'm sober now!" Tommy exclaimed. "That nap did the trick."

He drank a cup of black coffee at the kitchen table. Afterwards he hugged Dessie good-bye.

"Just you and me left now, kid," he said in a low, husky voice.

Orestes walked with him to the hallway. Tommy slipped into his coat and paused with his hand on the door.

"I know how hard it was for you and Dessie to have ma living with you all these years," he said in a low voice. "It will probably be a relief to have her off your back, but I'm going to miss her. Without her around to raise hell with me, I feel lost, like a kid who has become an orphan, you know what I mean?"

"I understand," Orestes said. "Now be careful driving home."

He waited in the open doorway and watched his brother-in-law brush the newly fallen snow from his windshield. Before entering the car, Tommy turned back toward the house and waved a final time, a morose flutter of his hand in the cold air.

When Orestes returned to the kitchen, Dessie was putting the last of the clean dishes into the cupboard.

"Poor Tommy," Dessie said. "Ma tormented him, and yet he had this strong bond to her. It's going to be hard for him."

"We'll make a point of having him over more often," Orestes said.

Dessie untied her apron and hung it on a hook.

"Carmela hardly said a word tonight," Dessie said. "And she barely ate anything. Every time I looked at her I found it hard to swallow my own food." She paused, her face reflecting her sadness. "Did you have a chance to talk to Paulie?"

"He told me he had no special date to leave, but it would be sometime in January. He said he'd come by the restaurant on New Year's Eve. I'll make an effort to talk to him then, but I'm afraid nothing any of us say will stop him now."

He stared at Dessie with concern.

"After the wake and funeral, I know how exhausted you must be," he said, "and you've been on your feet since early this morning. Why don't you go upstairs and rest for a while."

"You should be just as tired. Come up and rest with me."

As they walked through the dining room into the hallway, the gray, overcast afternoon had given way to twilight. The multicolored lights of the Christmas tree gleamed brightly in the darkened house.

"Shall I leave the tree on for Marika?" Orestes asked.

"She may forget to turn it off," Dessie said. "You better close it."

He pulled the plug from the wall, and the glittering tree

slipped into shadows. In the beam of the hallway light, they walked upstairs.

In the bedroom, Dessie took off her shoes and slipped off her dress. She put on a cotton robe and lay down on the bed. Orestes tugged off his tie and shoes and stretched out beside her. Her back was turned to him, and he slipped his arm about her waist, cradling her body against his own.

"Remember, Orestes," she said softly. "This is the way we always slept when we were first married."

"I remember," he said. He resolved to hold her that way more often.

In the stillness of the snow-locked house, he felt as if Stavroula's death had closed a door on a period in their lives. For the years she had lived with them, her brooding, acerbic presence had depressed their days and nights. He knew their lives would be less burdened without her. Yet in some enigmatic way, he also grieved for the loss of the strength and force with which she had lived.

He felt a sudden tremor sweep through Dessie.

"Are you cold?" he asked.

"I'm just thinking of mama," she said and turned on her back, staring wistfully at the ceiling. "You and Tommy were the last ones to see her alive. If I hadn't gotten that cold, I would have been able to see her at the end, as well."

"These last years you spent so many days and nights with her," Orestes said. "You played cards with her, drove her around, kept her company. Another few hours in the hospital wouldn't have made any difference."

"When you saw her that last night, what did she talk about?"

"She talked about Paulie. She reminded me that whatever we did or said, he was a grown man and would have to pay for his mistakes. She also asked me to look out for Tommy. I promised her I would."

Dessie twisted to face him. He felt her warm breath as she reached up and gently caressed his cheek.

"Tommy told me how you gave him the check after the funeral and how you offered to help him buy the store. You're a good and generous man, Orestes."

"I promised Stavroula I'd help him. Besides, the venture may even turn out to be profitable."

He felt her staring with a strange intensity into his eyes.

"That last night, did mom say anything about me?"

"She warned me if I ever mistreated you, she'd come back and cut off my balls."

"Be serious, Orestes. Did she?"

"Only at the end, when I kissed her good-bye," Orestes said. "She asked me then to forgive you."

Dessie looked away for a moment, her hand fumbling at the collar of her robe, her fingers tugging nervously at the cloth.

"Did you wonder what she meant?" she asked.

"I didn't really think about it," Orestes said. "Maybe she wanted me to forgive you because you don't peel the tomatoes for the salad the way she did."

He said it to tease her, expecting Dessie to smile, but her expression remained solemn.

"Maybe she wanted me to forgive you for bringing her into our house," Orestes said. "Hard as she was to get along with, you know I never complained to you about having her here."

Dessie remained silent. For the first time, he experienced a vague feeling of unrest.

"Do you know what she meant?" he asked.

Instead of responding, Dessie pushed herself up to sit on the edge of the bed with her back to him. Beyond her robed figure, through the bedroom windows, he saw that the snow had begun falling again.

She turned and looked down at him.

"You know I love you, Orestes," she said quietly. "You've been a good husband and a loving father to Paulie and Marika, and I love you very much. You know that, don't you?"

"Of course, my darling," he said firmly. "And I love you too."

In the silence that followed, he made an effort to recall Stavroula's face and the tone of her voice when she said "Forgive Despina." He had told Dessie the truth that he hadn't given her mother's words any credence. Yet Dessie's tense and serious face hinted at more.

"What is it, Dessie?" he asked. "What's wrong? I didn't take Stavroula's words seriously. I haven't even thought about them again until you asked."

Dessie continued to stare at him in an uneasy silence. "Mama always wanted me to tell you," she said finally, her words shaken in the flurry of her breathing. "I'd tell her that I didn't have the courage. When she was dying and asked you to forgive me, she knew I'd have to tell you."

Her somber voice caused a sudden ache in his shoulders and neck, a pressure that spiraled down to his stomach.

The phone on the bedstand rang, a loud intrusive ringing in the silent room. Neither of them moved to answer.

"Tell me what?" he asked, his own voice echoing strangely in his ears. "Dessie, tell me what?"

Dessie drew a deep, tight breath.

"You knew I wasn't a virgin when we married," she said. "I told you it had happened with a boy back in high school, that we were adolescents having sex to show bravado." She paused. "The truth is that I didn't lose my virginity in high school. It was later, during an affair that ended . . . not long before we married."

For an uncertain moment he wondered if she were teasing him. They had flirted about fantasy sexual partners in the past as a prelude to making love. But there wasn't anything flirtatious in Dessie's somber cheeks, or in her dark, serious eyes. He waited with a growing anxiety for her to go on.

"Remember the Norwegian boy, Jorgen? I told you that we had dated for a while."

Orestes recalled a faded snapshot he had seen among some of Dessie's old photographs, the image of a handsome youth with tousled blonde hair. He felt a quick pinch of jealousy.

"You told me you'd stopped seeing him a year before we married."

"We hadn't broken up," Dessie said slowly. "I was still seeing him while you and I were going out together." She hesitated, seemed to force herself to go on. "We were having sex together."

For a moment her words splintered in his ears. Then he swung his body violently off the bed, staring down at her in disbelief.

"Jesus Christ, Dessie!" he said in outrage. "You and I didn't have sex because we agreed that waiting was the proper thing to do! Now you tell me you were screwing him!"

"Forgive me, Orestes," she said, and her voice trembled. "It was only because I loved him."

He felt her words like an anvil against his chest, constricting his breath.

"Then why the hell didn't you marry him? If you loved him enough to screw him, you should have married him! Didn't he love you?"

"I think he loved me," she said and looked down at her hands in her lap. "But he wanted to be a doctor and go back to Norway to practice. His family had been sending him the money for his schooling. He knew how much he owed them and how much work there was ahead of him. He felt he couldn't take on the responsibility of a wife."

"It must have broken your heart that you couldn't be the wife of a doctor!" His voice sounded petulant and shrill. "You had to settle for a goddam restaurant man."

"It wasn't like that, Orestes," she said plaintively. "I cared for you! I really did!" She stared up at him, her face suddenly raw and stricken with despair. Finally, her eyes brimming with tears, she spoke again.

"God forgive me for having to tell you this, Orestes," she said, her voice fallen to a shaken whisper. "When I married you I was pregnant with Paulie."

A bombshell of pain exploded within him, sweeping violently through his body. He stared at her in shock, unable to accept that she could have concealed that stunning revelation for so many years. Then he recalled that when Paulie was born prematurely, everyone joked that Dessie must have become pregnant on her wedding night. Fool that he was, he had even accepted it as a sign of his virility.

He was struck suddenly by the monstrous enormity of what she had done to him, deceiving him into marriage, duping him into thinking the baby was his. His legs trembled and he reached to the bedpost for support.

"Jesus Christ!" The words came burned from his lips. "You're telling me that Paulie isn't my son! Twenty-two years after he's born, after we raised him together, and I cared for him as a father, twenty-two years later, you tell me he's not my son!"

"I'm sorry, Orestes," she said, her voice a burned whisper. "You have to understand I was desperate and in a panic. You had asked me to marry you, and I did care for you. I was afraid if I told you the truth I would lose you."

He wanted to feel the rage of a man betrayed, rage enough to assault and beat the woman who had deceived him. But all he felt was a terrible weakness seeping through his limbs, a crumpling and withering of his spirit.

"I wanted to tell you, I swear to God, so many times I wanted to tell you. But the years passed and it became harder and harder for me to speak up. You were everything a father could be to Paulie. I didn't want to hurt you. Dear God, Orestes, please try and forgive me!"

As he listened to her voice babbling the words, he became conscious of the furnishings in the room, the lamps, the paintings on the wall, the photographs on the dresser, long-familiar objects suddenly distorted and unsettling to him now. He felt that nothing in his life would ever be the same.

"Did the bastard know he'd made you pregnant?"

"I never told him."

"I guess you were lucky that you had old Orestes, respecter of a woman's honor, good old Orestes to fall back upon!"

"Orestes, it wasn't like that! Dear God, believe me it wasn't like that!

"What the hell was it like then?" he cried. "The bastard gets you pregnant and since he won't have you, you turn to me."

"I wouldn't have married just any man," Dessie said. "In the beginning I may not have loved you as much as I loved him, but you were a good and gentle man, and I knew you'd be a loving husband and a good father. I wasn't just looking for any man. I chose you!"

But nothing she said could lighten the frustration and despair that welled up in him then. He thought suddenly of the pride he had taken in his son, the years he'd spent watching Paulie grow from childhood to adolescence, driving him to Little League practice, sitting in the stands among other fathers cheering for their sons. He recalled attending Paulie's graduations, savoring whatever scholastic honors he had achieved. All that time, his son belonged to another man.

"Twenty-two years!" he said hoarsely, his voice trembling. "Twenty-two goddam years later, you tell a man that the son he raised and loved, fed and clothed, that son doesn't belong to him!"

"He does belong to you, Orestes! He was our son, and we loved him and raised him as our son!"

"Have you been in touch with the sonofabitch since then? Have you sent him snapshots of his son?"

"No! I swear I never did!"

"All this time Stavroula knew!" Orestes said. "How she must have been laughing at me! No wonder she thought me such a fool!"

"Orestes, it wasn't like that! Mama kept urging me to tell you . . . she knew the longer I waited, the harder it would be for both of us!"

"Who else knows? Your girlfriends? The ladies of Philoptochos? Did you take them into your confidence about how you fooled the stupid sonofabitch and got him to marry you?"

"Orestes!" she cried. "I swear on my life, I told no one! No one!"

He saw her then as if he were seeing her true face for the first time, the face of a woman made ugly by betrayal and deceit.

He also had a sudden lewd image of Dessie brazenly naked, the blonde-haired despoiler mounted on her, pounding his organ into her while she shrieked wantonly.

"Was he big?" he asked harshly. "Bigger than me?"

"Orestes," she begged. "Orestes, please . . ."

"Please what!" he said, his voice rising. He savored the emotions seething through him. Shock and rage at her betrayal. And yes, in that moment, the most perverse emotion of all, a thunderclap of desire. His entire body felt suddenly aroused, his genitals throbbing. He hadn't felt such rampant lust since the first days of their marriage.

He feared that if he revealed his desire she might see it as a sign of weakness, take it as evidence that she'd duped him again and gained his forgiveness. He had to get out of the room quickly, and he turned and started angrily for the door. She called his name plaintively a final time. He rushed out of the room and didn't look back.

Almost at once his rage and lust faded, and he was left feeling only futility and despair. He walked wearily downstairs and sat for a while in the darkened living room, in the shadow of the darkened tree. He had a senseless urge to begin dismantling the tree, tearing off the ornaments and tinsel, ripping out the lights.

Finally, he rose and took a pillow and blanket from the shelf of the hallway closet and carried them into the study. In the room, lit by the faint beam of a lamp on the desk, he made a bed for himself on the couch. He lay down wearily and listened for sounds from the bedroom upstairs, but he heard nothing.

Sometime later, he heard the front door opening, and a moment later Marika entered the partially open study door. Her cap was covered with snow and her flushed cheeks glistened in the lamplight.

"What's wrong, daddy?" she asked. "Why are you sleeping down here?"

"I'm coming down with a bad cold," he said. "I didn't want your mother to catch it." As she came nearer, he waved her away, "Don't kiss me good-night, my darling. You'll catch the cold too."

"Shall I close the lamp?" she asked.

"Yes."

She flicked the switch on the wall and closed the study door. As the room snapped into blackness, Orestes was hurled into the dark and lonely terror of his childhood nights.

Within that threatening darkness, he heard laughter, and then, like an apparition reclaimed from the dead, he saw the mocking and sardonic specter of Moustakas, his father, returned like a demon to feast on his despair.

Seventeen

O RESTES SPENT that Christmas night grieving because something treasured in his life had been lost. Through those sleepless hours, weariness plundered his reason and his despair turned to anger. He grimly recalled the transgressions of deceitful wives in the parish whose infidelity had destroyed their mates. Spyros Femelis, the grocer, had been driven to suicide after learning of his wife's numerous affairs. And there were the smirks and jokes about Peter Gatsis, a member of the board of trustees of their church. Although the entire parish knew the sordid details, the man remained foolishly unaware that his wife was cuckolding him. To his shame, Orestes himself had shared in the laughter at the poor devil's expense.

Although Dessie had confessed to only one lover before they married, she had lied about how she lost her virginity and dishonestly concealed her pregnancy into their marriage. Perhaps she still hadn't told him there had been other men.

The more he thought about it, the more the immensity of her deceit overwhelmed him. For as long as Orestes lived, he'd have to accept the reality that another man had fathered the son he had for so long considered his own flesh and blood.

When daylight rimmed the shade of the study window, he fell into an exhausted sleep. He woke with a start a short while later and, for a disoriented moment, let himself believe that Dessie's confession belonged to the world of his dreams. The slow, burdened throbbing of his heart confirmed that the nightmare was real.

When he heard movement on the stairs, he rose from the couch. As he walked through the hallway, he glimpsed Dessie moving about the kitchen in her robe.

Upstairs in the bedroom, after he'd dressed, he put underwear, socks, and toiletries into a suitcase and packed a suit and shirts into a garment bag. He carried the bags downstairs and slipped on his coat. Before entering the kitchen, he braced himself to resist lashing out at her again.

When he entered the kitchen, Dessie was sitting at the table with a cup of coffee. Her reddened eyes and swollen cheeks were evidence that her night had been as wretched and sleepless as his own.

"I had made reservations for New Year's Eve at the Congress Hotel downtown," he said stiffly. "I'll check in today and stay there for the next few nights."

"What shall I tell Marika?" Dessie's voice was low, drained of any strength.

"Tell her I'm staying near the restaurant to get ready for the party."

As he reached the door, Dessie spoke again.

"Orestes, what are we going to do?"

He was disappointed that she didn't plead for him to remain at home so he could have refused.

He didn't answer and started out the door.

On his drive downtown, he phoned the hotel to amend his reservation. He checked in, and, after shaving and showering, he collapsed wearily into bed. He slept instantly but woke an hour later with a brutal headache and called the desk for aspirin. Afterwards, he rang the garage for his car and drove west to the Olympia.

The snowfall had ended, and the day was crisp and clear. The windows of the downtown stores were adorned with holiday decorations that included smirking Santas and sly-faced elves, while the streets teemed with shoppers on their way to return gifts they didn't want or didn't need. He'd be grateful when the whole senseless hypocrisy of the holidays was over.

In the days that followed, leading to the end of the year, Orestes immersed himself in the turmoil and activity of the restaurant. Keeping busy allowed him less time to brood on the crisis in his life.

When Cleon learned Orestes was staying at the downtown hotel each night, he sternly rebuked him.

"You don't have to inconvenience yourself like this, partner!" Cleon protested. "You should be sleeping at home each night in your own bed. I've got everything here under control."

"Staying at the hotel works out fine. I don't have to drive as far each morning and night."

"That drive has never troubled you before," Cleon frowned. "Why should it bother you now?"

"Let's get ready for the damn party and not worry about where I lay my ass at night!" Orestes snapped.

Cleon stared at him in surprise.

"I was only thinking of you, Orestes," he said in an aggrieved voice and walked brusquely away.

Those hectic days before the start of the new millennium induced an excitement bordering on hysteria among the Olympia's young waiters. They gathered in small, noisy groups to gossip while customers fretted. After a series of futile warnings, Cleon had to threaten several of them with discharge.

"It's not really their fault," he muttered to Orestes. "With all this babble about water mains bursting, sewers backing up, and electricity failing, why should the brains of young men be exempt?"

In anticipation of impending disaster, a half dozen of the waiters approached Orestes and Cleon with plans to establish a militia.

"Why in God's name would we need a militia?" Cleon asked.

"In case of a Y2K disaster with lights going out and gas mains breaking, there will be general panic!" a tall waiter named Aristides said urgently. "Those of us who served in the Greek army can take charge and organize an orderly evacuation from the restaurant, if you know what I mean."

"Forget about militias," Cleon snapped. "If you don't concentrate on doing your work more efficiently, there won't be any patrons to evacuate, if you know what I mean!"

The premonition of some nameless catastrophe infiltrated the kitchen, as well, with Kyriakos warning the cooks and bakers about performing their duties in exemplary fashion.

The master chef stubbornly resisted the efforts of Cleon and Orestes to calm and reassure him.

"This may be the most significant menu I have ever created!" Kyriakos cried. "In place of the artisans I require to assist me, I have this motley crew of incompetents, and junk food castaways!"

"They haven't failed you before in crucial situations," Orestes tried to soothe him. "With you to lead and inspire them, they won't let you down now."

"The clod who fails me won't live to see the dawn of the New Year!" Kyriakos said ominously as he stomped off.

"That prima donna will be the death of me!" Cleon said grimly, as he and Orestes left the kitchen. "Will you believe I had to call the confetti dispersal engineer I had in before Christmas and cancel our plans for the shower of confetti at midnight? Kyriakos felt the particles of paper would contaminate his food!"

If plans for the great party preoccupied the restaurant waiters and kitchen staff, the advent of the millennium was also a persistent topic of conversation among the friends assembled in the Olympia on those final evenings before the New Year.

"All over the world people will be celebrating," Banopoulos, the editor, said. "They will be holding parties at the Acropolis in Greece, at the Pyramids in Egypt, and in Moscow's Red Square."

"Coussis, the travel agent, told me about a party that will take place at the South Pole," Lalounis, the realtor said. "A select group from the Union League Club will fly there to greet the millennium on a glacier. They'll carry with them vintage champagne, beluga caviar, lobster, foie gras, and oyster veloute. All this for only $25,000 a head, taxes and gratuities not included."

"I wonder how much of a gratuity is appropriate on $25,000?" Professor Platon said.

"The customary amount is 15 to 20 percent," Orestes said. "But for a party that expensive, some prior arrangement has probably been made."

"If we could convince Zografos to let us use that big freezer in his packing house," Cleon laughed, "it would be as frigid as the South Pole and we could throw a magnificent party for less than a hundred dollars a head."

"The arrival of the millennium won't cure injustice and inequity," Banopoulos said gravely. "As the New Year begins, Dr. Kevorkian will still be rotting in jail while the millionaire, Regis Philbrick, teases contestants with questions to also make them millionaires."

"His name is Philbin, not Philbrick," Lalounis said. "Regis Philbin."

"Philbrick or Philbin," Banopoulos said in disgust. "It's all part of the same madness. Even ideas for Christmas gifts this year reflect a society collapsing into decadence. How would you like to receive as a gift, cheddar-cheese flavored worms, a cremation urn shaped like a golf bag, or an alarm clock for masochists that wakes them in the morning with sixty seconds of verbal abuse."

"God help us," Karvelas made his cross. "We are entering the Apocalypse."

"Banopoulos is right," Dr. Savas shrugged. "I, for one, will be glad when the whole absurd charade is over. This coming millennium is a bonanza for scoundrels. Every con man and bunco artist is angling to get a slice of the cottage industry that has sprung up selling banners and medallions, minting coins and dispensing amulets. It's a disgraceful exhibition of duplicity and greed!"

"Don't forget the lists," Banopoulos said. "Everyone is preparing lists that I'm sick of reading. 'The one hundred best books of the millennium!' 'The one hundred best movies of the millennium!' 'Best actors, best actresses, best athletes, best serial killers!'"

"You're exaggerating, as usual," Karvelas snapped. "But I agree they're overdoing these lists. I saw one the other day cataloguing the one hundred most influential human beings of the last millennium. Mahatma Gandhi was rated second and Mother Teresa third. You'll never guess who was first."

"Albert Einstein for his scientific discoveries?" Professor Platon asked.

"Harry Truman for making the decision to drop the bomb and end the Second World War?" Lalounis said.

"It was John Lennon!" Karvelas said, his voice resonating with indignation. "Can you imagine the lout making up the list putting John Lennon above Gandhi and Mother Teresa?"

"He sold more records than either of them," Cleon said with a wink.

"You're an imbecile!" Karvelas said sharply. "I don't know why I bother coming in here to listen to your cynical, sarcastic remarks!"

"You come in here because it gives you a chance to escape from the odor of cadavers and formaldehyde!" Cleon chuckled.

In that time between Christmas and the New Year, Orestes decided that the crucial crossroads where he now stood in his life required he end his relationship with Sarah. At first, he considered pressing the affair to a sexual consummation as an act of retribution against Dessie. He savored the vengeful thought that he would show Dessie that two could play the game of infidelity. In thinking about it, however, he gloomily accepted that his own wretchedness left him with little desire for adultery.

He knew it would be a more valorous action to break off his relationship with Sarah in person. But he feared his resolve might fail him in the candlelit and incense-scented cloister of her apartment.

So one afternoon, secreted in his office, he phoned Sarah and told her, gently but firmly, that he believed it prudent they never see one another again.

"If when we're alone together, we weakened, and yielded to temptation," he said earnestly, "we'd never be able to forgive ourselves. It would dishonor both Dante and Beatrice."

"Does that mean we can never see one another again?"

He sighed loudly enough for her to hear.

"That would be best," he said. "Now, if we happen to meet by chance in the library, we can of course greet one another, and exchange a few words about a book or an author. But hard as it might be for both of us, we must never again risk being alone."

"My darling," Sarah said fervently. "I know you're being strong and noble for both of us, but the thought of losing you makes me terribly sad, as well."

"It's what Dante and Beatrice must do, my dear," he said gravely.

He lamented hearing Sarah crying softly as he hung up the phone.

Each evening around dinnertime, Orestes phoned home to speak to his daughter. Since Marika would have thought it strange for him not to speak to Dessie, at the end of their conversation, she put her mother on the phone. His exchanges with his estranged wife were brief and reserved.

"Are you eating all right?" Dessie asked.

"I'm fine."

"What are you doing for clean clothes?"

"I'm sending my shirts and underwear to the hotel laundry."

"They'll charge you a fortune."

"That's all right."

After a long silence he heard her voice, plaintive and muted.

"Take care of yourself, Orestes."

The most burdensome hours for Orestes began later in the evening after he arrived at the hotel. He found himself yearning for Dessie's presence and being able to share the experiences of the day with her. But remembering her betrayal plucked the scab on his wounded pride. He'd need to learn to live without her.

In spite of his weariness, rest and sleep eluded him. He lay awake in the dark hotel room, marking the sluggish passage of minutes and hours.

At times, frustrated by his sleeplessness, he fled from bed, and, with a quilt around his shoulders to protect him against the night chill, he sat in the dark room by the window.

From that high floor of the hotel, the glittering skyline of the downtown city was visible, a cluster of multileveled buildings marked by a patchwork of tiny, lighted windows. Above the glowing crests of the John Hancock and the Sears Tower loomed the night with its profusion of stars.

He had read somewhere that Mars contained networks of canals too regular and geometric to be only a chance creation of nature. If a form of life existed on that planet, he wondered whether the emotions of the Martians were the same as those of humans. Could they feel love, grief, anger, and betrayal?

As a respite from his cosmic musings, he turned on the TV with the volume low, until the folksy entreaties of the Home Shopping Network hucksters selling relentlessly through the night disheartened him, and he returned to bed.

Sometimes he managed to sleep for a while, but, for the most part, he remained wakeful and morose. He tried to focus on the affairs of the restaurant and on his portfolio of stocks. But his thoughts kept returning relentlessly to the impact of Dessie's confession. Pride allowed him no other recourse but to file for divorce. He'd begin that process right after the first of the year. At the same time, he wondered how the breakup of their marriage would affect Marika and Paulie.

He also spent time seething over the Norwegian seducer who decades earlier had exploited the emotions of an innocent young girl. Perhaps Dessie was still corresponding with him. If Orestes learned that was true, he'd insist on having the bastard's address so he might fly to Norway to confront the lecherous quack.

"You must think you're Clint Eastwood or Sylvester Stallone," he scoffed at himself. "You're Orestes Panos, restaurant man! You'd spend months locating the bastard, and if you threatened him, he'd probably call the police and you'd rot in a Norwegian jail."

There were other times when his anger wavered and he felt only the pain of betrayed love. He could never have imagined that the woman he felt he knew so well would be capable of such deception. And what about Paulie? Should he be told that Orestes wasn't his father? Was it fair to continue to deceive the young man, as Orestes had been deceived?

Yet, much as he would have wished to regard himself as blameless, an innocent victim trapped in Dessie's conspiratorial web, those sleepless hours he spent in the hotel room forced him to confront his own shortcomings.

As his thoughts ranged over the years of his marriage, he recalled an episode in the first summer after he and Dessie were married, on a day-long outing they had taken to a city park. They had strolled into a playground where a group of children frolicked and splashed barefooted in the shallow water of a fountain. In an impulsive moment, Dessie kicked off her sandals and joined the children in the fountain, holding her dress so high above her knees that the silk fringe of her panties were visible. Men and women walking past the fountain paused and stared, the women envious of her beauty and the men bewitched by her naked legs and thighs. Even the children paused in their playing to watch her high-spirited and joyful dance.

Orestes remembered feeling a little embarrassed because his young wife's naked thighs were exposed, but he also felt an erotic excitement and pride because other men were gazing with desire at what belonged to him.

He recalled nostalgically how beautiful Dessie had appeared to him on that summer day, her dark hair tumbling about her lovely face, her large, black eyes glowing with vitality and laughter, and, when she looked at him, her lips curved into a sensual, flirtatious smile that seemed to invite a kiss.

All the youthful beauty and sheer joy in life Dessie displayed on that summer day she danced in the fountain had been given into his care. And the stark truth was that he had proven a poor guardian of that treasure. While he had never been an abusive husband, he had often taken his wife for granted, ignoring her feelings and wishes. In addition to the most recent dinner with her he had canceled, he recalled all the other nights he had avoided taking her out. The absurd excuse he offered was that because he spent so many hours each day in the Olympia, he couldn't abide spending several hours at night in another restaurant.

Then there was the first trip to Greece they had taken five years earlier, a journey Dessie loved and enjoyed because in her family's village near Sparta, she had met cousins, nephews, and nieces she had never seen before. Every year since then, she had pleaded with Orestes for them to make a return visit. He invented one pretext or other to avoid making another trip.

And then there were the years Stavroula lived with them. Because of his loathing for the somber, acid-tongued woman, he often delayed coming home until late at night. That was in spite of his knowing his absence meant that, night after night, Dessie would have to endure those hours alone with her morose mother.

In his most serious transgression, as the years passed, he began more and more neglecting their sexual intimacy. Sometimes weeks passed when they did not make love. The fact that Dessie never complained encouraged his neglect. He convinced himself that the reason their lovemaking was so sporadic was because both of them were tired at the end of the day.

But there were other shameful reasons that he concealed from his wife. He had neglected their lovemaking because all too often he relieved his own desires through masturbation. He had acquired that baleful habit in his boyhood during those years of illness he had spent in bed. He had sustained the compulsion throughout his adolescence, and, even after he married, the obsession had proved impossible to break. He enjoyed the sex he shared with Dessie and many times vowed he would stop the self-abuse. He would manage to stop for a few weeks and even several months at a time. Then, stressed by problems at the restaurant, or simply because he was too tired to grapple with the arduous ritual of making love, he'd succumb to the noxious habit once more. His addiction had even intensified in the last few years when he discovered the sexual Websites on the Internet that indulged his fetishes of spankings and bondage, black silk stockings, black garter belts, and high heels. These fantasies proved more provocative and stimulating to him than the act of physically caressing his wife. He came to understand that he was guilty of what the ancient Greeks called *hamartia*, that flaw in a man's character that decreed his fate.

As he foraged into his grieving heart, he concluded that he had failed to mature into manhood. He and Dessie had made love and bred a child (he was momentarily tormented by a suspicion that his seed was impotent and that Marika might also not be his daughter), but in many ways he remained an adolescent imprisoned in a man's body. Perhaps that was the reason he had been faithful in his marriage and not because he was innately moral and devoted to his wife. Even his own stumbling attempts to prepare for the seduction of Sarah suggested immaturity.

However he twisted in an effort to understand why he had failed to mature as other men, the tortuous maze led back to his father, Moustakas. His childhood and adolescence had been lived under the domination and in terror of that fierce man. As Kronos in the old myth had devoured his children, so his carnivorous father had gorged on his flesh and spirit and impeded his growth into manhood.

"Goddam you, Moustakas!" Orestes cried into the darkness. "Are you happy now? Have I been humiliated enough to satisfy you? Are you perched on some crag in hell doubled up with laughter? Goddam you!"

Yet, cursing and condemning his dead father did nothing to lighten his pain or ease his despair.

Eighteen

B Y LATE afternoon on New Year's Eve, preparations for the party in the Olympia occupied all of Orestes' thoughts and his time. He spent an hour on the phone with Federal Express tracking a delayed shipment of lobsters from the East Coast. Afterwards, he made a hasty trip to the liquor distributor's warehouse on Orleans Street to bring back additional cases of imported champagne. He returned to Halsted Street in time to arbitrate a heated argument taking place outside the restaurant between Lefteris, in charge of parking for the Olympia, and a burly young Spartan named Vrakas in charge of parking for the Mykonos restaurant further down the block, which was also holding a New Year's Eve party.

"The south corner of the Jackson lot is ours!" Lefteris fumed. "It has always been ours!"

"If you think that's true, your father sired a moron!" Vrakas stormed. "We've been parking our cars there for years!"

"Liar!"

"Cretin!"

"Listen to me now." Orestes stepped between the two antagonists. "Lefteris, let the Mykonos boys use the Jackson lot. When our main lot is filled, we'll use the Pacific Mission Church lot on Green Street. I've already talked to the pastor."

With that armistice achieved, Orestes entered the restaurant to find Cleon delivering a final inspiring salvo to the assembled waiters and busboys.

"Someday when you're all married with blessed offspring," Cleon's voice trembled with emotion, "you'll be able to tell your family you shared this momentous celebration at the beginning of the new millennium! You served food prepared by Aristotle Kyriakos, one of the premier chefs in the entire country! And, yes, you'll also be able to tell your children that you heard the music of Bakalakis, the greatest lyre player in the world! Now, if all that weren't reward enough, I promise you that if this epic night goes well, you'll all receive a generous bonus in your pay envelopes!"

The waiters and busboys gave Cleon a rousing cheer and then, reinvigorated, dispersed to their duties.

"Magnificent, Cleon." Orestes gave his partner a slap of approval on his shoulder.

"The truth is sometimes I even astonish myself," Cleon said gravely.

Later that evening, Paulie came to the restaurant and found Orestes in his office. They had not seen one another since the dinner at Christmas, and Orestes stared poignantly at the young man, searching Paulie's features for resemblances to his Norwegian father.

"What did you and Carmela finally decide to do tonight?" he asked.

"She doesn't want to go anywhere," Paulie said quietly. "I guess we'll just see the New Year in at home." He shook his head ruefully. "I can't really blame her. She hasn't any reason to celebrate."

They sat in silence for a moment, and Orestes decided against making any last effort to convince Paulie not to leave his family. He was also disabled by the thought that his banishment as Paulie's father denied him any right to counsel the young man. He consoled himself that even parents by blood were only temporary guardians of the children they had begotten.

"Will mom and Marika be coming to the party?" Paulie asked.

"Marika is going to Jenny Vallas's New Year's party in the neighborhood," Orestes said. When he'd spoken to his daughter on the phone that evening, she'd also told him that her mother wasn't feeling well. Orestes suspected Dessie might be feigning illness as an excuse for not coming to the millennium party. "And your mother isn't well. She probably won't come down either."

"I talked with mom this morning." Paulie's voice was concerned. "She never said anything about feeling sick."

"She probably didn't want to worry you. Most likely it's only a touch of flu."

"It doesn't seem right," Paulie said. "You and mom should be seeing the millennium in together. It's a once-in-a-lifetime experience."

"We'll do something to celebrate together later on." As he spoke the words, Orestes wondered somberly how Paulie would take the news of their divorce.

"You look pale and tired yourself, pa. Maybe you're coming down with flu too."

"We've all been working hard getting ready for tonight's party. I'll relax when it's over."

Paulie spoke in a low, resigned voice.

"I know how much my leaving is going to hurt you and mom as well as Carmela. I wouldn't blame you if you never wanted to have anything to do with me again."

"How could you even think such a thing!" Orestes said earnestly. "We love you and will always want you to remain close to us!"

"I've never doubted that love," Paulie said. "Maybe I haven't told you how grateful I am because you've accepted all the crazy things I've done without throwing me out of the house the way other parents might have. I know I've disappointed you both. But mom never gave up believing in me, and no father could have done more for his son than you've done for me."

As if Paulie had sensed his anguish and reaffirmed his bond of fatherhood, Orestes was thankful for the reassuring words.

"You go now and make your journey!" Orestes said fervently. "We should have let you make that pilgrimage when you wanted to go, instead of forcing you into marriage. In my heart, I believe your love for Carmela and Catherine will bring you back. But make your journey now and for however long you're gone, I swear I'll look after your family with love and devotion!"

"I don't deserve parents like you and mom," Paulie said in a low, husky voice.

"You may deserve even better parents." Orestes made an effort to smile. "But you'll have to make do with us because we're all you've got."

Paulie stepped closer to Orestes and held out his hand. "Happy millennium, pa."

"Happy millennium to you, my son."

When he clasped Paulie's slim-fleshed fingers in his own hand, Orestes couldn't resist drawing him into his arms. For a moment, Paulie seemed startled, and then he welcomed the embrace. Orestes held him tightly for a moment before letting him go. Paulie walked slowly to the door. Before leaving the office, he turned and spoke to Orestes a final time.

"When I come back—" his voice was low and shy—"maybe you and mom can stop calling me Paulie . . . you know, I'd like to start the new millennium by having everyone call me Paul."

"We'll do that, my son!" Orestes reproached himself for failing to understand how that diminutive of childhood might have burdened the young man. "When you return, I promise everyone will call you Paul!"

After Paul had left the office, Orestes sat and recalled how even as a child the youth exhibited a seriousness that marked him as different from other children.

As memories of the boy's childhood swept through his mind, Orestes could not control his tears. He wept then for the fullness of the love he felt for another man's son.

Despite the clamor of voices from the restaurant indicating that patrons had begun arriving, melancholy and weary, Orestes resisted leaving the office. Finally, there was a flurried knocking on the door. Cleon burst in, his face flushed with excitement.

"Jimmy Damon is looking for you!" Cleon said. "And Judge Seymour Simon's party just arrived. He's asking about you, as well." He released a somber sigh. "Now I also have some unhappy news from the kitchen. I'm grieved to report that Kyriakos became so outraged at the little Macedonian cook, Barounis, for some real or imagined blunder, that he whacked him across the head with a copper frying pan. I sent the poor devil home in a cab with a promise of extra pay, but he'll probably sue us."

"What about Kyriakos?"

"I took care of it," Cleon said. "I promised that chef from hell that if he calmed down and resisted assaulting anyone else the balance of the night, after the first of the year, we'd give him a small percentage of ownership in the restaurant. I should have consulted with you first, but I was afraid if I left that culinary Gorgon still seething, there might have been a murder. If you don't agree, why I'll give him a couple points from my share of the business."

"I agree you made a smart move that should make it less likely that he'll jump to another kitchen."

"Thank you for that vote of confidence!" Cleon said fervently. He fell silent and frowned at Orestes.

"Now don't bite my head off, partner," he said anxiously, "but I'm worried as hell about you. It's obvious that you've been sorely depressed these last few days. You sit with the boys like your mind is off somewhere making plans for your funeral. Has the milestone of fifty hurled you into the cursed male menopause?"

"Dessie is down with what might be flu and won't be coming to the party," Orestes said. "I may be carrying the bug myself."

"If you're not feeling well, take a couple of aspirin and rest a while longer," Cleon said," but be sure you're in the restaurant by midnight for the millennium celebration. The Hellenic Trio plan a drum roll that will probably blow the roof off the building. Then don't forget that's when Bakalakis plays for the first time."

"I've rested enough." Orestes rose. "Let's look after our customers."

In the restaurant, he mingled with the growing crowd of patrons, greeting friends that included athletes, politicians, and entertainers. In the main dining room, he listened with pensive pleasure as Jimmy Damon sang one of his melodious ballads.

He made another round of the restaurant, briefly joining conversations among different patrons. At one table, a group of sports fans discussed the relative merits of the great athletes.

"Pound for pound, Michael Jordan was easily the best."

"Don't forget Wayne Gretsky."

"Professional hockey isn't a sport. It's legalized assault!"

"Did you watch Andre Agassi win the French Open last summer? He's a superb athlete."

"Better than Pete Sampras?"

"They're both great champions."

"Which athlete would you choose, Orestes?"

"If you're talking sheer skill and achievement against the best of his peers," Orestes said, "then Tiger Woods is probably in a class of his own. I don't play golf, and yet I began watching golf tournaments for the first time because of him."

At another table, Orestes greeted George Goritz, a childhood friend visiting from New York.

"Do you remember Tommy Zenakis from our class at school?" Goritz asked.

"Skinny boy," Orestes said. "A good baseball player."

"He's got testicular cancer," Goritz said. "He's going through a bad time. I'm sure he'd love to hear from you."

"Leave me his current address, and I'll drop him a line."

At an adjoining table, customers were discussing an innovative entrepreneur who was selling his urine on the Internet to help people pass their drug tests.

"That's one more example of how resourceful Americans can be," Tony Antoniou laughed. "It all began when the first pilgrims bartered worthless trinkets to the Indians in return for their furs."

At another table, the conversation centered on the environmental disasters occurring in Greece.

"It has devastated everything," Dr. Steve Economou said gravely. "Even the bees that droned in the tomb of Agamemnon are dead, destroyed by a chemical spray used on nearby crops."

Yet even as he greeted and spoke cheerfully to customers and friends, Orestes felt as if he were inhabited by a phantom, a mournful spirit moving him through meaningless gestures and idle speech without any will of his own.

About a minute before twelve, the Hellenic Trio of musicians, who had been playing Greek music all evening, launched a drum roll that rolled on and on and, finally, climaxed on the stroke of midnight. Its finale detonated a jubilant roar from the various dining rooms of the restaurant. The shouts and cheers crescendoed into a thunderclap that merged with the whistles and bells ringing from the other restaurants on Halsted Street. Orestes imagined the ear-piercing resonance whirling from the street into the sky, swooping through the firmament to blend with the bawl and bellow from the millions across the country heralding the arrival of the millennium.

Cleon embraced Orestes, tears running down his cheeks.

"I never thought I'd live to see this moment in time, partner," Cleon said, his voice choked with emotion. "A miracle . . . a bloody miracle."

Throughout the restaurant, men and women were kissing, hugging, and toasting one another. The waiters were also embracing and slapping one another's shoulders. Seeing so many euphoric men and women made Orestes think of Dessie, most likely sitting at home alone. He thought gloomily that phoning her would be a meaningless gesture. In view of the crisis in their lives, wishing one another a happy millennium seemed absurd.

As he resumed his rounds of the restaurant, one dining room more noisy and clamorous than the next, in a corner of the Olympia's long mahogany bar, he spotted Dr. Savas drinking alone.

"Why are you sitting here by yourself?" Orestes greeted him. "I'm sure any number of people would be delighted to have the skilled physician who delivered their babies and who takes care of their maladies celebrate with them."

"A few friends and patients did ask me to join them," Dr. Savas shrugged, "but I didn't want my brooding to spoil their celebration. I'd rather sit here and have a drink and then take myself home." He gestured at the crowd carousing, around them. "They greet the millennium as if it will change human nature"— his voice was low and resigned—"but hate, prejudice, and greed will remain the creed of contemporary life. The Palestinians will continue to kill Israelis and the Israelis will continue to kill Palestinians. The Serbs will go on killing Kosovans while Pakistanis and Indians continue threatening nuclear war over Kashmir. There will be five million more cases of AIDS around the world this year, and three million people will die of the disease. And there will be several third-world countries where millions of children will die of hunger. So when it comes to hate and killing, and callous indifference to the suffering of others, one millennium slips effortlessly into another."

"You paint a grim picture, my friend," Orestes sighed. "It's probably wise for you to drink alone. Your worldview is enough to scuttle any celebration."

"It's a realistic view," Dr. Savas said. "All this riotous celebrating is fantasy."

"Yet in spite of your catastrophic assessment," Orestes said, "you'll probably go on delivering babies and treating poor souls who are ill right into the new millennium."

Dr. Savas was silent for a moment.

"All of us who live the cycle of human experience understand how closely linked are the fates of the victims and the survivors," he said gravely. "Each day we survive we must offer what help we can to the victims, out of compassion but selfishly, as well. Since no man can know whose hands will stroke his last bubble of life, it is wise to be kind to strangers." He paused and waved Orestes away. "Now don't stand here listening to my laments. Go look after those fools who are paying your outrageously inflated prices and leave me to greet the millennium in my own way." He finished with a scowl. "And don't signal the bartender to skip my check. I don't need to start the millennium on your charity."

Shortly after midnight, the lyre player, Bakalakis, stepped onto the small stage in a corner of the main dining room. He wore the black garb of Crete, a dark shirt and beaded vest and a dark headband around his temples. As carefully as if he were cradling a child, the famed white-haired and craggy-faced musician clasped his lyre, a stringed instrument with a bowl-shaped body and a curved back made of shell, and a long, slim bow. He seated himself in the solitary chair on the stage, placed his lyre on his knee, and gazed solemnly at the jubilant crowd.

Cleon stepped up onto the stage and shouted for silence so he could introduce the artist, a plea which the boisterous patrons ignored. Finally, Bakalakis waved Cleon brusquely aside. He bent to his lyre and slowly drew the bow across the strings.

The patrons at the tables closest to the stage were the first to hush as the haunting strains of the lyre carried through the room. The music swept on, and when it encountered the laughter and babble from the other dining rooms and alcoves of the restaurant, it subdued that tumult, as well. Table after table of revelers fell silent, and as the sweet, plaintive melody extended into the furthest corners of the Olympia, even the most besotted drunks could not resist its beguilement.

Orestes recalled the old myth in which the god Apollo had given the first lyre to Orpheus, the hero with divine musical skills. When Orpheus played the lyre, the sound was so enchanting that even animals, trees, and rocks were driven to dance upon hearing its magic.

Now, as if the old musician were Orpheus reborn and his lyre a gift from a god, at the sound of the music, waiters paused in their serving, bartenders ceased mixing drinks, and busboys stopped rattling their trays of dishes. In the rear of the dining room, the swinging kitchen doors were opened, and the cooks and bakers crowded silently into the restaurant to listen.

The music banished the raucous artifacts of contemporary life, the buzzes and rings of the ubiquitous cell phones, the music videos, the droning of computers, the roar of jets taking off and landing in airports.

The lyre returned its listeners to a halcyon time when humans existed in innocence and amity, sang of joy in breathing sunlight and air, laced dreams and love in seamless harmony.

The melody quickened and evoked for Orestes the luminous light of Greece, sun-flamed islands awash in the foam of waves, graceful gulls soaring through winds from seas where sailors manned the masts of ships, dreaming of lovely, laughing girls in seaside ports.

The sorcery of the melody altered again, imparting a vision of fertile mountainsides on which flocks grazed, where shepherds slept beside newborn lambs to protect them from wolves. The music conjured up the rituals of planting and sowing, orchards bursting with sun-ripened fruits, the lush blossoms of mid- summer, the bleeding flora and fading foliage of autumn.

The tone of the lyre darkened, grew somber, beckoning its listeners along the journey each mortal begins with their first cry of terror at being ejected from the womb. The music paced their passages through darkness and divinity, crossing earth and traversing time.

Finally, the strings marked a transition from sunlight into shadows, entering that sunless land awaiting animals and humans, birds and fish, the inexorable flow of all life into death.

Deeply moved by the images and beauty the old musician's playing evoked, Orestes saw that the revelers at the tables had been profoundly touched, as well. Their faces were burned and reflective, their garrulous celebrations suspended. Even the applause when it began was at first tentative and troubled, and then slowly grew in volume and fervor as men and women came to understand the artistry and brilliance of what they had heard.

A little before five in the morning, his legs and back aching, his senses reeling with a surfeit of noise and celebration, Orestes walked through the restaurant a final time. He said good-bye to those remaining patrons waiting for the dawn, thanked the weary waiters still working, and praised Kyriakos and the cooks for their labor.

"Go and sleep in peace now, partner," Cleon told him as they embraced a final time. "Rest assured that I'll be the last man out of here to turn off the lights and lock the doors."

Orestes drove to the hotel through streets still teeming with celebrants transformed into maddened nymphs and satyrs by the arrival of the millennium. Some danced wildly under the streetlights, others stumbled in drunken stupors along the gutter. Within the span of a few blocks, he saw several police cars parked in the midst of small, rowdy crowds, their warning lights casting a ghostly glow over people's faces. An ambulance raced across an intersection before him, its siren wailing stridently across the night. He wondered if any of the dire Y2K predictions had proved true.

The hotel doorman took his car, and, as he entered the lobby, the strains of music and laughter from a raucous party in the adjoining ballroom pounded in his ears. He was weary suddenly of a world convulsed in the throes of a bacchanalian celebration.

He rode the elevator to his floor and walked slowly down the corridor, his exhausted body longing for bed and sleep. When he inserted the key card into the lock and opened the door, a streamer of light from the hallway swept into his room. He glimpsed movement in the shadows near the window, and he loosed a shrill, startled cry. He snapped the wall switch on and saw Dessie rise from a chair by the window.

"I'm sorry, Orestes," her voice was thin and shaken. "I didn't mean to scare you."

"How did you get here?" His voice trembled.

"When Paulie came to the house I told him I wasn't feeling well, but he wouldn't let me see the New Year in alone." She paused. "He wouldn't go home to Carmela and the baby unless I let him drive me to the restaurant first."

"Did you come into the Olympia?"

Dessie shook her head. "After Paulie left me, I took a taxi here. I told the desk clerk I was your wife, and he let me into your room." She made a small helpless gesture with her hands. "I didn't know where else to go, Orestes, I didn't know what else to do."

From a room further down the corridor, a door slammed and glass broke, the brittle sound cracking loudly in the stillness.

"If you don't want me here, Orestes, I'll ask for another room."

A silence drew out tensely between them as he tried to absorb the impact of her presence. He opened another lamp closer to where she stood. When the beam exposed her face, he was shocked at how the last few days had maimed her. She looked pale and drawn, her eyes looming blacker in the fatigued circles of her cheeks. For all the anguish he had endured the last few days and nights, he understood suddenly how much she had suffered, as well.

"The streets aren't safe tonight," he said. "You were right to come here."

A fine strand of her hair had fallen loose, cutting the paleness of her face. She fumbled nervously to push the hair off her cheek, and he saw the small gold circle of her wedding band that she'd never removed since the day they were married. They waited in silence and she was the first to speak.

"I tried to write you, Orestes," she said. "Tell you how sorry I feel about this terrible thing I've done to you. But my thoughts had blank spaces . . . I couldn't finish a sentence."

She waited for him to respond. When he didn't speak, she drew in a long, labored breath, and went on.

"I've held this secret inside me for so many years," she said, "always living in terror that you'd find out. As Paulie grew older, the fear stayed with me. What would become of us if you learned the truth? Whatever happens now, I'm thankful to finally have it out between us."

She stared at him, her eyes poignant and pleading.

"All I have any right to ask for now, Orestes, is for you to forgive me. I promise then I'll go away and never bother you again."

As her words, soft and forlorn, lingered in the air, he recalled his rage and the betrayal he'd felt when she first confessed. Those emotions had been scalded and consumed during his solitary, sleepless nights when despair had acted upon him like the flood in Genesis, washing away the illusions and hypocrisies that had existed in his own life. He had come to understand how fragile is the presence of man on earth and how vain and futile arrogance might be.

"There's nothing to forgive you for, Dessie," Orestes said. As he quietly uttered the words, he felt a great burden suddenly lifted from his heart. "You need to forgive me."

She stared at him in surprise.

"Forgive you for what, Orestes?"

"For the terrible things I said to you that night," he sighed. "For all my blunders and weaknesses, for all I should have done through the years and did not do. I've failed you, Dessie."

"Don't say that, Orestes!" Dessie cried. "You have been a good and loving husband! I'm the one who betrayed you!"

From the corridor outside their door a clamor of voices erupted as a party moved toward the elevators. The shrieks and laughter carried noisily into the room and then receded.

"You didn't betray me," Orestes said. "You loved this young man, and when the child was conceived, you did what you needed to do to protect your baby. For all these years, we both raised him and loved him. You were right when you told me that no matter who his father was, he became our son."

He heard her catch her breath, as if she were making an effort to hold back her tears. She moved closer to him then, staring with a sudden intensity into his eyes.

"No matter what you say now," she said, her voice trembling, "will you ever really be able to forgive me? Won't a day come, this year or the year after, when you'd start to resent me again, maybe even hate me for the way I deceived you?"

He wondered suddenly if she were right, whether he'd be able to remain as forgiving as he felt at that moment.

"We cannot know for sure what the future will hold," he said, "but if we don't make the effort now, Dessie, what will we do? Do we just give up all the years we've been married? Is that what Stavroula pleaded for when she was dying?"

She was silent for a moment, searching his face, trying to see behind his eyes.

"Tell me the truth now, Orestes. I couldn't bear thinking that you wanted us to stay together because you pitied me. I'm not asking for pity."

"Pity has nothing to do with it, Dessie," he said quietly. "I want us to stay together because I love you." He paused, smiled slightly to lighten the somberness of her face. "Of course, there are other reasons for us to stay together. Who would put out your vitamin tablets in the morning? And in the evening, who would I have to listen patiently to my stories of Kyriakos and Cleon and the young waiters in the Olympia?" He paused, a fervor entering his voice. "I cannot think of going through my days without you or consider growing old without having you beside me."

She let out her breath then and, with a soft cry, came into his arms. When he embraced her, it was as if part of his body that had been severed was joined again to his blood and bone. He trembled at how close he had come to losing that which he loved.

"How about it?" he asked gently. "Will you stay with me then?"

"Yes!" she cried. "Oh, my darling, yes!"

"I'm glad that's settled," he said and sighed. They hugged one another for a moment more in silence. "Now, my dearest," he said. "I feel as if I haven't slept in weeks, and you must be just as exhausted. Let's get to bed now, and in the morning, we'll go home. I've had enough of hotel rooms these last few nights to last me a lifetime. Tomorrow we'll have all day to talk again. But not now. Tomorrow and the day after tomorrow, we'll have time to talk. And when we talk, we'll also plan a trip back to Greece in the spring. No more damn delays. I promise this time we'll really go. But not now. Now let's have mercy on one another and go to bed and sleep."

"I haven't any nightgown," she said with a nervous laugh.

"I won't use my pajamas either," he said. "Remember how we slept naked when we first married?" They moved apart and began slowly to undress. As if she were suddenly feeling shy in his presence, she retreated into the shadows beyond the lamplight.

"Don't laugh at me, Orestes," she pleaded. "I know you've seen me naked so many times, but somehow I feel its different now."

He thought with surprise that she was right, as if a phase of their lives had ended and another period begun.

When he was naked, he shivered and hurriedly tugged down the spread and pulled back the quilt and sheet. He had a fleeting glimpse of Dessie's pale, lovely body as she slipped quickly into bed. He moved into the bed beside her.

He inhaled the pleasing, familiar scent of her, a faint trace of her cologne that carried the fragrance of flowers. Their cold arms and chilled legs slowly warmed one another.

"I was sure you were going to send me away," she whispered.

He could never have sent her away. It wasn't life and death that were the polarities but love and death. If one could not love, life was a wasteland.

After a few moments, Dessie turned her back to him and pressed her bare thighs against his naked loins. He cradled her waist with his arm.

"Do you think Paulie will come back?" Her voice seemed to be coming from far away.

"I think he will. I think his love for Carmela and the baby will bring him back."

She was silent for a moment, and then she spoke again.

"Did you mean it about Greece, Orestes? Can we really go in the spring?"

"Yes, we'll go," he said. "I'll make our reservations in the next few days. I promise . . ."

He felt her body relaxing, heard her breathing grow muted and drowsy and, after a moment, knew she had fallen asleep. Despite his own exhaustion, sleep continued to elude him. He became conscious of the clock on the end table, its barely audible ticking, the luminous numbers visible. He heard the soft rapping of snowflakes against the window.

In the serenity of that moment, he was suddenly conscious of the two of them, tiny particles of humanity embraced in a hotel room in the midst of the roistering city. From their small cloistered union, his thoughts ranged across the night. He thought of Father Anton, praying among the monks in the monastery in Greece. He thought of Bakalakis, his beloved lyre that was a gift from a god stored in its case, the old artist sleeping while his music lingered in the ears of those who had heard him play. He thought of the girl, Sarah, sleeping in the midst of her candles and her fantasies. He thought of Paul contemplating his journey while his wife Carmela grieved. He thought of Dr. Savas carrying his bleak vision into the millennium while healing those souls who needed his care. He envisioned Marika laughing among her friends, young girls and boys who could not yet understand how swiftly a lifetime could pass. He imagined sturdy and loyal Cleon turning out the last lights in the Olympia, the littered tables emptied of celebration, springing squarely into darkness.

And all the others who comprised his small world, Professor Platon, Banopoulos, Lalounis, Karvelas, all his friends who would continue to assemble at their table in the Olympia, arguing and assessing the foibles of contemporary life. And yes, in the mellowness and mercy of that moment, he even thought benevolently of Sam Tzangaris, Satan's representative on the church board of trustees, celebrating somewhere in the city, welcoming a new millennium in which he would continue to sow intolerance and hate.

From the living he moved to a vision of the dead entering the millennium, calling hoarse greetings to the corpses in graves surrounding their own. He thought of Stavroula, whom he'd despised while they lived together, but whose last whispered plea had lifted the dark burden of twenty years from Dessie's heart and helped him retrieve the healing power of forgiveness. He thought also of his quiet-hearted mother and his father, roaring Moustakas, now twin racks of sedate bones, lying in graves side by side. In that moment of his own fulfillment, irrevocably linked to the miracle of life and the wisdom of death, he forgave his father and sent the old unrepentant warrior his love across the night.

Beyond the bed in which he and Dessie lay, he glimpsed the first traces of the new day at the window. As the stars receded, the misted domes and towers of the city surfaced in the sky. And in a way he had never witnessed before, he saw the emerging light gird itself for battle with darkness, the day seeking dominance, the night reluctant to relinquish its power. In that confrontation as old as the earth itself, for the first time, Orestes grasped the beauty and power of the word humans called dawn.

In that way, their bodies nestled, souls and hearts in harmony, and their love reaffirmed, Orestes and Despina entered the new millennium.

Harry Mark Petrakis is the author of twenty books, including novels, memoirs, and collections of short stories and essays. He has twice been nominated for the National Book Award in Fiction, and his work has appeared in the *Atlantic Monthly*, *Harper's Bazaar*, *Playboy*, *Mademoiselle*, the *Chicago Tribune*, and the *New York Times*. In 1992, he held the Kazantzakis Chair in Modern Greek Studies at San Francisco State University. For the past forty years, he has also been a lecturer and storyteller, often reading his stories to college and club audiences in the old bardic tradition. He and his wife, Diana, live in the Indiana Dunes overlooking Lake Michigan. They have three sons and four grandchildren.